"Y O... nna said challengingly. "Why?"

"No, I am not." Philip came across the room towards her as he spoke. "How could I be vexed, when only kindheartedness prompted your visit? I am concerned because you have come seeking me here with only a servant to attend you. Surely you know that such conduct is unwise?"

Joanna's expression cleared as if by magic, and she gave a little ripple of laughter. "Oh, you are thinking of my reputation," she exclaimed merrily, "but what harm, pray, have I done to that? No one in the village will think any the worse of me for calling upon you. Why, they have known me all my life!"

"Yes, but they have not known me," he retorted ruefully. . . .

Fawcett Crest Books
by Sylvia Thorpe:

THE SWORD AND THE SHADOW

THE SCANDALOUS LADY ROBIN

THE GOLDEN PANTHER

ROGUES' COVENANT

CAPTAIN GALLANT

ROMANTIC LADY

THE RELUCTANT ADVENTURESS

TARRINGTON CHASE

THE SCARLET DOMINO

THE SCAPEGRACE

THE SILVER NIGHTINGALE

ROGUES' COVENANT

A NOVEL BY

Sylvia Thorpe

A FAWCETT CREST BOOK

Fawcett Publications, Inc., Greenwich, Connecticut

ROGUES' COVENANT

THIS BOOK CONTAINS THE COMPLETE TEXT OF
THE ORIGINAL HARDCOVER EDITION.

A Fawcett Crest Book reprinted by arrangement with Hutch-
inson Publishing Group

ISBN 0-449-23041-4

Printed in the United States of America

10   9   8   7   6   5   4   3   2   1

I

The House of Varne

In a handsome bedchamber with tall windows embracing a view of the rolling Cotswold hills, Charles Granville Colyton, fourth Earl of Varne, lay dying. In another part of the great house, three of his lordship's closest relatives awaited his passing with indifferently concealed impatience.

The eldest of the three, a large, middle-aged gentleman somewhat inclining to corpulence, sat squarely in a high-backed chair, his elbows resting on its arms and the tips of his fingers pressed lightly together. He still favoured the now declining fashion of the periwig, and the heavy curls of powdered hair framed a face bland and unrevealing, with heavy-lidded eyes and full, slightly pursed lips. He had an air of solid well-being, and a calm assurance of his own worth.

By the window, but with his back to the noble prospect it offered, stood a young man in his early twenties, tall, and a trifle too slender for his height. He was remarkably handsome, with an olive-skinned face almost too perfect in its beauty, and long-lashed, lustrous dark eyes. He stood there quietly enough, but his glance moved restlessly about the room, and one hand plucked continuously, in nervousness or febrile excitement, at the heavy curtain beside him.

The third man was seated by a small table midway between the other two, and might have been a contemporary of either, for though his lean, rather harsh-featured face was smooth and unlined, its expression, and the hard, cynical grey eyes, were those of a much older man. He was dressed with a kind of careless elegance, and lounged very much at his ease, his left hand thrust into his pocket, his right arm resting on the table as he cast and gathered up a pair of dice. The rattle of the ivory cubes on the polished wood was the only sound to break the silence until the youth by the window, as though goaded beyond endurance, said violently:

"For God's sake, Gregory, put those damned things away! This is not one of your cursed gaming-hells."

The other swept the dice up into his hand, held them for a moment while he shot a sardonic, upward glance at the speaker, and then cast them again with a flourish. A faint smile which was almost a sneer touched his lips.

"I am aware of it, my child," he replied mockingly, "and God send I find more profit here than I have yet found in them."

"Profit!" The young man made a gesture of distaste. "Can you not at least assume a decent gravity, even if you do not feel it?"

"I am no hypocrite, Francis," the other replied equably, "and I will not pretend that our noble relative's imminent decease causes me any great distress."

The third occupant of the room turned his head a little so that his sleepy gaze rested upon the last speaker. He said quietly:

"You have found some generosity here in the past, I believe. Varne has paid your debts more than once."

"Not lately, my dear cousin, not lately," Gregory Trayle retorted. "It is all of five years since Varne's purse-strings were loosed on my account."

"Yet now you expect to profit by his death!" There was scorn and anger in young Francis Colyton's voice. "Faith! you're sanguine."

"Why not?" Gregory spoke softly, but with some meaning. "My kinship with Varne is as close as yours, and I have not stepped into a dead man's shoes."

A silence which had in it something of tension followed these words. The dice rattled again on the table as Trayle cast them, but he was not looking at them. His hard glance was intent upon Bertram Colyton's face.

"I am well aware," the elder man said after a moment, "that our cousin resents the fact that I am his heir, but that was no more a matter of my choosing than of his. Only the sad fact of his son's death placed me next in succession to the title, and that no one could have foreseen."

"Oh, no one in the world," Trayle said ironically. "That, as I recall it, was not Varne's opinion, then or now."

Francis took a hasty step forward, but his father checked him with upraised hand.

"I mislike your tone, Gregory, but let that pass. It is true that at the time of Ashmore's death, and during the five years which have since passed, Varne has harboured a groundless suspicion against me, but I bear him no grudge on that score. The shock of losing a dearly-loved only son, in the prime of his youth and vigour——"

"And less than a month before his wedding-day," Gregory struck in mockingly. "Do not forget the most pertinent fact, I beg of you."

Mr. Colyton ignored the interruption.

"Such a shock, as I say," he continued calmly, "may well give rise to such disordered fancies as Varne entertains. It is also true that, to my lasting regret, I did introduce the boy to Colonel Trevor, but that cannot be held to make me responsible for what followed. Why, I was not even present when they quarrelled!"

"I was," Gregory said with a hint of grimness, "and ever since Varne has coupled me with you in bearing the blame."

There was a pause, while the thoughts of all three went back to the time when young Charles Colyton, Viscount Ashmore, had accused one Colonel Trevor of cheating him at cards, and two days later had died at the Colonel's hands in the inevitable duel. Gregory Trayle had been his young kinsman's second at the fatal meeting, which had made Bertram Colyton heir to the earldom of Varne, but if he had ever shared Lord Varne's suspicions he had given no hint of it, until today.

Trayle was the first to break the silence. He had stopped casting the dice and was now balancing them one on top of the other in the middle of the table, his whole attention apparently absorbed in the foolish task. In a tone almost pensive, he said reflectively:

"Trevor did cheat that night. I perceived it before Charles did."

"Then why the devil did you not say so?" Francis demanded with mingled indignation and perplexity. "Why keep silent while your own kinsman was being fleeced?"

"Because I was curious." Trayle's reply was addressed to Francis, but he was once more looking at Bertram. "I had seen Trevor play before, you see. He was one of the most skilled card-sharps I have ever encountered—and my experience, you will admit, is wide and varied. Yet that night, after he had won a considerable sum from Charles, he suddenly became so clumsy that not even a child would have been deceived." A pause, and then he added slowly, "Trevor was also, though this was not generally known until later, a quite exceptional swordsman."

The implications of this speech were unmistakable, but Mr. Colyton's calm remained unimpaired. He regarded his cousin blandly, almost, it seemed, with amusement.

"If you shared Varne's suspicions, my dear Gregory, you should have said so at the time. Your word would have carried some weight, and he would have been grateful for your support."

"No doubt!" Trayle's faint smile touched his lips again. "By the same reckoning you should be grateful to me for keeping silent. Of the two, I fancy your debt is the greater."

The elder Mr. Colyton smiled gently.

"And now you deem the moment ripe to reap the profits of your silence," he remarked. "Do I read your thoughts correctly?"

"Let us say that I trust to the strength of family affection," Gregory replied sardonically. "When you are Earl of Varne, you will be in a position to give your cousinly fondness for me full rein."

Francis had listened to this interchange with a bewilderment which gradually gave place to horror as its full meaning dawned upon him. He loosed his hold upon the curtain and took a step forward.

"It is not true?" he said in a strangled voice. "Father, you do not admit——"

"Like the wise man he is, he admits nothing," Gregory broke in shortly. There was a hint of contempt in his voice, and more than a hint of it in his eyes as he looked at his young relative. "Charles died in fair fight at the hands of a man he had insulted, and whether or not the insult was deserved matters less than nothing. The affair placed you in direct succession to wealth and honours, so keep a still tongue in your head and give thanks for——" he paused and then with a low laugh once more cast his dice. "For the whims of unpredictable fortune," he concluded drily.

For a few seconds Francis continued to stare at him, his face white and shocked, and then he swung abruptly away to where a heavy silver tray bearing decanters and glasses had been placed on a nearby table. With shaking hands he poured himself a generous measure of brandy and gulped it down, while his cousin watched him with scornful comprehension.

"God preserve me from a tender conscience!" he sneered. "I should have known better than to broach the matter before such a weakling."

Francis paid no heed to the gibe. He had dropped into a chair by the table and buried his face in his hands, and for an instant the eyes of the two older men met above his bowed head in a glance of impatience and derision. Silence fell again, and was broken only when Francis looked up to say wretchedly:

"Has it occurred to neither of you that your crime may have been committed in vain? Varne had a brother, had he not? If he still lives, he is the heir and may return to claim his inheritance."

Mr. Colyton regarded his son with some annoyance.

"Nothing has been heard of Richard Colyton since he left England three-and-thirty years ago," he said shortly, "and it is not likely that he will return now. Even Varne himself assumes him to be dead, or he would have made some effort to trace him when Ashmore died."

Gregory laughed softly.

"He would indeed!" he remarked. "What satisfaction it

would have given him to place a fresh obstacle in your way, Bertram."

He swept the dice into his pocket at last, and, rising, strolled across to the table by which Francis sat. He filled a glass for himself, and, with decanter poised, glanced inquiringly at Mr. Colyton. Bertram shook his head, and Trayle picked up his own glass and returned to his chair.

"I have often marvelled that Varne never thought to marry again," he said idly. "A young bride might have given him a second son to take Charles's place, and he need not have looked far afield for a match. There was Alison Stonehurst, for instance."

Bertram raised his brows.

"Miss Stonehurst was betrothed to Ashmore," he pointed out.

"What matter?" Gregory's expression was saturnine. "Do you imagine that old Stonehurst would have cared whether the girl married the father or the son, if he could have realized his cherished ambition for an alliance with the Colytons?"

"It is an ambition which may yet be fulfilled," Bertram informed him gently.

"To be sure! The fair Julia!" Gregory glanced over his shoulder at the huddled figure of his younger cousin. "How speeds your wooing, Francis?"

"Well enough!" The young man spoke sulkily, without looking up. "Julia is not indifferent to me."

"And her father is not indifferent to your brilliant expectations! Cousin, I predict that you will call her wife before the year is out."

This time Francis did raise his head, a dark flush spreading across his handsome face, for though the words were innocuous enough, the tone of Trayle's voice transformed them into a subtle insult. He stared resentfully at his kinsman, whose hard grey eyes returned the gaze with mocking comprehension above the rim of the half-empty glass.

"It is said in the village," Francis remarked at length with apparent irrelevance, "that Oliver Stonehurst is soon to marry Joanna Selbourne."

If he had hoped to trick Gregory into some show of feeling, he was disappointed. The gamester's face remained inscrutable, his steady glance did not waver.

"Mr. Stonehurst is a notable matchmaker," Trayle said carelessly. "The new Viscount for his younger daughter, and Selbourne's heiress for his son. A remarkable achievement!"

Neither of his companions replied, though both knew that there was some truth in Gregory's remark. Mr. Stonehurst of Foxwood Grange passionately desired an alliance with some noble house and, his earlier matchmaking having come to naught, was now doing all in his power to encourage Francis Colyton's courtship of his younger daughter. Of his son's possible marriage to Joanna Selbourne, Francis knew no more than anyone else, but he had spoken out of malice, for Gregory himself had for some time been laying unsuccessful siege to the heiress's heart and hand.

Another half-hour dragged by, marked by the steady ticking of the handsome timepiece above the hearth; a half-hour of sudden silences, and spurts of desultory, trivial conversation between the two elder men. Francis remained slumped in his chair, his hands gripped tightly together, and stared blankly before him with eyes in which horror still lingered. He had always known of Lord Varne's suspicions concerning his son's death, but he had never for one moment supposed that they were justified.

At last, unable to be still any longer under the goad of his thoughts, he thrust back his chair and rose restlessly to his feet. He moved back to his former position by the window, but after staring for a minute or two at the gardens beyond, where the shadows of evening were now beginning to gather, he swung round once more to face the room.

"In God's name, how much longer are we to be kept kicking our heels here?" he demanded desperately, and Gregory gave a short laugh.

"Impatient to assume your new honours, Francis?" he sneered. "In truth, our noble kinsman is an unconscionable time a-dying."

As though to belie the callous words, footsteps were heard approaching the door, and a lackey ushered into the room his lordship's physician, a neatly-dressed small gentleman of grave aspect. The three men turned towards him, but it was left to Bertram to voice the question in all their minds.

"How fares his lordship, Dr. Towne?"

The doctor pursed his lips and shook his head.

"He has rallied a little, sir, though I fear it is but the final flicker of an expiring flame. I can do no more to aid him." He sighed deeply, and then added on a brisker note: "His lordship desires to see you, gentlemen. Permit me to advise you not to delay."

"To see us?" Francis spoke with surprise, and some dismay. "All three of us?"

"All three of you, Mr. Francis," the doctor assured him. "His lawyer, Mr. Coleford, is with him."

Bertram rose ponderously from his chair and moved towards the door, beckoning to his son and his cousin to follow him. The great house seemed very silent as they went, without speaking, across the hall and up the broad staircase, and so at length to the door of the Earl's bed-chamber. As they reached it, it was opened from within by his lordship's personal servant, an elderly man whose face was marked now by weariness and grief, and so they passed into the presence of the dying man.

The huge fourposter in which Lord Varne lay was set on a dais in the middle of the room, and candles were burning on either side of it. A chair had been placed on the dais close to the head of the bed, and from this, as the cousins approached, John Coleford rose and bowed. Bertram inclined his head in grave response, Gregory gave a careless nod, but Francis was staring apprehensively at the Earl and seemed unaware of the lawyer's presence.

Lord Varne was in his sixty-third year, though he looked much older; a big man, gaunt now to the point of emaciation, and, like all the Colytons, dark of complexion and of hair. He lay motionless, watching his kinsmen with dark eyes which, sunken and shadowed though they were, revealed that the mind was still clear and active in his failing body. The sombre gaze rested on each in turn, and then came back to the eldest of the three.

"A day of triumph for you, Bertram, is it not?" His voice was very weak, a mere thread of sound in the stillness of the great room. "The day which brings you your long-desired inheritance. I fear you have come a trifle early to claim it."

"I came, cousin, because it was your wish," Mr. Colyton replied quietly, "just as it has been your wish to have no traffic with me these five years past. In both cases, I have respected your desires, for had you not expressly summoned me, I should not have thrust myself upon you."

"Nor I, cousin, depend upon it!" Gregory leaned one hand against the bed-post; his tone was casual, almost flippant, but there was a wary expression in his eyes. "Why did you send for us, Varne? Not, I'll wager, to give us your blessing."

The Earl looked at him reflectively.

"You always were an impudent devil, Trayle," he said musingly, "but I liked you well enough until you lent yourself to your cousin's murderous schemes." He closed his eyes for a moment, and when he opened them again there was a glimmer of malicious amusement in their dark depths. "I sent for you because there is something you should know." He moved his head slightly on the pillow, and added to the lawyer, "Tell them, Coleford."

"Certainly, my lord." Mr. Coleford cleared his throat, and spoke in a dry, matter-of-fact voice. "Gentlemen, the matter to which his lordship refers concerns the succession. You are aware, of course, that, failing a direct male heir, the title must revert to Mr. Richard Colyton, his lordship's younger brother, who left this country at an early age. Since that time, no news of him has reached his family, but, after his son's tragic death, Lord Varne realized that some effort must be made to trace him, if the question of the succession were ever to be satisfactorily settled."

"After more than thirty years?" Bertram broke in. "Impossible!"

There was an undertone of alarm in his scornful voice, and Varne looked at him with sardonic understanding. The lawyer inclined his head in grave agreement.

"That, sir, was my own opinion, and for a considerable time it appeared to be justified. My agents sought in all the principal cities of Europe for some trace of Mr. Colyton, but in vain. I would have abandoned the quest, but his lordship insisted that as a last resort the search should be transferred to the Americas. There, at last, we met with some success."

He paused, and a silence which was almost palpable filled the room. Bertram Colyton was breathing hard, his hands clenched tightly at his sides, an ugly expression about his mouth. Francis was staring at the lawyer in blank dismay, but Trayle, still leaning against the bedpost, smile with grim appreciation.

"Some months ago," Mr. Coleford resumed tranquilly, "my agent arrived in Barbados. He discovered that Richard Colyton had come there four years after leaving England, and found it so much to his liking that he purchased a property near the principal town. He attained a position of some influence in the colony, and remained there until his death three years ago."

Francis gave an audible gasp of relief, and his father imperceptibly relaxed, but this reaction proved to be premature. Mr. Coleford went on:

"Within a year of his arrival in Barbados, Mr. Colyton took to wife a niece of the then Governor, who bore him two children. A daughter, Penelope, now married to a gentleman of the island, and a son, Richard."

"Who will succeed me as Earl of Varne!" The faint voice from the bed was eloquent of the deepest satisfaction. "Your villainy will bring you no profit now, Bertram, no profit at all."

This time Mr. Colyton made no attempt to deny the allegation, or even to dissemble his fury and chagrin. His plump face livid, his mouth distorted with rage, he took a pace forward and spoke in a rasping voice.

"Damn you, Varne! What trickery is this?"

"There is no question of trickery, sir," Mr. Coleford interposed in a tone of cold rebuke. "As his lordship's nephew, the younger Richard Colyton is naturally his lordship's heir. Your own claim to the title must give place to his."

"Give place?" Colyton repeated furiously. "Do you imagine that I will stand aside in favour of some young jackanapes from the colonies, who cares so little for his English kin that he has not even troubled to inform them of his existence? By heaven, sir, I will not!"

"You have no choice!" The lawyer's voice was, if possible, even more frigid than before. "There is not the smallest doubt that Richard Colyton is his lordship's closest surviving relative, and therefore the next in succession to the title. He has been informed of this, and of his uncle's wish that he should come to England, and he sends word that he will do so as soon as he has settled his affairs in Barbados." He paused, and then added in a lower tone, "At that time, no one was aware how great was the need for haste."

Quietly though the last words were spoken, they reached the ears of the dying man. He moved his head again on the pillow, and gave the ghost of a laugh.

"I shall not be here to welcome him," he murmured, "but it is enough to know that he will come. My brother's son, to take the place of my own murdered boy! The place that you, Bertram, thought to fill! I have outwitted you, for all your scheming." His eyes closed, and he made a slight, disdainful gesture of dismissal. "Leave me now. I am very tired."

For a moment or two longer Bertram stood glaring down at him, and then without another word turned sharp on his heel and strode out of the room. Gregory Trayle watched him go, and then with a short, sardonic laugh looked again at the Earl.

"I make you my compliments, Varne," he said lightly. "You have turned the tables with a vengeance."

He grasped the stunned and petrified Francis by the arm and thrust him in Bertram's wake. When the door had closed behind them, Varne opened his eyes once more and signed to the lawyer to come closer.

"You believe me now, John, eh?" he whispered.

"I do, my lord, and if I have ever doubted your judgment in this, I crave your pardon for it. Yet, even now, there is no proof of his guilt. He admitted nothing."

"But we know that he caused my son's death, and he may well attempt to cause Richard's also. The boy must be warned, John, and convinced of his danger. You have the letter safe?"

"It is here, my lord. He shall have it as soon as he reaches England."

"I have cautioned him to trust no one, save yourself and Forester." A movement of the hand summoned the servant from his place at the head of the bed, and brought him to the Earl's side. Varne's hands moved again, and sensing his wish, each of his companions grasped one between their own. "I would I could see him!" The faint voice was wistful now. "Richard's son! His father should never have left England, but he was ever a law unto himself. As well try to cage a whirlwind." The words faltered, and for a space there was silence in the room; then, with an obvious effort, the Earl opened his eyes once more. "My friends," he whispered, "I trust you to serve him as loyally as you have served me."

He did not speak again.

II

Wind from the West

Mr. Bertram Colyton walked in his garden, and surveyed it, and the house beyond, with a gloomy and disparaging eye. It was a pleasant garden, but it lacked the spacious elegance of those he had expected to inherit, and his solid, comfortable house compared unfavourably with the country seat of the Earls of Varne.

That beautiful and dignified edifice, hidden from him by some three miles of intervening countryside, but ever present in his thoughts, stood empty now, awaiting its new master. Five weeks had passed since the fourth Earl had been laid to rest in the crypt beneath the village church, and ever since, the whole district had hummed with gossip and speculation concerning his successor. Many of the older folk remembered the elder Richard Colyton, and anecdotes concerning him, forgotten for thirty years, had been resurrected for the benefit of a later generation.

Bertram Colyton neither needed nor desired such reminders. His memories of Richard were all too vivid, and not in the least endearing, for he had disliked the younger brother even more than the elder, but he had been denied even the meagre consolation of giving vent to his bitterness and fury, for the only man to whom he could safely have disclosed it was Gregory Trayle, and Gregory had not lingered in Brinkbury village after the last rites had been observed. He had taken himself off to his own impoverished estate at Marwood, some miles to the south, where he was no doubt engaged in evolving some scheme whereby he could reap the greatest possible profit from the unexpected turn of events provided by the disclosure of a new heir to the earldom. Failures were of no interest to Mr. Trayle.

Francis had never made any reference to Gregory's disclosure on the day of Lord Varne's death, either to his father or to Trayle, and seemed preoccupied now with the unpalatable discovery that he was no longer a welcome guest at Foxwood Grange. He was taking his dismissal hard, but Bertram had no sympathy to spare for his son's misfortunes. His own occupied his mind to the exclusion of all else.

His aimless pacing brought him near to the house, just as a servant came into the garden in search of him. Mr. Colyton paused, and watched his approach with a jaundiced eye. No good news, he felt, was likely to be coming to him.

"There is a gentleman asking to see you, sir," the man informed him, and Bertram frowned.

"A gentleman?" he repeated. "You mean a stranger?"

"Yes, sir, a Mr. Digby by name. He says the matter is important." He hesitated, regarding his master somewhat doubtfully, for Colyton's temper was unpredictable. "He told me to say that it is blown here by a wind from the west."

Mr. Colyton had opened his lips to utter a curt refusal, but at that he paused, an arrested expression in his eyes. Then he turned his head and looked towards the rim of the hills bounding the western horizon, while his thoughts went leaping far beyond, to a tropical island which had been much in his thoughts of late. The cryptic message might mean much, or little, but "a wind from the west" could have arisen in Barbados.

"I will see him," he said abruptly, and went towards the house.

When he entered the room where the visitor was waiting, he found a slim gentleman of medium height standing with his back to the door as he studied the painting above the hearth. His plain, dark brown riding-dress clothed a well-knit, muscular figure, and his thick, waving hair, confined by a black ribbon at the nape of his neck, was a flaming red. Then the stranger turned, and Mr. Colyton's first thought was that never before had he seen a man who gave an impression of such intense vitality; even in repose, the impact of it was almost physical.

Mr. Digby was young, certainly not more than thirty, with a lean, expressive face which was deeply bronzed, as though he were accustomed to being out of doors in all weathers. His clear hazel eyes were curiously flecked with green, and remarkably brilliant and direct, and there was strength as well as humour in the firm lines of his mouth. A sword more serviceable than fashionable swung at his side, and in spite of the neat elegance of his attire, an indefinably swashbuckling air clung about him. Young Mr. Digby, in fact, looked capable of dealing with any situation.

"Mr. Colyton?" His voice was crisp and pleasant, in keeping with his looks. "Permit me to present myself, sir. I am Philip Digby, entirely at your service."

A courteous bow accompanied the words. Bertram inclined his head in response, but said, with a civility which was faintly mocking:

"I am honoured, Mr. Digby, but since you have given

yourself the trouble of seeking me out, it would seem more likely that I am to be of service to you. I am right, am I not, in supposing that you are not a native of these parts?"

"Quite right, Mr. Colyton." Digby's tone matched his engaging smile for frankness, but there was an intent look in the hazel eyes. "I was born in Barbados."

"Indeed?" Bertram waved his guest to a chair, and moved deliberately to seat himself in another. "You roam far afield, Mr. Digby."

"There is one who travels as far, sir, and to some purpose, if half of what I hear is true," Digby retorted quietly. "Your kinsman, Richard Colyton, now the Earl of Varne. To tell the truth, I thought to find him here before me."

"Ah!" Bertram placed the tips of his fingers together, and regarded Digby across them with bland curiosity. "You are a friend of my young relative, no doubt?"

There was a pause, so slight as to be scarcely perceptible, and a hardening of the lines of the young man's face. Then he replied lightly:

"I know him, sir, and have done so all my life. My father was his tutor, and we were educated together."

"I see!" Bertram's smile was benign. "This is excellent, Mr. Digby. If you are at liberty, I beg that you will stay to dine with me, so that we may talk of Richard. Beyond his name, and the place of his birth, I know nothing of the boy, nothing at all."

"And you are interested, sir, of course?" There was a mocking inflection now in Digby's voice. "You are overflowing with affectionate eagerness to make the acquaintance of the son of your long-lost kinsman, the new head of your family?"

Mr. Colyton frowned.

"I am naturally curious concerning him," he replied with dignity, "but I dislike the tone of that remark, Mr. Digby. Perhaps, after all, it would be better if I restrained my curiosity until Richard himself is here to satisfy it."

"I doubt it, sir! I doubt it very much!" Mr. Digby, unabashed by the rebuke, spoke flippantly. "Perhaps I should tell you that I have taken the trouble to acquaint myself with the present situation, and that I am aware that by the mere fact of his existence, Richard Colyton has deprived you of an estate, a fortune and a title. My dear sir, if you cherish any kindly feelings towards him, you are more saint than human."

There was another, longer pause, while Bertram's sleepy eyes met the brilliant, penetrating gaze of his visitor, a pause in which each seemed to take the measure of the other. Then, as though that silent exchange of glances had established some kind of understanding between them, Colyton permitted himself to relax a trifle.

"I will confess," he said slowly, "that it was a severe shock to me to learn that I was not, after all, heir to the Earl of Varne. I will even admit that it would give me pleasure rather than pain to hear that a fatal accident had befallen the present Earl. Are you answered, Mr. Digby?"

"Certainly, sir. It is the answer I would expect from any man of sense."

"You flatter me!" Bertram's voice was ironic. "And now perhaps you will answer me in your turn. What is the nature of your present business with Richard Colyton?"

Philip Digby smiled, but it was not the frank and engaging smile which Bertram had previously seen. It touched his lips but not his eyes, which remained as cold as ice. It was a smile more deadly than a frown.

"That is soon told," he said softly. "I am going to kill him."

The words dropped quietly into the silence, like pebbles into a deep, still pool, stirring the placidity of that pleasant room with dark ripples of violence. Bertram's hands went to the arms of his chair, and gripped them, as though he would have risen, and when he spoke his voice was scarcely more than a whisper.

"Why?" he said hoarsely.

Digby got abruptly to his feet. He moved with supple grace, as though every muscle of his body were under perfect control, and as Bertram watched him it passed fleetingly through his mind that the young man was probably a formidable swordsman. At the time, he was scarcely conscious of the thought, for his whole attention was centred upon the incredible statement his visitor had just made.

"The cause is common enough," Digby replied at length. "Too common for me to weary you with the details. There was a woman concerned in it, the young lady I hoped to make my wife. Richard Colyton also admired her, but she had neither birth nor fortune to commend her to him as a bride."

He was standing now by the window, his back to the room and his hands clasped behind him. His voice, though bitter, was controlled, but the observant Mr. Colyton could see how tightly his fingers were gripped together.

"Business took me away from Barbados," Digby went on, "and a series of mischances delayed my return. By the time I reached home again, all was over. My poor Louise, betrayed and deserted, had taken her own life, and Colyton already found a new light-o'-love."

"So you have pursued him to England to call him to account?" Bertram hazarded after a moment, but Digby shook his head.

"That I have already done," he replied. "We fought, and I was defeated. It almost cost me my life, for though I have some skill with a sword, Richard Colyton has greater. Yet kill him I will, by foul means since I cannot achieve it by fair."

A short silence followed this grim pronouncement. Bertram Colyton leaned back in his chair, and with a complacent smile on his face studied his companion's straight shoulders and fiery head. Yet it was a complacency tempered with caution, for though this implacable young man was clearly the gift of a kindly Providence, Mr. Colyton had no intention of committing himself immediately.

"Your feelings, Mr. Digby, are understandable," he remarked at length, "and pray believe that you have my sympathy. I cannot, however, suppose you to be serious in that threat."

"I was never more serious in my life!" Digby swung round to face him. His face was pale, his lips tightly compressed, and the quiet, deadly tone of his voice carried more conviction than any amount of ranting. "I mean to kill Richard Colyton. I have travelled half across the world to do it."

"He is not here," Bertram pointed out mildly.

"I can wait!" Digby came away from the window, and stood looking down at the elder man with those curiously brilliant eyes. "Sooner or later he will come."

"True, but it does not follow that you will be here to greet him. You have threatened my kinsman's life, and it is only reasonable to suppose that I shall take measures to protect him."

"It is not reasonable at all." Mockery leapt in the hazel eyes, and twisted the firm lips. "Firstly because there is only your word against mine that a threat was uttered; secondly because Richard Colyton is an obstacle in the way of your own ambition."

"Mr. Digby," Bertram was softly, "the fact that I have admitted to you that I should be glad to hear of Richard's death does not mean that I will connive at his murder. If you intended to meet him in fair fight I would wish you well, and even give you any aid that lay within my power——"

"Would you?" Digby broke in. "Yet it would seem a trifle suspicious, would it not, if yet another heir to the earldom were to perish in a duel, leaving you to take his place?"

Bertram's plump, white hands closed again on the arms of his chair, and though his heavy lids drooped more sleepily than before, the eyes beneath them glittered dangerously.

"By Heaven, young man," he said in a low voice, "for a stranger from another land, you are oddly familiar with the history of my family!"

Digby shrugged.

"Only that part of it which is common knowledge," he replied carelessly. "I lodged last night at the village inn, and you must be aware that the whole district is alive with rumour and with gossip. It seems that the late Earl made no secret of his suspicions." He paused, studying with ironic comprehension the chagrin in the other's face, and then added more briskly: "Now, sir, shall we leave this wordy warfare, and come to business? It was not idle mischief-making which brought me here today."

"Go on, Mr. Digby," Bertram said quietly. "I make no promises, but I will hear what you have to say."

Philip Digby drew forward a chair and sat down beside his host, leaning towards him and speaking softly and decisively.

"I came to you, sir, because we both have good cause to hate Richard Colyton, and because my purpose can be achieved more easily with your help. Not in the deed itself, for that I will delegate to no man, but in the planning which must go before. I am a stranger here. I know neither the country nor the people, and I have no means of obtaining the information I shall need. You, on the other hand, are known and trusted, and as Colyton's kinsman will be the first to learn of his arrival in England."

"That may be so," Bertram agreed, "but what of it?"

"Once I am informed of his movements, I shall waste no time, for if he discovers my presence here he will realize his danger. Let me but know at which port he lands, and the road he must travel to reach this village, and I give you my word that he will not live to claim his inheritance."

"And if I am not informed of his intentions? He will see Varne's lawyer first, and John Coleford, I believe, trusts me as little as did my kinsman. He may warn Richard against me."

"You will be told of his coming," Digby replied with scornful assurance. "If I know Richard Colyton—and, believe me, I know him as well as any man—he will expect to be greeted with pomp and ceremony. He was always vain, but it seems that since he discovered himself to be a future peer of the realm he has grown insufferable. Many of his old friends in Barbados were antagonized by his coxcomb ways."

"One thing puzzles me, Mr. Digby," Bertram remarked. "Why did you not settle your score with Richard before he left the Indies?"

"I had no opportunity, for he left Barbados while I still lay sick of the wound he dealt me when we fought."

"Yet you are here before him. How comes that?"

Digby shrugged.

"Simple enough! He did not come direct to England. You may not know it, Mr. Colyton, but your upstart kinsman is already a wealthy man, and there would be many affairs for him to settle before he could leave the Indies for good. I am told that the Barbados plantation was made over to his sister, Mrs. Warren, but there were other properties, in Jamaica and St. Kitts, which would have to be disposed of. Rather than chase him from island to island through the Caribbean, I chose to come here and await his arrival."

"I see. Then we may presume Richard to be at present on his way to England?"

"It is most likely. He would not need to wait long for a ship. His brother-in-law, Edward Warren, owns several merchantmen, and would doubtless place one at Richard's disposal." He paused, looking steadily at the elder man. "I have been frank with you, sir. May I depend upon your aid?"

Bertram did not reply at once, but sat silent, drumming his fingers on the arms of the chair, and studying Digby's face with a searching glance. The young man bore the scrutiny without wavering, and Colyton was struck once more by his air of forcefulness and purpose.

"I can afford no further suspicion to fall upon me," he said at last.

"Nor would it," Digby replied promptly. "All that the world need know is that Richard Colyton and I are friends of long-standing. Learning by chance of his good fortune, I have come to greet him, and because he is tardy, I await his coming. When I learn that he is on his way hither, what more natural than that I should ride out to meet him? Depend upon it, I shall not return."

"It would serve, I suppose," Bertram agreed dubiously.

"Of course it will serve. 'Tis the tale I meant to tell before I learned how matters stood between you and your cousins."

"But do you seek no reward? I confess that I would more readily accept your proposal if I could see wherein lay your hope of profit."

Digby's face hardened.

"I am not a hired assassin, sir," he said shortly, "and to know that Louise is avenged will be reward enough. For the rest, if you are disposed to furnish me with the means to return to America, I shall be grateful. My resources are slender, and this venture has already taxed them to the uttermost."

"That I will do," Colyton replied with sudden decision. "I agree to your proposal, Mr. Digby. Here is my hand on it."

He stretched out his hand, and Digby took the plump, white fingers in a grip which made Mr. Colyton wince. He freed them as speedily as possible, and rose from his chair to summon a servant.

"We will take a glass of wine to seal the bargain," he said, and waited until the footman had appeared, and been despatched again upon his errand. Then he went on: "You speak of returning to Barbados. Will you not stand in some danger there, when news comes of Richard's death, and the quarrel between you is remembered?"

Mr. Digby chuckled. The prospect of danger seemed to amuse him.

"It is a risk I would be willing to take, sir, but it is unlikely that I shall return to Barbados. The New World is large, and I have ever had a taste for roving. In fact, since I have already seen some service along the frontiers of the northern colonies, I shall probably return there. In those vast plains and forests, a man can be truly free."

For the rest of his visit he spoke entertainingly of those same wild frontier-lands, and no further mention was made of the real purpose behind his presence in England. When the time came for him to take his leave, Bertram Colyton walked with him to the door, and stood there while he got to horse. The servants thus observed that cordiality had been established between their master and his visitor, and were able, from remarks dropped with apparent carelessness in their hearing, to discover that this dynamic young man was a close friend of the new Earl. That this information was being deliberately presented to them they did not guess.

Philip Digby bade his host a courteous farewell, and rode decorously along the short avenue to the gates. The road on to which these opened was deserted, and a stretch of grass beside it offered better going than the rutted surface of the highway itself. Philip spurred his horse to a canter and headed away from the village, sitting easily erect in the saddle, a gay snatch of song on his lips.

III

Encounter on a Hilltop

After a short distance he left the highway for a narrow lane which led in the direction of the uplands, and dwindled gradually until it lost itself amid the sheep-cropped grass on the higher slopes. When at last he had reached the crest of the tallest hill in the immediate vicinity, he drew rein and sat looking thoughtfully at the countryside spread out before him.

The village where he had slept the previous night lay far below him in a fold of the hills, its grey-gold Cotswold stone half hidden by clustering trees, and a mile or so beyond, the great house of the Earls of Varne lifted its graceful gables and chimneys from the midst of a timbered park. The mansion and its attendant buildings formed a second, miniature village, bowered, like its larger neighbour, in trees now beginning to show the first golden tints of autumn, and between the two he could see the flash of the broad stream over whose old stone bridge he had passed on his way to visit Bertram Colyton.

He turned slowly, tracing the course of the road, but Colyton's house was hidden by a lesser hill between. Philip's gaze passed on, lingered for a moment on another house, apparently of some size, glimpsed fleetingly on a hillside some way off, and so came back to Brinkbury village and the noble mansion beyond.

It lay there at his feet, like a map unfolded for his inspection, the broad domain of Varne. Windswept hilltop and wooded valley, fields of golden stubble and rich pasture, village and farm and cottage, threaded with the silver gleam of water beneath the blue September sky.

For a considerable time he remained at that point of vantage, studying the scene before him and imprinting it deliberately upon his memory. Presently he would ride down again to the valley and begin to explore it at closer quarters, for the time might soon come when an intimate knowledge of the countryside would prove invaluable.

So intent was he upon this self-imposed task that not until his horse lifted its head and gave a low whinny did he become aware of a muffled thunder of hoofs somewhere close at hand. He looked up, frowning, seeking the source of the sound, which an instant later burst into view around the shoulder of the hill below him. A great, powerful grey horse racing at a mad gallop across the hillside, and all too clearly beyond the control of the slight, feminine figure in the saddle, who was making valiant but unsuccessful attempts to check its headlong career.

Digby set spur to his own mount and plunged recklessly in pursuit. The slope of the ground was in his favour, and only a few moments elapsed before he drew alongside the grey and leaned over to grasp its bridle. Beneath the steely pressure of his grip the terrified animal gradually slackened its pace, until at last both horses had come to a standstill, the grey sweating and trembling, and Philip had leisure to spare a glance for its rider.

His first reaction was astonishment that she should ever have attempted, or been permitted, to ride such a horse, for she was the daintiest little creature imaginable, and certainly not more than seventeen or eighteen years old. She had lost her hat, and strands of fair hair had broken loose from the confining ribbon to curl enchantingly about a heart-shaped face, pale now in the reaction from her recent danger. It was a sweet face, with large blue eyes and a *retroussé* nose, but an exceedingly wilful one. The lady did not lack spirit, he reflected with some amusement, even if it were for the moment in abeyance.

"You ride recklessly, madam," he remarked. "May I,

with all deference, suggest that in future you choose a mount which you can control?"

She had seemed for the moment to be on the point of tears, but the bantering tone which he had deliberately adopted checked the inclination at once. A flush of mortification rose in her cheeks, and the blue eyes flashed indignantly.

"I am exceedingly grateful for your assistance, sir," she replied coldly, "but it does not give you the right to censure me. My horse was startled, and bolted. It was the merest stroke of ill fortune."

As though to refute this statement, the grey, resentful of the firm hand on the bridle, snorted and tossed its head. Then, finding itself still held in check, began to stamp and sidle, so that Philip wondered afresh who had been mad enough to mount the girl on this wild, half-broken brute. Skilled horsewoman though she undoubtedly was, she had not the strength to control such an animal.

"Oh, no doubt," he retorted mockingly, "but it must have caused your companions a good deal of alarm. So, since you appear to have outdistanced them, I will escort you until they come up with us."

"Thank you, but I am alone," the lady informed him frigidly, "and I have no need of an escort."

Philip's brows shot up in assumed surprise.

"You astonish me, madam," he said cheerfully. "I did not realize that it was the custom in England for a lady to ride unattended. It is a practice which seems to me both inadvisable and dangerous."

It was not the custom, and they both knew it. The realization that he was rallying her served to increase a vexation which had its root in fright, and was insensibly aggravated by the knowledge that with every word she was putting herself more completely in the wrong. He had rescued her from an alarming and perilous plight, and if his bearing lacked that respect which she was usually accorded, her own behaviour was largely to blame. Irked beyond measure by every aspect of the situation, she said sharply:

"I am not interested in your opinions, sir! Please be

good enough to take your hand from my bridle, and let me go on my way."

He laughed and shook his head.

"A sorry plight you would be in if I did," he retorted. "No, my child, I have no intention of allowing you to endanger your pretty neck any further on the back of this ill-tempered brute, however eager to do so you may be."

"Indeed?" She was all haughty disdain now, though the pose accorded ill with her dishevelled appearance. "May I ask how you propose to prevent me?"

"Certainly you may," he agreed cordially, "and I will tell you with all the pleasure in the world." He urged his own horse forward as he spoke, the grey and its rider accompanying him perforce. "When we reach those two thorn-trees yonder I shall tether the horses and change the saddles. Then I shall restore you to your home."

She looked at him with quick suspicion, beyond which there seemed to be a trace of dismay.

"You know who I am?"

"Not yet," he admitted, smiling, "but you are going to tell me, are you not?" He saw wrathful refusal gathering in her eyes, and added before it could take shape in words, "If you do not, I shall have no choice but to take you to the village, and find someone there who is willing to do so."

She was left to consider this ultimatum, which she did in silence until the thorn-trees were reached. When the horses had been tethered, and he came to help her to the ground, she ignored his outstretched hand and said furiously:

"I will not! You have no right to treat me in this fashion. You are rude, and overbearing, and I hope——"

The hope was destined to remain unuttered. Mr. Digby, losing patience, laid hold of her without ceremony and swung her out of the saddle, so that the words ended in a gasp of mingled surprise and indignation. As he set her on her feet, she struck at him wildly, but he caught her wrist in a hard grip, and she saw that he was laughing.

"So you can curb your temper no more than you can curb your horse," he said lightly. "Upon my soul, I do not know which of you stands in the more urgent need of schooling!"

For a moment she faced his amused regard, and then the blaze of anger in the big blue eyes was drowned in sudden tears; her head drooped, and a heart-rending sob broke from her lips. Mr. Digby's heart was not rent. Retaining his grasp on her wrist, he led her to a mound of moss-grown stones at the foot of one of the trees, seated her, none too gently, upon it, and then without a second glance at her busied himself with the task of exchanging the two saddles.

The young lady lifted her drooping head and looked at him with unmixed astonishment. Never before had she found tears an ineffective weapon. Any other man of her acquaintance would have been cast into the most complete disorder, abjectly begging her pardon and beseeching her to dry her eyes, but this masterful, red-headed stranger with his infuriating smile could not have been more completely indifferent to her woe. He had treated her like a sulky child, and the knowledge that she was behaving like one did nothing to soothe her feelings.

She sat there in silence, ill-humouredly poking the ground with the toe of one foot, until the exchange was completed and he came to stand before her. Even then she did not look up, and after a moment or two he said pleasantly:

"Well, madam, have you made your choice? Will you tell me your name, and the way to your home, or must we advertise your tantrums by riding to the village?"

She lifted her head and looked at him speculatively. He was smiling with obvious amusement, but nothing in the lean, brown face or green-flecked eyes suggested that he would hesitate to carry out his threat. She had a vivid and unwelcome vision of the sensation which would be created if she were escorted into the village by a strange young man who requested passers-by to tell him her identity, and though she was generally impatient of convention the mere thought of such an experience made her feel hot with embarrassment. Inwardly seething, she capitulated with as good a grace as she could muster.

"I am Joanna Selbourne," she said curtly, "and my home is at Greydon Park. It lies in that direction, about two miles from here." She pointed towards the south as she spoke. "I will show you the way."

"Now you begin to show good sense," he said briskly, stretching out his hand to help her to her feet. "My name is Philip Digby, and, in spite of what you may believe, I desire only to be of service to you."

She acknowledged this with no more than a slight, incredulous lifting of her brows, but suffered him to take her hand, lead her to the horses, and lift her on to the back of his own fine roan. She watched him mount the grey, which immediately began to signify disapproval of the change by every means in its power, but any hope that he would meet with ignominious defeat was soon banished. With grudging admiration she watched his expert handling of the big horse, until the grey, realizing that it had met its master, at last permitted them to proceed in a reasonably decorous manner. Mr. Digby seemed unperturbed by the struggle, giving, in fact, the impression that he was enjoying it, and Miss Selbourne concluded that he had often dealt with obstreperous horses in the past.

Her resentment burned with unabated force, but now an almost involuntary curiosity was beginning to mingle with it. Strangers were rare in that quiet corner of Gloucestershire, and she wondered who the mysterious Mr. Digby might be, and what business could have brought him to Brinkbury. It had been her intention to complete the journey in stony silence, but by the time they reached the road at the foot of the hill, curiosity had become too profound to be borne.

"I think you are a stranger to these parts, sir," she said abruptly, and was immediately furious with herself for being the first to speak.

"That is true, Miss Selbourne," he admitted gravely, but with an amused glance which told her that no information would be volunteered. She tossed her head and pressed her lips tightly together, determined to say no more, but after only a minute or two of silence found herself asking:

"Perhaps, even, a stranger to England?"

He nodded.

"You are quite right. I recently arrived in this country from America."

"America!" Her eyes widened with astonishment. "Why, that is where—are you acquainted with the new Earl of Varne, sir?"

"I am, madam, though it is some while since we met. We were boys together in Barbados, and when I learned by chance that he was coming to England, I resolved to seek him out for old times' sake. It appears, however, that his arrival has been delayed."

Miss Selbourne was regarding him with new interest, and more friendliness than before. He had realized within an hour of his arrival in Brinkbury how eager everyone was to learn something of the new Earl, and he guessed that curiosity was even greater among the ladies of the district than among their menfolk. As though to confirm this opinion, Miss Selbourne said eagerly:

"What is he like? Everyone expected Mr. Colyton to succeed to the title, after Lord Ashmore was killed. Oh, perhaps you do not know Mr. Colyton! He is the Earl's cousin, and lives at Brinkbury House, just outside the village."

"Thank you, I waited upon Mr. Colyton today, in the hope that he had some tidings of his kinsman, but he could tell me nothing."

"You have told me nothing, either, sir," Joanna pointed out after a pause.

He did not reply at once, and, glancing at him, she saw that he was frowning.

"Varne is a man like any other," he said abruptly at length. "Were I to say more, I might well give you a false picture, since no two people ever see in a third the same qualities of good or evil."

She was disappointed, and pouted a little.

"Is that all you will say, sir?"

He shrugged.

"What more can I say? He is—let me see—twenty-seven years old, is accounted by some to be not ill-looking, and is tolerably well acquainted with the ways of the world. He is also, at present, a bachelor."

The last words were spoken in so significant a tone that Joanna looked at him with quick suspicion. He returned the glance with seeming frankness, and after a moment she replied lightly:

"Your words imply, sir, that his lordship is contemplating marriage."

"It is unlikely, I think," there was scorn now in Digby's voice, "but I'll wager the thought will be put into his mind soon enough when he arrives here, and finds every marriageable girl in the district being flung more or less willingly at his head."

"Willingly?" Joanna's slight figure stiffened; her voice was indignant. "You judge us hastily, Mr. Digby!"

"Women are women the world over," he replied cynically, "and there is no lure more potent for them than a high-sounding title, particularly when it carries wealth with it, as this one does. Believe me, I am sorry for Varne!"

"He will be grateful for your sympathy, no doubt," she retorted cuttingly, "but may I ask why you think he deserves it?"

He smiled, but less pleasantly than before; almost he seemed to sneer.

"Because all the fair maidens and their scheming parents will be concerned merely with the Earl of Varne, and not with the man who bears the title. Would you, for instance be questioning me so eagerly about him if he were coming here as plain Richard Colyton instead of 'my lord the Earl'?"

She stared at him in speechless indignation, wrathful colour rising again in her cheeks. Then, as though not trusting herself to speak, she compressed her lips and urged her mount to a brisk trot. The ready laughter leapt again into her companion's eyes, but he said no more, and allowed her to ride half a length ahead of him for the rest of the short journey. His tactless words had been uttered deliberately, and had apparently achieved their purpose, for the new Earl of Varne was not a subject he wished to discuss with anyone.

Save for some men at work in the fields, they saw no one until Greydon Park was reached. Joanna had soon forsaken the road to follow byways which apparently were little used, and Philip suspected that she had deliberately chosen the least frequented road to her home. Whether this was because she did not wish to be seen in his company, or because she had ridden the grey horse without permission and was fearful of the consequences, he could not decide.

The path they followed brought them at length across a strip of parkland to an avenue of fine old trees, which sloped gently down to serve a big, rambling house built of the prevailing, grey-gold stone. The main door of the house was open, and on the few broad steps that led to it two men were standing, at sight of whom Miss Selbourne gave a stifled exclamation in which Philip thought to detect both annoyance and dismay.

The two gentlemen had been staring fixedly at the riders from the moment they came into view, and when they drew near enough, Digby could see that their expressions combined relief with astonishment and some misgiving. He drew rein at the foot of the steps, but before he could speak the elder of the two, a stout old gentleman with shrewd blue eyes beneath bushy white brows, demanded sternly:

"What is the meaning of this, Joanna? Will you have the goodness to explain?"

She flushed and bit her lip, but before she had time to reply the second man, a well-built, pleasant-faced youngster only a few years older than herself, hurried to lift her down from the roan's back, saying, with a somewhat possessive solicitude:

"Thank God you have come safely home, Joanna! I was about to come in search of you."

She gave him a fleeting smile, but said nothing. His obvious concern apparently reassured her, for she turned again to the other man.

"I know I did wrong, Father," she admitted meekly, "and I am truly sorry. Please forgive me."

She spoke with a pretty air of sincere repentance, but not as though she had any real dread of punishment, and Philip concluded that she was accustomed to every indulgence from her parent. The old gentleman's present anger was probably no more than the reaction from concern on his daughter's behalf.

Both gentlemen were eyeing him suspiciously. He dismounted, handed the grey over to a groom who had come running around the corner of the house, and waited with outward gravity for Miss Selbourne to introduce him, wondering humorously with what version of their meeting she would choose to regale her parent.

He was not kept long in suspense. Having admitted her own fault, Joanna lost no time in diverting attention to his. Mounting the steps to her father's side, she said hurriedly:

"Sir, this gentleman"—the vicious emphasis on the last word showed how little she thought he merited the description—"has insulted me in every conceivable fashion. Let him deny it if he dare!"

Philip laughed softly, but his appreciation of the humour of the situation was not shared by the young man hovering so solicitously at Miss Selbourne's side. His face darkened, and he took a pace forward, groping for the hilt of his sword.

"So you find that amusing, do you?" he said savagely. "Why, you——!"

"Oliver!" Selbourne spoke sternly to check him. "Be good enough to keep silent. I will deal with this." He looked at Digby. "Well, young man?"

"The explanation is simple, sir," Philip replied frankly. "Your daughter was having some difficulty with her mount. Since the horse was obviously too strong for her, I lent her my own, and escorted her home."

"Oh!" It was a cry of indignation from the lady. "Father, he commanded me to change horses with him, and when I refused, dragged me by force from the saddle, and said that——that——"

"That you could no more curb your temper than your horse," Philip struck in, grinning. "A statement which I can see no reason to retract."

A strangled exclamation of rage came from Oliver, but Selbourne's lips twitched and he raised a hand rather quickly to his mouth. His daughter's bosom swelled, but she appeared for the moment to be bereft of words.

"I do admit, sir," Philip went on, addressing himself now to Sir Andrew, "that my conduct was a trifle high-handed. I was concerned more with Miss Selbourne's safety than with her feelings."

"I am deeply grateful to you for your intervention, sir," Selbourne replied cordially. "May I know your name?"

"It is Philip Digby, sir," he answered, bowing slightly. "As for any small service which I may have rendered Miss Selbourne, it has been amply rewarded by the privilege of making her acquaintance."

Miss Selbourne, ungratified, tossed her head.

"Do not trouble yourself to make pretty speeches now, Mr. Digby," she said coldly. "They cannot efface the memory of your earlier incivility."

"Joanna, that will do!" Sir Andrew reproved her. "Mr. Digby has rendered you a great service. Your disobedience might well have cost you your life, for if that horse had bolted you could have had no hope of regaining control over it."

Philip said nothing, but could not resist the temptation to glance quickly at Miss Selbourne. The swift colour had mounted again to her cheeks, though that might have been caused by the reproof administered to her, and her eyes were downcast. To his surprise, however, and after only the briefest hesitation, she said reluctantly:

"It did bolt, sir. That is what Mr. Digby meant when he said I was in difficulties."

"Upon my soul!" Sir Andrew stared at her with astonishment and deepening displeasure, while even Oliver looked shocked. "Then our debt to him is even greater than I supposed, and it would become you, Joanna, to express your gratitude to him in proper terms."

"I did thank him!" Angry tears sprang into Joanna's

eyes, and her voice trembled indignantly. "And I see no reason to do so again. He teased and bullied me until there was no bearing it, and now you are taking his part against me! It is unjust!"

Oliver Stonehurst intervened. He had watched uneasily the effect of this speech upon Sir Andrew, and now made a praiseworthy but unsuccessful attempt to divert the anger gathering in his eyes.

"Miss Selbourne is overwrought," he said quickly. "I am sure Mr. Digby realizes that, and——"

"Miss Selbourne is an ungracious and ill-mannered hoyden," Sir Andrew broke in wrathfully, turning an angry glance upon his daughter. "Go to your room, Joanna, and do not leave it until I give you permission. I shall have something to say to you presently on the subject of obedience and proper conduct."

This, clearly, was a command which admitted of no denial. Joanna's lip quivered, and then, with head defiantly erect, she turned and went into the house. As she passed out of sight Philip addressed himself to Sir Andrew.

"Permit me to take my share of the blame, sir," he said quietly. "My raillery was perhaps ill-timed, for I believe that Miss Selbourne was more badly frightened than she will admit."

"Very probably," Selbourne agreed, "though that does not excuse her conduct. However, enough of that! Come into the house, my boy, and let me present you to my wife. She will be eager to add her thanks to mine."

He gave Philip no chance to decline the invitation, but led him at once indoors, Oliver following them in disgruntled silence. It was plain to Digby that Mr. Stonehurst had taken an instant dislike to him, for reasons which were not far to seek, but he was undisturbed. He had other enemies, more dangerous by far than Oliver Stonehurst could ever be, and he never permitted the thought of them to cause him any disquiet. He was a born adventurer, and revelled in danger.

IV
Activities of Mr. Philip Digby

Since Philip had other and more important matters to occupy his thoughts, his meeting with Miss Selbourne, though not forgotten, was thrust to the back of his mind. On the following morning, however, when he was on the point of sending for his horse in order to continue his exploration of the countryside, the hostess of the inn ushered into the parlour a man whom she announced as the bearer of a message from Greydon Park.

Philip took the note held out to him, and observed with some surprise that it was addressed in a feminine hand. Its contents were brief, and even more surprising. Miss Selbourne would be obliged if Mr. Digby would wait upon her at his earliest convenience.

"Tell Miss Selbourne that I will come immediately," he said, but when the servant had left him, Philip remained where he was, still holding the paper and looking down at it with humorous perplexity.

What mischief, he wondered, was the vivacious Joanna plotting now? Well-bred young ladies did not usually send a peremptory summons to gentlemen whom they had met only once, but his brief experience of Miss Selbourne had convinced him that where propriety clashed with her own wayward wishes, it was propriety which went to the wall.

He realized, with a sense of mild surprise, that he was by no means averse to pursuing the acquaintance which had begun so inauspiciously. She was, of course, atrociously spoiled, but that was not unusual in the only child of elderly parents, and there was a streak of frankness in her character which he found oddly attractive. What this new start might portend, whether some dark scheme of vengeance had taken shape in the lady's undoubtedly fertile imagination, he could not guess, but if her message was in reality a challenge, he would accept it, and let fortune decide who came off best from the encounter.

He rode straight to Greydon Park, but before he had traversed more than half the length of the avenue he saw Miss Selbourne walking towards him. Philip dismounted and bowed, looking appreciatively at her, for against the background of sunlit grass and trees she made a charming picture. She greeted him with a sunny smile and an outstretched hand, which he carried to his lips before releasing it.

"It was good of you to come, sir," she said frankly. "I want to ask your pardon for behaving so badly yesterday. You were quite right to make me change horses with you, for I could not have held the grey, you know. Indeed, I was hardly out of the stableyard before I realized what a foolish thing I had done, and it was very lucky for me that you were at hand. I hope that you will forgive me for treating you so rudely."

This had so much the sound of a prepared speech that Philip's lips twitched involuntarily, but the expression in Joanna's big blue eyes was guileless enough, and he decided to accept her words at face value.

"I had already forgotten it, Miss Selbourne," he replied courteously, "and I trust you will believe that had I thought for one moment that you would have attended to me, I would have suggested that we changed horses, rather than ordering you to do so."

"But I would not have attended," Joanna confessed candidly. "I never do when I am in a rage, and yesterday, to make matters worse, I knew all the time that I was in the wrong, and that vexed me more than ever. Besides, you did try to provoke me, did you not?"

Philip laughed.

"Deliberately," he admitted. "I thought that it might help you to recover from the fright you had had. I make you my apologies."

"And I accept them, sir, so now we may be comfortable." Joanna turned as she spoke and began to retrace her steps towards the house, Philip falling in beside her. "I had no wish to appear ungrateful," she went on, "and I was even more angry with myself than with you. That is why I wanted to ask your pardon."

"Is it?" He looked at her, amusement in his eyes and in his voice. "I thought perhaps this was the punishment inflicted upon you by your father."

"Oh no, nothing of the sort!" Instead of the resentment he half expected, laughter to match his own sparkled in her eyes. "He knew I would do that without being told, once I recovered my temper. My punishment is much, much worse. As long as the grey remains in the stables I am forbidden to ride anything but the old pony I had when I was a child—which means, of course, that I shall not ride at all."

"It also means, does it not, that because of your pranks Sir Andrew feels himself compelled to part with a remarkably fine horse?"

"But he never intended to keep the grey," she said defensively, "although he was bred in our stables. That is why I took him out yesterday. I wanted to ride him just once, before he was sold."

"Even though it was forbidden?"

"Because it was forbidden," she replied earnestly. "Mr. Digby, did you never feel compelled to do a thing, simply because you had been told not to?"

Philip, casting his mind back over a scapegrace boyhood, was obliged to admit that he had, a confession which won him a smile of warm commendation from his companion. He refrained from voicing his opinion that this was a risky philosophy for a lady, and they continued on their way in an atmosphere of cordiality which would have seemed incredible the previous day.

This was immediately obvious to the three riders who presently overtook them, and it afforded one of them no satisfaction at all. The newcomers were Oliver Stonehurst and his sister, and Francis Colyton, whom they had encountered at the gates of Greydon Park and who had fallen in immediately with the suggestion that he should accompany them on their visit to Joanna. They rode at a leisurely pace along the avenue, conversing with the familiarity of life-long friends, but as soon as they came in sight of the couple ahead, Oliver uttered a furious exclamation.

"Hell and the devil! That infernal coxcomb is here again! The fellow who claims to be a friend of your West Indian kinsman, Francis," he added in explanation.

"Digby, do you mean?" Colyton said with some surprise. "Is he acquainted with the Selbournes? I thought my father said that he had only recently arrived in England."

"He has been here long enough to scrape an acquaintance with Joanna," Oliver retorted, and gave him a hasty account of the events of the previous day. Julia, who had already been obliged to listen to a great deal of the same strain, waited with some impatience for him to finish, and then said in her soft, tranquil voice:

"If Joanna was in a temper, Oliver, she was not likely to listen to reason, but she appears to have recovered her spirits now. For pity's sake, try to be civil to Mr. Digby, even if you do not like him."

If Mr. Stonehurst endeavoured to follow this excellent advice, his efforts were not crowned with success. Forthright by nature, he could no more conceal his dislike of Philip than his admiration for Joanna, and the combined effect of these two powerful emotions was disagreeable enough to bring its own punishment upon him. Inexperienced though she was, Joanna infinitely preferred Mr. Digby's easy address to the sullen taciturnity of her old playfellow, and she made no attempt to disguise the fact.

Philip was glad of the chance thus afforded him to make the acquaintance of young Colyton. Francis was something of a surprise to him, and he wondered how deeply the boy was involved in his father's scheming. From village gossip he had already learned something of the situation between Francis and Julia, and realized that more hopes than Bertram's had been dashed by the news of Richard Colyton's existence, though what Miss Stonehurst felt about it he could not guess. She was a statuesque beauty, brown-haired and brown-eyed, with a slow, indolent smile. No more striking contrast to the volatile Joanna could be imagined, and yet they appeared to be the best of friends.

After a while Digby politely but firmly took his leave of

the four young people, and went to pay his respects to Sir Andrew. He did not return, and with his departure a flatness settled over the party. The four of them had been friends from early childhood, but now the easy course of that familiar, close-knit companionship had been disrupted by the intrusion of a new and vigorous personality, and Digby's withdrawal left a curious sense of anticlimax. Julia became pensive, Joanna perverse, and when at length Francis diffidently suggested that it was time to depart, no one made any protest.

Farewells were said, and Miss Stonehurst and her companions rode away, but before the end of the avenue was reached, Oliver was seized by an idea so brilliant that he felt impelled to act upon it without delay. Requesting Francis to escort Julia home—a charge which Colyton accepted with alacrity—he hurried back to the house and asked to see Sir Andrew.

He was pleased to find Joanna with her father, for he fancied he had hit upon a way to restore himself to her favour. The punishment earned by her escapade of the previous day was an irksome one, but it lay in his power to bring it to an end.

"I came back to speak to you about that grey horse, sir," he said, when he had replied to Sir Andrew's greeting. "I should like to buy it from you, if you are agreeable."

Selbourne stared.

"What, another of you?" he exclaimed. "Confound it all, my boy, why did you not say so before? I have just sold the brute to young Digby."

Oliver's lips parted, but for a moment he seemed incapable of speech. A dark flush of mortification spread across his face, and after opening and shutting his mouth several times he said in a strangled voice:

"To Digby? What the devil does he want it for?"

"Presumably to ride." Sir Andrew's surprise was swallowed now in amused comprehension, and though he spoke gravely, his eyes were twinkling. "If he had any other reason for buying it, he did not disclose it to me." He glanced at his daughter, who was looking both surprised and gratified. "Joanna, my dear, your gallants seem determined that you shall not pay the price of your naughtiness."

"I am very grateful to them both," she said decidedly, "but I am glad that Mr. Digby came to you first. I would rather he had the grey than Oliver."

"Would you, Joanna?" Oliver's voice was hurt and reproachful. "May I ask why?"

"Because he is the better rider, and that grey is the very devil to manage," she informed him candidly, but softened this blow to his pride with a smile and an outstretched hand. "I would not like to see you hurt on my account, Oliver."

He took the hand and kissed it fervently, deciding that after all he had had the best of the bargain, since she was obviously indifferent to any risk which Philip Digby might incur in riding the grey. Sir Andrew, viewing this by-play with an indulgent eye, was less certain of the implications of his daughter's words, but chose to hold his peace. He had been mildly irritated of late by Oliver's air of calm possession where Joanna was concerned, and felt that it would do him no harm to be jolted out of it.

During the days which followed, Mr. Digby became a familiar figure in the neighbourhood as, on horseback or afoot, he explored the countryside around Brinkbury village. His interest and energy alike seemed boundless, and his easy, pleasant manners made him welcome wherever he went, so that he was just as likely to be encountered in the kitchen of a labourer's cottage as in the drawing-room of one of the great houses. He was accepted by everyone as a friend of the new Earl whose coming was awaited with such lively curiosity, but any who sought to question him concerning Lord Varne were answered as he had answered Joanna Selbourne; they must wait to form their own judgment.

Bertram Colyton, hearing how completely Digby had fitted himself into the life of the community, was very well pleased, and congratulated himself upon acquiring so resourceful a confederate. When the blow had been struck, and the truth concerning the young man became known, there would be none who dare point an accusing finger in his direction, since they would all have been equally deceived. One thing did cause him a twinge of suspicion, and that was Philip's purchase of the grey horse, for Bertram had supposed him to be too short of money for extravagances of that kind. When challenged, however, Mr. Digby informed him confidently that when the time came, the success or failure of their plot might depend upon the quality of his mount, and that he looked to Mr. Colyton to reimburse him. Bertram, relieved and a trifle amused, agreed without further argument.

The following day saw Philip once more abroad, but this time on foot. He left the inn in the chill crispness of the autumn morning and went at a steady and seemingly tireless pace through the countryside which was already becoming familiar to him, until, an hour or so later, he found himself on the further slopes of the hill where he first encountered Miss Selbourne.

From this side of the hill, where the lower slopes were clothed in extensive woodland, the roof and chimneys of Greydon Park could be clearly seen, and a reminiscent smile touched his lips as he recalled his first visit there. Although since the day of his meeting with Francis Colyton and the Stonehursts he had not been there again, the memory of the daughter of the house had never been far from his thoughts, and now he was conscious of a compelling need to see her again. For a moment or two longer he stood looking towards the distant house, a faint crease between his brows, and then with a shrug and a little laugh started at a brisk pace down the hillside.

In the woods the morning mist still lingered, and the first leaves were falling. Philip found a narrow, winding path which brought him presently to the foot of the hill, and a broad ride which cut through the woods in the direction of Greydon Park. He turned left-handed along it, striding briskly and whistling as he went, and so deep in thought that he passed without observing it a hollow beside the path, screened from it by a clump of bushes, where two men lay stretched beside the dead ashes of a fire.

The sound of his whistling had roused them, but because they had no wish to be discovered they remained silent and motionless until he had passed. Then one of them rose cautiously to his knees and, parting the protecting branches, peered after the merry wayfarer. A muttered oath broke from his lips, and with an urgent gesture he summoned his companion to his side, in time to catch a glimpse of Digby before he passed out of sight around the next bend. They exchanged startled glances.

"By thunder, 'tis him—and alone!" the elder of the two said softly. "There's luck for you, my lad!"

Without waiting for a reply he turned to snatch up the heavy cudgel which had lain all night within reach of his hand. His companion, a pallid, sharp-featured youth in a scarecrow assortment of rags, pulled a pistol from his pocket, but the other saw it and scowled.

"Not that, you fool," he said savagely. "We don't want no noise! Use your cudgel, and be quick about it. If we lose this chance we might not get another."

He pushed through the bushes on to the path, and with his companion at his heels started at a shambling run in the direction Digby had taken. On the grassy track their footsteps were muffled, and they were within a dozen yards of their quarry before the sound of their approach pierced his preoccupation. He wheeled round then, and almost in the same movement dragged his sword from its sheath, and the cold gleam of the steel checked them in their headlong rush.

So for a moment or two they measured each other in silence and utter stillness, and then the elder man leaped forward with cudgel raised. The sword flickered out like the tongue of a snake, driving him back with a red stain on his sleeve, but the wound was no more than a scratch, for at the last moment the stout staff had been shifted from attack to defence, deflecting the deadly point.

Again he advanced, more cautiously this time, and again was forced to retreat, but all the while the pale youth was edging his way round towards Digby's rear, watching for an opportunity to strike while the intended victim was engaged in defending himself from the frontal attack. He

saw his chance at last and darted in, but Philip, glimpsing
the movement from the corner of his eye, swayed aside,
so that the blow aimed at his head instead crashed sicken-
ingly upon his right shoulder. An involuntary cry was
jerked from his lips and he dropped to one knee, the
sword slipping from his numbed fingers.

With an exultant oath his first attacker surged forward,
but in the same instant a piercing scream rang out to halt
him in his tracks. There was a flurry of hoofbeats close at
hand, and a girl's voice cried urgently:

"Father! Oliver! Come quickly, Mr. Digby is being attacked!"

V

The Crossroads

Philip staggered to his feet as a rider dashed past him,
and saw his assailants give way and turn to flee before the
charge of a mounted groom. Then another horse was
brought to a standstill beside him, and he looked up into
Joanna's pale face and wide, frightened eyes. He smiled
wryly at her, and laid his hand on the pommel of the
saddle.

"So you play rescuer in your turn, Miss Selbourne," he
said rather breathlessly. "Believe me, I am grateful."

"Are you hurt?" There was a tremor in her voice, and
she laid her free hand fleetingly upon his. "I saw them
strike you down."

He moved his arm and shoulder cautiously and shook
his head.

"A bruise, no more. Your intervention came in the nick
of time." He looked about him, frowning. "Did I dream
it, or did you call to your father and Mr. Stonehurst as
you rode up?"

"I called to them, but they are not here," she explained. "I thought that if those men believed there were
others behind me, they would run away."

"And thanks to your quick-wittedness, run they did,"
he said, smiling, "but I trust your servant will abandon

the chase before they guess the truth. They may be armed with weapons more deadly than cudgels."

"Who are they, then?" she asked. "Why did they set upon you?"

He shrugged, wincing a little as the movement sent a stab of pain through his shoulder.

"Footpads, no doubt, plying their usual trade," he replied lightly. "I shall walk more warily in future."

"Footpads? Here?" There was astonishment and incredulity in her voice. "Oh, surely not!"

"Poachers, then, fearing to be caught red-handed." Philip turned away to pick up his sword and replace it in the scabbard; his tone was flippant. "They gave me no opportunity to inquire into their identities."

She looked indignant, but any comment she might have made was forestalled by the return of the groom, who informed them with some chagrin that the two men had made off up the hill, where the trees grew too thickly for a horseman to follow.

"I was half minded to go after them on foot, Miss Joanna," he concluded, "but then I thought I'd best come back to see if the gentleman was hurt."

"Just as well that you did," Philip said briskly. "I am not hurt, but your place is with Miss Selbourne." He glanced up at Joanna, laughter glinting in his eyes. "Do not imagine that I am rash enough to forbid it, but I would be a deal easier in my mind if you did not ride through the woods this morning. In fact, unless your errand is important, it might be wiser to go straight home."

"Then to show you, sir, that I am not always self-willed, I will go straight home," she retorted, "but only if you will come with me." He hesitated, and she bent towards him, speaking more seriously. "Please! Those men may still be skulking in the woods."

There was the tiniest pause, and then the swift smile flashed again across his face.

"How can I refuse so charming an invitation? If you are willing to go at walking pace, I will gladly avail myself of it."

"Take my horse, sir!" The groom dismounted, and of-

fered the reins to Philip. "I can walk back by way of the
keeper's cottage, and warn him to keep watch for those
two rogues."

"Yes, do that, Tom," Joanna said approvingly before
Philip could make any reply. "Whoever they were, it is
plain that they are dishonest, and my father will wish every effort to be made to discover them."

The servant touched his forelock and strode away,
while Philip mounted and rode with his fair companion
towards Greydon Park. Joanna appeared to have recovered from her alarm and chattered gaily, but though
Digby maintained an easy flow of conversation, his
thoughts were busy with the morning's adventure.

He was well aware that it had not been an ordinary attempt at robbery, for the elder of his two assailants was
no stranger to him. It had been a considerable shock to
see the stocky figure and ugly, mahogany-coloured face of
Ned Mullett in the incongruous setting of an English
woodland, for their last encounter had taken place against
a very different and far more exotic background, although
it had much the same purpose and outcome as this morning's meeting. Philip realized that he had been guilty of
carelessness, born of a false sense of security, but he
would not be so again. If Ned Mullett had successfully
trailed him as far as England, others might well have
done the same, and he could expect some lively moments
in the immediate future.

He saw difficulties looming ahead, and a gleam of
reckless anticipation stole into his eyes. Difficulties were
made to overcome, and it was fruitless to tax one's mind
with unanswerable questions.

At Greydon Park, where at Sir Andrew's insistent invitation he stayed to dine, he dismissed the attack upon him
as a matter of no importance, a trifling mishap which
could have happened to anyone, but his host could not
agree with him. Outraged by the thought of such an incident occurring on his land, almost at his very gates, and
involving a man to whom he considered himself deeply in-
debted, Sir Andrew lost no time in taking measures to discover the miscreants. Lady Selbourne, meanwhile, was

filled with concern for the hurts which she felt sure Mr. Digby had sustained, and was with difficulty convinced that these were negligible. Philip, doing his best to soothe both the indignation and the anxiety, could only hope that Ned Mullett was sufficiently wily to evade capture.

He accepted the loan of a horse to carry him back to Brinkbury, and, more reluctantly, the escort of the groom who was to bring the animal home again. When he reached the inn he went straight to his bedchamber and took from a locked drawer a pistol which he primed and loaded before slipping it into his pocket. That morning he had been taken unawares for the first and, he hoped, the last time.

He could see no reason to abandon his systematic exploration of the countryside, and next morning sent for his horse as though nothing had occurred. The animal was already at the door, and Philip himself descending the stairs on his way out of the inn, when to his surprise the door opened and Miss Selbourne came tripping into the narrow, stone-flagged passage.

She paused when she saw him and gave him a dazzling smile, colour rising faintly in her cheeks. He went quickly down the remaining stairs to greet her, but his own smile of welcome faded as, looking beyond her in the expectation of seeing Sir Andrew, he glimpsed through the open door only the servant who had attended her the previous day, in charge of his own horse and Joanna's black mare.

"I am on my way to visit Julia Stonehurst," she informed him airily, "but I could not pass without inquiring whether you had recovered from yesterday's misadventure. Ellen told me that you were just about to ride out."

Ellen was the landlord's daughter, a pretty, empty-headed girl of about Joanna's age, who chattered incessantly. Philip had no doubt that within a matter of hours the whole village would know that Miss Selbourne had come alone to visit him, and be commenting upon such unconventional conduct. In the faint hope of saving the situation, he said, with more formality than he had ever used with her before:

"Such concern, madam, does me too much honour. I

am deeply grateful to Sir Andrew and Lady Selbourne, but they need not have burdened you with such an errand for so trifling a cause."

Some of the radiance faded from Joanna's face, to be replaced by a look of hurt bewilderment. She said quickly, with the air of one correcting a misapprehension: "Oh, they did not tell me to come, though they will be glad to know that all is well with you. I wanted to be sure of it myself."

It was clear that the warning which he had tried to convey by words and manner had been either ignored or not understood, and while he was trying to think of some way of repeating it, the clatter of hoofs and wheels in the street outside indicated that a coach was drawing up before the inn. The sound spurred him to swift action, for it was plain that Miss Selbourne's disastrous frankness would not be curbed by any considerations of discretion. The door of the parlour was close at hand, and without hesitation he flung it open and ushered her into the empty room, hoping as he did so that the occupants of the coach did not intend to enter the inn.

He closed the door and turned to face his companion, who was standing rather stiffly in the middle of the room. She met his eyes with a look of mingled indignation and reproach in her own.

"You are vexed with me, Mr. Digby," she said challengingly. "Why?"

"No, I am not!" He came across the room towards her as he spoke. "How could I be vexed, when only kindheartedness prompted this visit? I am concerned because you have come seeking me here with only a servant to attend you. Surely you know that such conduct is unwise?"

Joanna's expression cleared as if by magic, and she gave a little ripple of laughter.

"Oh, you are thinking of my reputation," she exclaimed merrily, "but what harm, pray, have I done to that? No one in the village will think any the worse of me for calling upon you. Why, they have known me all my life!"

"Yes, but they have not known me," he retorted ruefully. "My dear child, do you not realize that while you might treat Oliver Stonehurst or young Colyton with this informality, you ought to use more discretion where a stranger is concerned?"

She looked up mischievously beneath her lashes, but before she could utter whatever reply was hovering on her lips, a brisk step sounded in the passage, the door opened, and after one instant of silence a man's voice said with icy mockery:

"A thousand pardons, Miss Selbourne! Your servant told me that you were within, but neglected to warn me against intruding upon you."

With Joanna's startled gasp in his ears, Philip spun round to face the speaker. Framed in the open doorway, one hand still upon the latch, stood a tall man dressed with careless elegance, a silk-lined cloak hanging loose from his shoulders. Powdered hair formed a striking contrast to a dark, harsh-featured face, and hard grey eyes cynically regarded the couple before him. He and Philip looked at each other, and antagonism, instant and bitter, leapt like a flame between them.

"Sir?" Digby spoke quietly, but there was a note of deadly inquiry in his crisp voice which even Joanna recognized as a danger signal. She laid a restraining hand on his arm.

"There is no question of intrusion, Mr. Trayle," she replied, and Philip glanced at her in quick surprise, for though she spoke with a hint of breathlessness, there was a composure in voice and manner which was oddly mature. "This is a public room, and you have every right to walk into it if you choose."

"I stand corrected, madam." Gregory Trayle strolled forward, the faint, half-sneering smile which she had always detested just curving his lips. "I should be disconsolate if I thought that I had caused you any embarrassment."

"I do not know why you should think it," she retorted lightly. "Now permit me to make Mr. Digby known to you. He is a friend of your kinsman, Lord Varne."

"Indeed?" Trayle's hard glance had been fixed upon the small hand still resting on Philip's sleeve, but now he looked up quickly at the other man's face. "Am I to infer from that that my colonial relative has arrived to claim his inheritance?"

"No, sir, you are not," Philip replied shortly. "It is not yet known when Lord Varne will reach England. I merely await his coming."

"And beguile the time most pleasantly meanwhile," Gregory murmured. "You are to be congratulated, Mr. Digby."

There was a brief pause. Philip's temper, which when roused was of a violence to match his colouring, was rising rapidly, but for Joanna's sake he forced himself to control it. Harmless village gossip was one thing; to allow himself to be provoked into a quarrel on her account was quite another, and would be anything but harmless.

"Miss Selbourne is on her way to Foxwood Grange," he said carelessly, "and knowing that I was also bidden there, was kind enough to offer to guide me, since I am a stranger to the village. I fear, however, that I have been guilty of the discourtesy of keeping her waiting."

"Which accounts for her presence in this room," Trayle concluded softly. "There is an explanation for everything, is there not?" He turned to Joanna. "Miss Selbourne, I must not detain you longer, or I shall incur Miss Stonehurst's displeasure. I am bound for Brinkbury House, but I shall give myself the pleasure of waiting upon Lady Selbourne tomorrow, if that is agreeable to you."

"Of course, sir. You are always welcome," she replied civilly, though without enthusiasm, and the mockery deepened in his face as he bowed an acknowledgment, and then turned again to the door to open it for her.

He followed them from the inn and stood watching while they mounted their horses. Philip had told the ostler to fetch out the grey horse, which he had named El Diablo, and Trayle ran a shrewd, appraising eye over the animal as the younger man swung up into the saddle. Then he lifted his gaze to the rider's face, and once more the hostility which had been born in their first exchange of glances quivered like a tangible thing between them.

"I am delighted to have made your acquaintance, Mr. Digby," he said sardonically. "No doubt we shall meet again."

"No doubt," Philip agreed pleasantly, and smiled, cold-eyed, into the sneering face. Then he touched El Diablo with the spur and rode after Joanna along the village street.

She looked up with a fleeting smile as he reached her side, but neither spoke until the last houses had been left behind. Then the groom fell back out of earshot, and after another moment or two of silence Joanna said vehemently:

"I dislike Gregory Trayle more than anyone I have ever met. How dare he say such things, and look at me in such a way!"

"His manner is certainly not conciliatory," Philip agreed.

He had deliberately banished all expression from his voice, but Joanna looked at him with quick understanding.

"And because *I* was there you had to bear with him, instead of answering him as he deserved," she said. "I put you in an intolerable position, and I am truly sorry."

His expression relaxed a little, and he glanced humorously at her.

"Prove it by using some discretion in future," he suggested. "Tell me, Miss Selbourne, does Trayle come often to Brinkbury?"

"Oh yes, quite often," she replied with a sigh. "His home is not far from here, you know, although he used to spend a great deal of time in London. I once heard my father say that when Mr. Trayle came to Gloucestershire it meant either that his creditors had grown too pressing or his affairs of honour too numerous, but during the past year he has been here nearly all the time."

"Is he a close friend of his cousins at Brinkbury House?"

Joanna looked doubtful.

"Of Mr. Colyton, perhaps," she said slowly, "but Fran-

cis does not like him, I know. Mr. Trayle is always jeering
at him, and trying to make him look foolish."

Philip found no difficulty in believing this. Though a
man of Trayle's type might have a good deal in common
with the elder Mr. Colyton, the dreamy, sensitive Francis
would seem to him a natural target for mockery. Instead
of pursuing the subject, however, he said briskly:

"The road to Foxwood Grange, I believe, joins this one
a short way ahead. I will leave you at the crossroads, for
if Trayle is bound for Brinkbury House he will not come
this way."

"Why not come with me?" Joanna suggested. "Mr.
Stonehurst, I know, is anxious to make your acquaintance."

"The devil he is!" Philip spoke between amusement
and disbelief. "May I ask why?"

Miss Selbourne chuckled.

"Because you are Lord Varne's friend, and he still has
hopes of seeing one of his daughters a Countess," she replied candidly. "He is one of the scheming parents you so
despise."

"So I have already heard," Philip said with a grin, "but
what of Miss Stonehurst herself? Is she a willing pawn in
her father's game?"

"I do not know," Joanna confessed reluctantly. "She
made no protest as long as Francis was the husband
chosen for her, but now that he is no longer the heir, Mr.
Stonehurst will scarcely permit them to meet. Perhaps she
is waiting to see what Lord Varne is like."

"Perhaps she is," Philip agreed. He laughed softly, as
though at some secret jest. "If he is not to her liking, do
you suppose that she would refuse him, in spite of his ex-
alted rank?"

"No, never in the world!" Joanna replied with conviction. "She would weep, and plead with her father, but she
would never defy him. She is a dear creature, but with no
spirit at all."

"Whereas Miss Selbourne, having a great deal of spirit,
would never submit so tamely to parental tyranny?"

Philip glanced sidelong at her as he spoke, and saw her lift her head defiantly.

"Indeed I would not," she said emphatically, "but my father would never compel me to marry a man I disliked, just because he had a title to offer me. He has promised me that I shall choose my own husband."

Digby was startled, and showed it, for this was contrary to every notion of what was proper. He had heard Sir Andrew described as eccentric, and knew beyond all doubt that he spoiled his daughter, but this was carrying indulgence to the last extreme.

"A rash promise," he murmured. "You might so easily choose unwisely."

"Well, I do not say that he would let me marry a man of whom he disapproved," she admitted, "but at least he would not force me into marriage against my will. Take Oliver, for example. He wants to marry me, and Father would be quite pleased if I accepted him, but he does not try to influence me in any way."

The crossroads lay only a short way ahead. With his gaze intent on the crest of the hill high above them, Philip said quietly:

"Let us suppose that Varne has the good taste to seek your hand. Can you say truly that his rank and honours would mean nothing to you?"

"Yes, I can," Joanna answered firmly, without hesitation. "Of what use would these things be to me, if I did not love him?"

"And if you did?" Philip's eyes were still lifted to the hilltop, and he did not see the look she turned towards him, or the wise little smile that touched her lips for a moment.

"If I did," she said softly, "nothing else would matter at all."

He did not reply, and they rode on without speaking until they reached the spot where four roads met, on the side of the hill above the village. There they drew rein, and Joanna pointed along the road to the right.

"That leads to Foxwood Grange," she said. "Do you come with me, sir?"

His brows lifted.

"To help Miss Stonehurst to a coronet?" he asked lightly.

"No!" Joanna's eyes lifted to meet his; there was a heightened colour in her cheeks. "Because I want you to come."

There was a moment of silence. The groom had halted a discreet distance away and was lost in contemplation of a nearby flock of sheep; the wind raised little swirls and eddies of dust from the four white roads, and swift flying clouds bathed the scene alternately in sunshine and shadow. Philip felt a sudden conviction that this was a moment of decision, that without warning he had been confronted with a choice of great import and far-reaching consequences.

He looked to the right, along the road that climbed and dipped and climbed again towards the gates of Foxwood Grange, and then at the other ways, along any of which he would have to ride alone. Finally his gaze returned to Joanna's face and found anxiety in her eyes, as though she, too, was aware of the importance of the choice. Suddenly he smiled.

"I will come with you," he said simply, and swung El Diablo to the right. Side by side, the grey horse and the black moved forward along the same road.

VI

The Cousins

Gregory Trayle stood in front of the inn and watched Miss Selbourne and her companion until they passed from sight. Then, with a curt word to his servants, he re-entered his coach, and the journey was resumed.

Within a very shore while he alighted again at the door of Brinkbury House, where he was informed that though Mr. Colyton was at present from home, Mr. Francis could be found within. Trayle nodded, and strode through the house with the air of one long familiar with his surroundings.

He found Francis seated at a table, a pen in his hand and a half-written letter before him. He looked up quickly as his cousin came into the room, and an expression which was anything but welcoming crossed his handsome face.

"So you are here again, are you?" he remarked. "What is it this time, money you owe or a man you have killed?"

"Charming as ever, eh, Francis?" Gregory said sardonically. "You must not overwhelm me with the warmth of your welcome, you know."

He strolled forward to lean against the table, and with a swift, defensive movement Francis swept his letter out of sight. Trayle's lips twisted mockingly.

"Be easy, I do not wish to read your amorous vapourings," he sneered. "They may possibly amuse Miss Stonehurst, but I am reasonably sure that they would nauseate me."

"You are always so successful in these matters, are you not?" Francis retorted. He leaned back in his chair, brushing the feather of his pen to and fro against his chin, studying the other's face with thoughtful eyes. "It seems to me that you are in an even more unpleasant mood than usual. What's amiss?"

There was a brief pause. Gregory took an enamelled snuffbox from his pocket, held it, unopened, in his hand, looking down at it with a slight frown. At length he said abruptly:

"What can you tell me of a man named Digby? An impudent, red-headed fellow who claims to be a friend of our unknown and unwanted kinsman?"

"Oh, so you have fallen foul of him already, have you?" Comprehension and a glimmer of malicious amusement crept into Francis's eyes. "What happened?"

Gregory's lips tightened.

"I found him at the inn, in close and very private conversation with Joanna Selbourne. I saw her servant waiting with the horses as I came past, and halted to say a word of greeting. My arrival was obviously ill-timed."

"You mean she had gone there to see him?" There was more resignation than surprise in Francis's voice.

"Froward little baggage! What will she be at next, I wonder?"

Trayle took a pinch of snuff, and shut the box with a snap. He said curtly, "I am still waiting for you to tell me who Digby is, and why he is here."

Francis told him, but as his knowledge was no greater than that of anyone else in the village, his father excepted, the information left Mr. Trayle little wiser than before. The frown still lingered in his eyes when Francis had done, but it held more perplexity than ill-humour.

"If Digby, too, had come from America," he said slowly, "how does it happen that he is here so far ahead of Varne?"

Francis shrugged.

"He set out before Varne did, I suppose."

"Then why, if they are such close friends, did they not travel together?"

"Oh, devil take it, Gregory, how should I know? I have not met the fellow above twice. If you are curious concerning him, take your questions to my father."

Gregory's eyes narrowed.

"So Bertram also is on terms with Mr. Digby," he said softly. "Now how comes that about?"

"When Digby found that Varne had not yet arrived, he came seeking news of him here. That was natural, of course, since we are Varne's kinsfolk."

"Of course," Trayle agreed smoothly. "What then?"

"I was not here at the time, but it seems that they were closeted together for some while, and no doubt Digby gave my father the full story then. I met him the next day at Greydon Park, and a few days later he dined with us here. I must confess that I find him likable."

"And you are not alone in that opinion?" Trayle's voice was still soft, but there was an edge to the quiet words. "It seems to me that you have all been singularly credulous. What proof have you that Digby is in fact what he pretends to be?"

Francis stared.

"If he is not, I'm damned if I can see what profit he looks for in his masquerade."

"You can never see anything, Francis, unless it is made so plain that an imbecile child could understand it! It is obvious that Digby has some sort of claim upon Varne. He is a creditor, perhaps, or he knows something which Varne would prefer to keep secret. Good God! did it occur to none of you to seek below the surface?"

During this speech the door had swung softly open, revealing Bertram Colyton upon the threshold, and when Gregory paused, the elder man said with some amusement:

"You are heated, cousin! What makes you suppose that we are so easily duped?"

Francis chuckled.

"Gregory has discovered, sir, that Philip Digby finds favour in Joanna's eyes, and so he will admit nothing to his credit," he explained maliciously. "He is in a rare ill-humour, as you can see."

"The pangs of jealousy, Gregory?" Bertram inquired with mock concern, closing the door and coming farther into the room. "Upon my soul, I never suspected that your heart as well as your head was concerned in that affair!"

"This is to be humorous, I suppose!" Trayle's voice was contemptuous, but his eyes, fixed upon his cousin's plump, pale face, held a deepening glimmer of suspicion beneath the mockery which filled them. "You may find less cause for jesting if it transpires that you have given countenance to an imposter."

"If he is an imposter, he is a singularly harmless one," Bertram replied mildly, "for he has neither used Varne's name to obtain credit, not attempted to gain access to his house."

"He has not been slow, however, to gain access to every other house of note in the neighbourhood," Gregory said with a sneer. "Suppose that Varne and Digby do know each other as intimately as he claims. How do you know that Varne is glad of the acquaintance? It will be a trifle awkward if you find that you have made welcome some by-blow of his father's, whose sole aim is to establish a kinship which Varne himself is only too eager to deny."

"That is possible, I suppose," Francis said dubiously. "If it were so, his purpose would be to establish himself so securely before Varne's arrival that he could not be easily denied, and that, without doubt, he is in a fair way to achieving."

There was dismay in his voice, but his father's calm remained unimpaired. He lowered himself into a chair and regarded his two companions with tolerant amusement.

"All things are possible," he said easily, "even that Digby is precisely what he says he is—a close boyhood friend of Varne's. I find nothing incredible in his story, and neither did anyone else until Gregory came here with wild surmises born of a sense of pique." He shook his head with mock regret. "It is not worthy of you, cousin! I had always supposed your methods of dealing with a rival to be far more direct."

A saturnine smile touched Trayle's lips.

"I can be direct when the occasion demands it," he said shortly, "as Digby may yet learn to his cost. This is not, however, a mere question of rivalry. I have every intention of establishing cordial relations with Varne, and as the first step towards them I mean to discover more concerning this fellow Digby than you have troubled yourself to ascertain. He has the stamp of an adventurer."

"And what if you are mistaken?" Francis queried derisively. "It will scarcely make for cordiality if Varne discovers that you have been hounding his best friend with impertinent inquiries."

"If Digby is honest, I will admit it," Gregory replied with a shrug, "and if he is not, I shall see to it that he does no harm. In either event, Varne will perceive that I have his interests most sincerely at heart."

"Well, in my opinion you will succeed only in making a fool of yourself," Francis said frankly, rising to his feet and picking up the letter he had been writing. "To my mind, it would be a good thing if Digby did get the better of you. You are too damned sure of yourself, and that's the truth!"

"Envious, Francis?" Trayle asked softly as his cousin went past him and out of the room, but he spoke absently, the baiting of Francis being a habit with him. His thoughts were elsewhere. Bertram had not spoken since Gregory announced his intention of proving the truth or falsity of Philip Digby's story, and the younger man had not failed to observe the expression of annoyance and mild dismay which had passed across his face for one incautious moment. Suspicion grew within him, and to put it to the test he continued carelessly: "Now how to set about this business, I wonder? A word dropped in Coleford's ear, perhaps? If there is trickery afoot, Varne's lawyer should be warned of it."

He was watching Bertram closely as he spoke, and had his reward in a perceptible deepening of the dismay in the sleepy eyes. Colyton said shortly: "You are determined, are you not, to stand well with Varne when he arrives? May I ask why?"

"I should have thought my reasons were obvious. Varne is young. He will not desire to spend all his time in this Godforsaken spot, and when he goes to London he will need a friend who is familiar with the way of the world. Who better fitted for that rôle than I?"

"You are certainly in a position to introduce him to all the more expensive pleasures of the town," Bertram agreed caustically. "So you would play bear-leader to this cub, would you?"

"Adviser, mentor and friend," Gregory replied lightly. "You know as well as I do, cousin, that if this raw lad from his barbaric island is left to his own devices, he will become the prey of every adventurer and trollop in London. Do you wish to see the Colyton fortune dissipated in such a manner?"

"No," Mr. Colyton admitted, "but neither have I any desire to see it flowing into your pockets. I am still Varne's heir."

Gregory laughed shortly.

"Heir to a man young enough to be your son, who is presumably in the best of health," he retorted. "A barren prospect, my friend, the more so since it is unlikely that he will remain unmarried. No, Bertram, if you are hoping to inherit our kinsman's rank and fortune, I fear you will be disappointed." He paused, and then added softly, "Unless, of course, you intend once more to unsurp the function of destiny."

There was a little silence, and then Colyton said quietly: "You mean. . . ?"

"I mean that Charles, too, was young and healthy and on the point of marriage when your minion, Trevor, crossed his path; and Charles died. Now another young man stands in your way, and you have found a new henchman in this fellow Digby." His eyes, shrewd and penetrating, were upon his cousin's face, and the sneering smile twisted his mouth. "A perilous heritage, this earldom of Varne!"

This time the silence was more prolonged. Bertram sat motionless, his chin sunk upon the folds of his neckcloth, the heavy lids hiding whatever expression was in his eyes. After waiting several moments for him to speak, Trayle went on:

"My suggestion that Digby's story should be investigated was unwelcome to you. Why, unless you have something to hide? Digby is a friend of the new Earl, we are told. You accept him as such, and it follows that others accept him also. Selbourne and Stonehurst make him free of their houses. Everyone agrees that he is a pleasant fellow. I will own that as yet I do not see clearly what purpose you have in mind, but that it bodes anything but ill for Varne I cannot believe."

"Tell me one thing!" Colyton spoke without looking up. "Where do you stand in this?"

"Midway between the pair of you at present," Gregory replied frankly, "waiting to discover in which direction lies my greatest hope of profit. I have told you my intentions where Varne is concerned, but I am willing to alter my plans if you can prove to me that it would be worthwhile to do so."

"And if I cannot, or will not prove it?"

"Then I must set inquiries afoot concerning Philip Digby. Suspicion is never hard to arouse." He leaned back in the chair into which he had thrown himself, regarding the other man with hard, mocking eyes. "You know, Bertram, it would really be more prudent for you to tell me what scheme you have in mind."

Bertram raised his head and looked at him with acute dislike. He had not the smallest desire to admit a third person to the plot hatched by Philip Digby, but, as Gregory had pointed out, suspicion was fatally easy to arouse and he could afford no doubts to be cast on Digby's integrity. Reluctantly, and with deep misgivings, he outlined the plot against the Earl's life.

"So Digby nurses a grudge against Varne, does he?" Gregory remarked when the tale was told. "Do you suppose he is to be trusted?"

Bertram shrugged.

"I find his story likely enough."

"Oh, I have no quarrel with his story. The only inconsistency I perceive lies in the fact that though he is ready to risk the gallows to avenge his dead love, he is not averse to pursuing Joanna Selbourne meanwhile."

"Look for his motive in your own. She is heiress to Sir Andrew's wealth."

"True, but how can he hope to make himself master of it while he is engaged in this other business? Even if Digby makes his escape, Selbourne will never permit their marriage once the truth is known, and Digby would not risk burdening himself with a woman on such an errand as his."

"Joanna Selbourne is wilfulness itself," Bertram replied drily, "and when she resolves to marry a man, marry him she will, no matter what obstacles stand in the way."

"Selbourne might disown her."

"Never! He might threaten it, but to him and to his wife Joanna is the whole world. They would go to any lengths for her sake, and to avoid a lasting estrangement from her."

"To any lengths," Gregory said as though to himself. "Yes, I believe they would."

His tone was pensive. Bertram looked at him with grave misgiving, and said shortly:

"This matter to which you have forced me to admit you is one of extreme delicacy, and I will not have it imperilled by any hare-brained scheme of yours involving Digby or the girl. Oblige me by remembering that."

Gregory looked at him in silence for a moment or two. There was a dangerous expression in his face, the eyes cold and slightly narrowed, the sneer more pronounced than ever on his thin lips.

"I will do nothing to imperil your precious plot," he said contemptuously. "You have convinced me that the greater profit lies with you. Only understand one thing, Bertram. Where Joanna Selbourne is concerned I permit no one to dictate to me; not you, nor Digby, nor Selbourne, nor even Joanna herself. Remember that!"

With unshaken calm Colyton's sleepy gaze met the cold, hard, menacing eyes of his kinsman. He said reflectively:

"For once I find myself in complete agreement with Francis. You are too sure of yourself, too sure by far. One day you will underestimate an opponent, and that will be your ruin."

Trayle laughed, quietly and confidently.

"Not wrought by you, Bertram," he retorted softly, and Colyton shook his head.

"No," he said, and smiled with a hint of grimness, "we know each other too well for that, I fear. I was thinking rather of Philip Digby. It is my belief that you would be well advised to walk warily in your dealings with that young man."

VII

Rendezvous at Sunset

The visit to Foxwood Grange was not an unqualified success. Mr. Stonehurst and his stout, indolent wife were certainly delighted to welcome the uninvited guest, but their son made no attempt to hide his disgust at the intrusion. He had been looking forward to Joanna's visit, supposing that in his own home at least he would be safe from the unwelcome presence of Mr. Digby, and his disappointment found an outlet in a display of ill-humour acutely embarrassing to his companions.

Mr. Stonehurst, eager to learn all he could about Richard Colyton, endeavoured to draw Mr. Digby out upon that subject, but though the young man was willing enough to talk of life in the New World, he skilfully avoided introducing a more personal note into the conversation. To Oliver, this suggested that Digby had something to conceal, and presently, some matter having taken his father from the room while his mother fell into a doze beside the fire, he said abruptly:

"It would seem, sir, that though you are willing to deliver a lecture upon the geography and inhabitants of America, you are less ready to tell us anything of your own past history. I wonder why!"

There was a brief and somewhat startled silence, and then Philip replied easily:

"I was not aware, sir, that I was delivering a lecture, but if that is how my conversation appeared to you, I make you my apologies. There is only one thing more tedious than a man who holds forth at length upon some subject with which he happens to be familiar."

"And what is that, Mr. Digby?" Julia inquired, casting a reproving glance at her brother.

There was a hint of mockery now in Philip's smile.

"A man, Miss Stonehurst, who can talk of nothing but himself. It is only those with too great an opinion of their own importance who imagine that their quite unremarkable life-stories are of as much interest to others as to themselves."

Julia looked amused at this swift rejoinder, but it was Joanna's ripple of laughter which caused Oliver to lose his precarious hold upon his temper. That laughter, he knew, was at his expense; it was the final humiliation.

"And it is only those with something to hide who so constantly avoid any mention of their past," he sneered. "Better to be an honest fool than a clever rogue!"

Philip continued to smile, but his direct and brilliant

gaze, now fast upon Oliver's face, held more scorn than amusement.

"You speak with authority, I am sure," he said softly. "Your honesty can never have been in doubt."

"Never, thank God!" Oliver retorted hotly, and then broke off as the deeper implications of Digby's words dawned upon him. Rage and mortification darkened his face, and one hand clawed at the hilt of his sword. "Hell and the devil, do you call me a fool?"

"Oliver!" Julia spoke sharply, in indignation and alarm. "Mr. Digby is our guest."

The reminder checked his blind fury for a moment, and in that moment Philip rose and turned courteously towards her. His manner was perfectly composed, but she could see with what difficulty he was restraining his temper.

"That is a fact which I was myself in danger of forgetting, Miss Stonehurst," he said quietly. "Perhaps it will be best if I take my leave."

She looked distressed, but made no effort to dissuade him. With another reproachful glance at her brother, she replied in a low voice:

"You must do as you think best, sir. I can only tell you how sorry I am that you should have met with such discourtesy in this house." She got up, and went across to her mother's chair. "Mama, Mr. Digby is leaving us now."

Mrs. Stonehurst awoke with a start, to find her visitor already bowing before her. Too flustered to perceive the atmosphere of strain which pervaded the room, she gave him her hand, assuring him in the same breath of her regret at the brevity of his visit and the pleasure she would derive from a repetition of it. He made some civil reply, and turned to take leave of Miss Selbourne, while Mrs. Stonehurst overwhelmed her son and daughter with conflicting instructions concerning the departing guest.

Philip was bowing over Joanna's hand; she tugged at his fingers and said in a fierce whisper:

"I will come with you."

He gave a quick, decisive shake of his head. He was

frowning, and for once she could see no laughter in his eyes.

"It would make matters worse," he replied briefly in the same tone. Joanna looked mutinous, but something in his manner warned her of the futility of argument or defiance, and she said no more. A moment or two later the door closed behind him.

On leaving Foxwood Grange, Philip turned El Diablo towards the high, bare crests of the hills, letting the great horse have its head and finding, in the exhilaration of that wild gallop, an outlet for the anger seething within him. At last, when his temper had cooled, he checked his headlong pace and began to reflect upon all that had occurred since his arrival in Brinkbury.

At least his brief stay had not proved uneventful, he mused, the irrepressible laughter creeping again into his eyes. Bertram Colyton's readiness to join in the murderous plot against the new Earl; the unlooked-for arrival of his old enemy, Ned Mullett; the acquisition of at least two new enemies in the persons of Oliver Stonehurst and Gregory Trayle. All these things combined to create the sort of situation he most enjoyed, his own wits against the world, with a spice of danger thrown in for good measure; and if he had made enemies, he had also made friends.

Joanna! A rueful smile touched his lips for a moment at the thought of her, for that was a complication he had not foreseen. He had not guessed, when he came to the pleasant, placid village among the hills, that he would find there the prize for which, almost without knowing it, he had been seeking throughout his adventurous career. The one woman in the world for him, who had swept from his heart and from his mind even the memory of others whom he had thought he loved. An impulsive, headstrong child with, at times, a quaint dignity all her own, and with courage and honesty looking out of her clear blue eyes. Joanna, he felt certain, would follow her heart's call to the ends of the earth, but Sir Andrew Selbourne would not give his daughter to a stranger, and if he guessed the truth it might well mean an end to their meetings. Yet

guess it he must, sooner or later; how long, in a small
country village, could such a secret be kept?

He rode far afield that day, halting to dine at an inn in
one of the little grey stone towns scattered among the
hills, and not returning to Brinkbury until after darkness
had fallen. Next morning he set off again, and though
temptation was strong upon him to visit Greydon Park, he
forced himself to resist it, for he remembered that Gregory Trayle had spoken of calling there that day. The less
he saw of both Trayle and Oliver Stonehurst, the safer it
would be, for to become embroiled in an open quarrel at
this stage would be disastrous.

So, resolutely, he turned his back upon Greydon, and
rode instead towards Bristol. It seemed likely that when
Varne arrived to claim his inheritance, it was from this
direction that he would come, for it was in Bristol that
John Coleford, the lawyer, lived.

Philip came back to the Colyton Arms midway through
the afternoon, and found a messenger awaiting him. In
accordance with his usual custom, he had ridden straight
into the stableyard so that he might supervise the tending
of his horse, but as he was about to follow the ostler into
the stables, a hand plucked at his sleeve, and he turned to
find a round-faced lad of about fifteen at his side. The
newcomer introduced himself as Jem Roberts, a stable-lad
at Greydon Park, and informed Philip that Miss Joanna
had sent him with a message which she dare not set down
on paper. Would Mr. Digby meet her at sunset at the
Queen's Oak?

He was palpably nervous, and for a moment or two
Philip stood looking at him in frowning silence. The
whole business savoured strongly of a plot, and yet the
message was certainly one which Joanna might have sent,
jestingly, in response to his advice to her to be more
discreet, or in earnest, if some sort of trouble had befallen
her.

Suddenly he remembered Gregory Trayle's intended
visit to Greydon Park. If, out of malice, Trayle had spoken of their encounter the previous day, and hinted at a
budding intrigue between Joanna and Digby, Sir Andrew's

suspicions might have been aroused. With a silent male-
diction on the chance which had brought Mr. Trayle upon
them, Philip turned his attention once more to the boy.

"Where is the place you call the Queen's Oak?" he
asked abruptly.

" 'Tis in the woods just north of the Park, sir," Jem explained, "not far from where you was set on two days
ago. About half-way between there and the edge of the
woods a path leads away to the right. Follow that for a
quarter of a mile, and you come to a great oak tree standing by itself in a hollow. That's the Queen's Oak, sir."

Philip nodded, still watching him narrowly.

"Does the path end there?"

"Oh no, sir. It goes on as far as a gate in the orchard
wall."

"And that is the way Miss Joanna will come?"

"I—I suppose so, sir. 'Tis only a step, as you might
say."

"Very well. You may tell her that I will be there."

He took a coin from his pocket and offered it to the
boy. Jem accepted it with an odd reluctance but made no
move to go. Philip's brows lifted.

"Have you more to tell me?"

"No, sir." Still he hesitated, and then added with a
rush: "You'll need to go afoot from the Broad Ride, sir.
The path's not fit for a horse."

He made off without waiting for a reply, and Philip
shrugged and turned away. If the message was a trap
there were several people in the neighbourhood of Brinkbury who might have set it, and the only way to learn the
truth was to keep the assignation.

He reached the Broad Ride without incident, and passing the place where Mullett and his crony had attacked
him, came after a little while to the path Jem Roberts had
described. It sloped steeply down through the woods, a
narrow track, dark and forbidding, thickly overgrown
with trees and already almost in darkness, although the
sinking sun was still gilding the topmost branches with a
ruddy glow. Philip tethered his horse at the edge of the
ride, and after standing for a few seconds to listen in-

tently, stepped forward into the mouth of the uninviting path.

The shadows closed softly about him, and it might have been perceived, had there been any to see, that a surprising change had come over the debonair Mr. Digby. In the woods he moved as though he were as completely at home there as any animal, going forward silently as a wraith, with never the rattle of a stone or snap of a broken twig to betray his passing. Not for nothing had he lived and fought along the wild frontiers of the American colonies, and if the message which brought him here was indeed the bait in a trap, those who had set the snare might learn that they had chosen an ill place for it. He came at length to the edge of the hollow where the Queen's Oak stood, and halted there, still hidden among the trees, to study the scene before him with keen, appraising eyes.

He had seldom seen a likelier place for an ambush. The little depression was not more than a score of yards across and surrounded on every side by steep slopes thickly clothed with trees and undergrowth. The vast, gnarled oak tree stood, not in the centre of the hollow as he had expected, but to the left of it, so that the tangled greenery grew right up to one side of its massive trunk. On the other, the path went winding beneath the spreading branches to climb the far slope, where almost at once it was lost to view among the trees. The silence was profound, and the shadows already so thick that only by looking straight up through the twining boughs could Philip tell, by the golden light at their crests, that the sun had not yet set.

How long he stood there, motionless as the trees about him, he could not tell, but suddenly a sound which was not natural to the woodland reached his ears. Someone was coming along the path from the direction of Greydon Park, and coming, it seemed, with more haste than caution. Philip's hand slid into his pocket, and closed about the butt of the pistol there. He drew the weapon out, and cocked it with infinite care.

The hurrying footsteps drew nearer, checked to sudden

stillness, and then after a moment of aching suspense advanced more hurriedly than before. A shower of loose earth, scattered by a hasty foot, pattered among the leaves, and then Joanna appeared at the turn of the path on the far side of the hollow, and halted there, in surprise or disappointment at finding the rendezvous deserted.

For perhaps ten seconds she stood there, a hand at her throat, her gown glimmering faintly through the shadows below the dark cloak caught about her, and then she came forward again, but slowly this time, with hesitation in her steps. Philip moved at last, and with the pistol still in his hand stepped clear of the trees, and softly spoke her name.

She gave a little cry in which gladness and dismay were strangely mingled, and then suddenly she was running again, stumbling forward with such headlong speed that he was not half-way to the oak tree when she reached him, hurling herself upon him and flinging her arms about his neck.

"Philip," she gasped incoherently, "it is a trap! There is a man in the bushes by the oak tree—I saw him as I came down the hill! Oh, take care!"

A movement of the undergrowth confirmed her words. Philip levelled his pistol, and the sound of the shot was echoed by a strangled yell of rage and pain. A dark figure dropped from the overhanging branches of the oak and disappeared behind the tree's great trunk, and after a few moments there was the sound of a laboured retreat, though little could be seen in the gathering darkness.

Philip was torn between the desire to go in pursuit and reluctance to leave Joanna unprotected. She had given a whimper of fright and buried her face against his shoulder as the shot crashed out beside her, and now she was sobbing and trembling in his arms. He could not leave her alone while the men who had sought to ambush him were still at large, even though one of them was wounded and it seemed unlikely that they would return to the attack that night.

He listened to the sound of their retreat die away in the

distance, and then he returned the empty pistol to his
pocket and looked down at Joanna.

"It is over," he said quietly. "They have gone."

She raised a pale and tear-stained face from his shoulder, a sob fluttering in her throat.

"I was so frightened," she whispered. "I thought he
meant to kill you, and I did not know what to do."

He realized then why she had rushed to meet him,
flinging herself between him and the supposed assassin,
making her own body a shield for his protection, and he
was filled with wonder and pride and a great humility. He
bent his head and kissed her, tasting her tears salt against
his lips.

Always she had seemed to him a child, but it was no
child's kiss she gave him, her lips warm and yielding, the
clasp of her arms tightening about his neck. It was an
avowal of love which had no need of words, of a trust
which was boundless, and of a certainty that they belonged to each other. For a space the world was forgotten, and time had no meaning at all.

At last he let her go, and reality rushed upon them
once again. They stood in the darkening woods where a
murderous trap had so recently been set, and the cold autumn mist rose about them. Joanna shivered, and Philip
drew her cloak more closely around her.

"Wait here," he said softly, and moved silently away
from her towards the oak tree.

In the bushes close by it he found a patch of flattened
leaves and broken boughs where the unseen watcher had
crouched, and leading from it the trail which marked the
line of his retreat. That the trap had been set by Ned
Mullett, Philip did not doubt, and though the cry which
had greeted his shot suggested that one of the rogues had
been wounded, the speed with which they had made off
indicated that the injury was not a serious one.

He went back to Joanna, who was standing rigidly
where he had left her, watching him with wide, apprehensive eyes. She breathed a sigh of relief as he reached her
side again, and he looked down at her with a smile.

"Come," he said gently, "I will take you home, and

you shall tell me as we go how you discovered what was afoot tonight."

"Jem Roberts told me," she replied, slipping her hand into his as they went forward along the path. "That ruffian had bribed him to carry a message to you, and though he did it, he knew it was wrong. He was so frightened of what might happen that in the end he could bear it no longer, and confessed to me what he had done."

"Why not to your father?"

"He was afraid to do that in case he was turned off. As it was, I had to promise that I would tell no one else before he would say what he had done. This is why I had to come alone to warn you."

"Cowardly little knave!" Philip said angrily. "How dare he let you take such a risk? He should have come himself if he was afraid to seek help elsewhere."

Joanna's fingers tightened upon his.

"Do not be angry with him, Philip," she said. "He is so afraid of what those men may do to him if they find out that he has played them false."

"He has good cause to be afraid," Philip replied grimly. "It is not their way to let betrayal go unpunished."

There was silence until they reached the top of the farther slope, and then she said in a low voice:

"So you do know who they are! I thought from what Jem told me that they must be the men who set upon you two days ago, even though you said then that they were either footpads or poachers."

"They were neither," he replied. "The name of the young one I do not know, but his leader, Ned Mullett, has followed me from America. He is a thorough-paced villain."

"Oh, if only I could have brought help with me tonight!" she exclaimed. "Then they might have been caught, and you would be safe." She shivered, and moved closer to his side. "I cannot bare to think that they used my name to lure you into a trap! How could they have guessed that I might send you a message? They are strangers here."

Philip shrugged.

"Mullett is a resourceful rogue, and in a place where you are so well known to everyone, such information is not hard to come by."

She did not reply, and they walked on in silence until the trees became more widely spaced and then ceased altogether, and Sir Andrew's orchard wall loomed before them beyond a strip of meadow-land. Here in the open some light still lingered, and the sky in the west reflected a rosy glow. They crossed the grass to the gate, and passed through it into the orchard. There Joanna halted and turned to face him. She was still pale, but her eyes met his steadily.

"Philip," she said quietly, "why do those men seek your life? Tell me, I beg of you!"

"It is not my life they seek, Joanna," he replied after a pause, "though no doubt they would kill me once they had obtained what they desire. I have something in my possession which they covet very greatly. That is all."

"All?" she repeated in a whisper. "When it may cost you your life? Whatever it is cannot be worth such a risk."

"To a man like Ned Mullett, life is the cheapest thing on earth," he replied with a wry smile. "I would not be the first man he had killed."

She made a little gesture of anger and dismay.

"Do not talk so of killing," she said unsteadily. "What is this thing he is so greedy to possess?"

For a moment he hesitated, and then, as though coming to a sudden decision, he loosened his neckcloth and unfastened a cord which hung about his sunburned throat. Joanna saw that the cord supported a tiny bag of soft leather, curiously worked in faded colours and securely fastened. Philip undid the clasp, and then took her hand and tipped the contents of the bag into her palm.

"That," he said quietly, "and many men have died for it before now."

Joanna gasped. In her hand lay an enormous emerald, larger than any jewel she had ever seen, which even in the dim light of evening glowed with a magnificent and baleful fire. A thing of beauty which yet seemed redolent of evil, and charged with a mysterious, sinister power.

VIII

The Star of Death

"Philip!" she said in an awe-struck whisper. "It cannot be real?"

"It is real enough, my dear," he replied quietly. "The story goes that that jewel came out of Peru with Pizarro's conquistadores, and it is a fact that for more than a century it adorned a statue of the Virgin in one of the great churches of New Spain. Then the city was sacked by buccaneers, and the emerald was part of the plunder they brought back with them to Port Royal in Jamaica. After that it changed hands many times, and always violence and bloodshed followed in its wake, until it became something of a legend among the islands, and people spoke of it as a thing accursed. They called it 'the star of death'."

Joanna shuddered, and with a gesture of distaste held the stone out to him.

"Put it away, Philip, please," she said. "It frightens me."

He smiled, but took it from her and held it up between finger and thumb so that the last of the light stirred green fires in its depths.

"Yet it is a lovely thing," he said reflectively, "and harmless enough in itself. The evil springs from the passions it arouses in men."

"Philip!" There was a new note in Joanna's voice, the faintest trace of apprehension underlying the breathless words. "How did it come into your possession?"

He looked at her, still smiling, and she had the odd fancy that some of the jewel's colour was reflected in his eyes. He seemed amused, yet when he spoke it was in a tone of the utmost seriousness.

"Honestly, Joanna, that I swear, even though I received it from the hands of a dying man."

He returned the emerald to its covering, and while he restored the bag to its former hiding-place he told her how, many years before, the ill-fated jewel had disappeared, nor did anyone know what had become of it until he himself stumbled upon it in one of the little frontier settlements of the northern colonies.

It had happened a year ago. Arriving in the village, he learned that an old man lay dying, feared and shunned by his neighbours because, they said, he was mad. Philip had given him what aid he could, and in return the dying man bestowed the emerald upon him and told him the story of its disappearance. He had been one of a pirate crew in his youth, and having by treachery and murder possessed himself of the jewel, he had fled from the Indies in an attempt to reach Europe. His flight took him to one of the more northerly ports, and there he was discovered by two of the comrades he had betrayed. He killed them both, and to escape the consequences of the crime was forced to flee into the wilderness.

What befell him thereafter Philip had been unable to discover, but he had come to that place with the first settlers and dwelt there ever since, dreaming always of wealth and power, and fearful that his neighbours would learn his secret and steal the jewel.

"They made game of him, and laughed at his wild words," Philip concluded quietly, "as I might have done had I not held in my hand the proof that he spoke the truth."

The shadows were crowding closer now, silent and menacing, and even the western sky was dark. Joanna glanced uneasily over her shoulder and moved closer to him.

"It is an ugly story," she said in a low voice, "and I think they were right who named that jewel accursed. What did it bring to that man save fear and mockery and harsh usage, and now it endangers your life also. It is a hateful thing!"

There was a note almost of hysteria in her voice. Philip took her in his arms, holding her in a comforting embrace.

"Sweetheart, you are tired and overwrought," he said gently. "It was not the emerald, but his own crimes, which haunted that poor rogue and drove him mad. As for myself, if it has brought me into danger, that is due to my own folly in letting others learn of my possession of it. Had I been more careful of the secret, no harm would have threatened me on that account."

"But it has threatened you, and does so still," she insisted anxiously. "Would it not be wiser to sell the emerald? It must be worth a great deal."

"A fortune," he agreed laconically, "and it was to sell it that I brought it to England, but it is not easy to find a purchaser for such a gem. Besides, who would take the risk of buying so costly a jewel from a stranger? Some person of unimpeachable integrity would be needed to stand surety for me."

"Lord Varne!" Joanna spoke triumphantly, as one who has discovered the answer to a perplexing question. "That is why you have come seeking him, is it not? That he may vouch for you in this matter?"

He hesitated for an instant before he replied, and then he said briefly:

"The name of Varne would certainly be surety enough."

So evasive an answer might have aroused her suspicions had she been less preoccupied, but, confident that her supposition was correct, she had already let her thoughts leap to a matter of greater urgency.

"But until Lord Varne comes you will be in danger from this man you call Ned Mullett," she said, "and you cannot hope always to escape him. Oh, Philip, do not carry the jewel about you. Hide it in some safe place until it can be sold."

"Willingly, my love, but where? I dare not leave it at the Colyton Arms, for an inn is a public place into which anyone may walk, and I have no wish to find my chamber ransacked and the emerald gone. Nor do I fancy the notion of burying it in the earth. I would rather carry it with me and trust to my luck and my sword to keep it safe."

There was a brief, and on Joanna's part somewhat

crestfallen, silence, and then she exclaimed triumphantly:

"I know what to do! You must ask my father to take charge of it for you. He can lock it away in his strong-box, and no one need ever know of it save we three."

"It is a possible solution, certainly," Philip agreed slowly, "but would he be willing to undertake such a charge? It is no small thing to ask."

"He will do it if I ask it of him," she replied confidently. "Come to him now."

"No!" he said firmly. "I may ask this favour of your father, but he must not be allowed to suspect that the suggestion came from you."

"Why not?" Her voice was puzzled. "I do not understand."

"Oh, Joanna!" He laughed softly, but it was rueful laughter, with the faintest undertone of bitterness. "If Sir Andrew were to come upon us now, he would be more likely to kick me off his land than to grant me favours."

"No, no!" she said earnestly. "He likes you, Philip, truly!"

"Not so much that his liking would survive that discovery," Philip replied wryly. "No, my dear, your part in tonight's affair must remain a secret between us. Can you trust young Roberts to keep silent?"

"Oh yes, for he will be too frightened to tell anyone what he did, but I cannot see the need for secrecy. Not from my father."

"No!" Philip was staring above her head into the darkness, and the bitterness had deepened in his voice. "An honest suitor would have sought his leave to address you, would he not? Even now, the only honourable course would be to go to him and tell him that I love you."

There was a little silence, and then she said shyly:

"Only if you want to marry me, Philip."

"Of course I want to marry you. Did you ever doubt that?" He was looking down at her now, and with one of the lightning changes of mood she was learning to expect, the laughter was back in his voice. "Did you, Joanna? If you did, it is even more improper for you to be here than if you had been certain of my honest intentions."

"I was not sure," she replied candidly. "I have never known anyone like you before." She paused, her fingers rearranging the folds of his cravat, smoothing them into some semblance of neatness. "If you say we must be secret I will do my best, but I wish you will tell me why it is necessary."

"Because I am not in a position to ask for your hand in marriage. Think for a moment, Joanna! What does your father know of me, save what I have told him myself? He would have every right to forbid us to meet again. Be patient for a while, my love, and trust me."

"Oh, I do!" She spoke without hesitation, for she thought now that she understood. He would not approach her father until his friend was there to vouch for him, and until the fabulous, ill-fated emerald had been sold to provide wealth which, if not comparable with her own, was at least sufficient to save him from being thought a fortune-hunter. "I will do whatever you think best."

"Then you will go indoors now, and say nothing to anyone of what has happened tonight," he said firmly. "If your absence is noticed you will be hard put to it to think of a convincing excuse for walking abroad after dark on an autumn evening. Come, I will walk with you through the orchard."

In her new-found docility she made no protest, but allowed him to lead her under the laden fruit-trees towards the house, her skirts whispering across the grass. After a little she said softly:

"You will take the emerald to my father, will you not? I cannot be easy while you carry it about you."

"I will, I promise," he replied. "This very night, if that is what you wish. As soon as I have fetched my horse from the Broad Ride, I will come to the house, but remember, you and I have not met since we parted yesterday at Foxwood Grange."

She nodded, though without paying much heed to the warning, and her hand tightened on his arm.

"Philip, you cannot go back through the woods alone! You may be set upon again."

He laughed and shook his head.

"Mullett and his crony are no woodsmen," he said
lightly, "and I should be aware of them before they could
see or hear me. Be easy, my love, they will not take me
unawares."

"But you may lose your way," she insisted. "It is so
dark."

"No, there is starlight, and the moon is rising." They
had reached the far side of the orchard now, and the
lighted windows of the house could be seen across the
gardens. "Go now, sweetheart. I will see you presently."

He kissed her again, swiftly, and so left her, disappearing into the darkness as silently as a shadow. There was
something almost uncanny about that abrupt and soundless departure, and for several moments Joanna stood
motionless, straining her ears yet hearing only the faint
whisper of the breeze in the dying leaves, and the ham-
mering of her own heart. Then she turned and sped
through the familiar gardens towards the lights of her
home.

She made an unobtrusive entrance and contrived to
reach her own room without being seen. There she laid
aside her cloak, and, having removed all outward signs of
her recent errand, went sedately down to join her parents
in the drawing-room.

There she busied herself with a piece of needlework
and tried to take an intelligent part in the conversation,
though heart and mind alike were away in the dark
woods, and every minute seemed like an hour. Reason
told her that it was impossible yet for Philip to have re-
traced his steps to the Broad Ride and then have ridden
to Greydon Park, but she was consumed by an anxiety
which no logic could allay.

At last, after what seemed an eternity, the brisk rhythm
of approaching hoofbeats reached her straining ears. The
sound grew until the hoofs crunched on the gravel before
the house, and then a peremptory knocking fell upon the
front door.

Sir Andrew, who had been on the point of dropping
into a doze, opened his eyes in surprise, and Lady Selbourne placidly wondered aloud who the belated caller

might be, but their daughter bent her head low over her sewing, trying to set stitches with fingers trembling with relief and something, too, of apprehension. Then a servant came to inform his master that Mr. Digby begged the favour of a word with him in private, and Sir Andrew, in even greater surprise, heaved himself up out of his chair and went away, nodding in response to his wife's command to bring Mr. Digby to the drawing-room when their business was concluded.

Sir Andrew received his guest in the library on the other side of the house, and when greetings had been exchanged Philip said abruptly:

"Forgive me, sir, for waiting upon you at this unseasonable hour, but the matter which brings me here admits of no delay. I have come to seek your help."

For the second time that evening he produced the leather bag and tipped the emerald into the light. Sir Andrew leaned forward to stare incredulously, and Philip, putting the jewel into his hand, recounted again the story of the fabled star of death and the crazed old man who had given it to him.

From that he passed to an account of the attack upon him that evening, letting Selbourne assume that only now had he recognized his assailant, and concluding with the hope that Sir Andrew might take charge of the emerald for a time.

"Though I would not have you do so unwillingly, sir," he said frankly. "That stone is a charge which few men would accept on another's behalf."

Sir Andrew shrugged this aside with some impatience.

"I do not shrink from accepting the responsibility, my boy," he said testily, "and you may leave the jewel in my care for as short or as long a time as you choose. It seems to me, however, that if these would-be robbers expect to find it upon your person, you stand in grave danger of being murdered before they discover their mistake."

"I think not, sir," Philip replied easily. "They are none of them fools, and though it has always been my habit to carry the emerald with me, habits can be changed and they know it. They will not risk killing the one man who can tell them where it may be found."

"If they succeed in laying hands on you, they may well use force to extract that information," Sir Andrew reminded him grimly.

"I will go warily, sir, never fear," Philip assured him with a laugh, "and with the emerald in safe-keeping I can devote all my wits to the task of evading capture. Moreover, should the worse befall, they will find that I do not take kindly to persuasion of that nature. An answer they might succeed in forcing from me, but it is not likely to be a true one."

He spoke lightly, but there was an undertone in his crisp voice, and a glint in the green-flecked hazel eyes, which convinced Sir Andrew that the words were no idle boast. This dynamic young man, with his tremendous vitality and air of living every moment to the full, was of a fibre which would toughen under adversity.

"I do not think there is any danger of Mullett guessing where I have bestowed the jewel," Philip went on, "even if he realizes that it is no longer in my possession. Being thoroughly unscrupulous himself, it will be inconceivable to him that any man exists honest enough to have it in his care without desiring to acquire it for his own. If at any time I have reason to suppose he does know of its whereabouts, I shall, of course, relieve you of the charge without delay."

Sir Andrew chuckled.

"That would not be necessary," he said genially. "The rogue would be hard put to it to steal the jewel while it lies in this house."

Philip had been looking at the emerald, which Selbourne had placed carefully on the table beside him, but at that he lifted his gaze sharply to meet the elder man's. There was no laughter now in his eyes, and the lines of his face had hardened perceptibly.

"You do not fully comprehend the power of this jewel, Sir Andrew," he said gravely. "Believe me, not for nothing is it called the star of death, for the number of men— yes, and women, too—whom it has lured to destruction can only be guessed. If Mullett learns that it is here, then not only you, but your wife and daughter also, would stand in danger." He took up the stone as he spoke, and in the candlelight it winked like a mocking and baleful eye. "I tell you this because I wish you to realize the magnitude of the favour I am asking."

"Since neither of us will speak of this matter to anyone, the danger is not likely to arise," Sir Andrew retorted cheerfully. "Put the confounded thing back into its case, my boy, and let me lock it away. Then we will go join the ladies. I'll wager they are wondering what business is keeping us for so long."

Philip obeyed, and so presently followed his host into the long, candle-lit drawing-room, where Lady Selbourne accorded him the warmest of welcomes. He had been a trifle dubious of the wisdom of meeting Joanna again so soon after their parting, under her parents' eyes and with no other company present to distract attention from them, but he soon saw that he had no cause for anxiety. Miss Selbourne never dealt in half-measures. She gave him her hand, and a friendly smile, and made some remark about their last meeting at Foxwood Grange. As he replied, she met his laughing glance with complete composure, and if there was something behind the laughter to deepen the colour in her cheeks and wake a response in her own eyes, only she perceived it.

He did not prolong his visit beyond the time demanded by common courtesy, and half an hour later was again in the saddle, riding back to Brinkbury by the light of the now risen moon. He came without further adventures to the Colyton Arms, and having seen El Diablo stabled, made his way into the inn. A murmur of voices came from behind the closed door of the tap-room, but the narrow passage was deserted; Philip went into the parlour, where candles were burning and a bright fire added its cheery light to theirs.

He pushed the door shut with a backward thrust of his hand and went towards the fire, but he had not taken more than a couple of paces when a voice spoke softly behind him in ironic greeting.

"Good evening to you, Mr. Digby," it said. "I was wondering how much longer I'd need to wait for you."

Philip spun round with his hand flashing to his sword, and then as swiftly froze into stillness again. The man who had spoken was leaning against the wall, in such a position that he had been hidden by the opening door; a tall, looselimbed young man, with a bronzed, reckless face and very clear blue eyes. He leaned there negligently, completely at his ease, a glass of wine in one hand, and in the other a pistol which was levelled at Philip's heart.

IX

Mr. Digby Strikes a Bargain

For perhaps ten seconds there was silence in the room, a silence emphasized by a burst of laughter from the tap-room, and the distant barking of a dog. Then slowly Philip relaxed, and he said softly:

"Simon Halliard, as I live! Now how the devil did you find your way here?"

Mr. Halliard grinned.

"I followed a star," he replied impudently. "A small green star that has twinkled beguilingly in my mind's eye these many months."

Philip shook his head.

"Not a star, Simon," he retorted mockingly, "a marsh-light! A jack-a-lantern, leading you on a vain journey."

"Vain?" Hilliard's brows lifted. "I have found you."

"That does not mean that you have also found the star, but even supposing that it were still in my possession, by what means did you hope to persuade me into parting with it? Not these, surely?"

He nodded with good-natured contempt towards the pistol, and then turned his back on it and walked across the room and threw himself down in a chair before the fire. Leaning back comfortably, legs outstretched and crossed at the ankle, hands clasped behind his head, he continued amiably:

"You cannot shoot me in a public inn, you know, with

half the village in the next room. That would mean that you followed me out of this world in a very short space of time."

There was a pause, and then Halliard shrugged and lowered his weapon.

"True enough," he admitted cheerfully, moving away from the wall. "To be honest, the pistol was merely a gesture, to discourage any rashness on your part when you first saw me. I am not fool enough to rouse the whole place with the noise of a shot." He perched himself on the edge of the table, laying aside the weapon and lifting his glass in mock salutation before putting it to his lips. "There's noise of another sort, however, that I could make with small risk to myself, but which would cause you a deal of embarrassment. I fancy I know rather more concerning Mr. Philip Digby than do the inhabitants of this charming village."

"You know at least that I do not take kindly to threats." Philip still spoke pleasantly, but there was a challenge in his eyes. "This is simply another way of holding a pistol to my head, and I like it no better than the first."

"Who spoke of threats?" Simon asked reproachfully. "I am making you a fair and reasonable offer. Give me the emerald and I will be away with the first light of morning, before my tongue has a chance to wag too freely concerning you."

Still lounging in his chair, Philip considered him in silence. He had known Simon Halliard for a number of years, and felt for him a genuine liking which was in no way diminished by the knowledge that he was an incorrigible rogue. Halliard was the youngest son of a wealthy Jamaican planter, but his highly respectable family had cast him off while he was still in his teens, and thereafter he had drifted from place to place in the Americas, sometimes affluent, more often in a state of cheerful indigence, and always ready to plunge headlong into any excitement that offered. He and Philip had recognized one another as kindred spirits within an hour of their first meeting, and had shared some rollicking adventures during the course of their acquaintance, but this would not prevent Simon from using any method to possess himself of the emerald. He was utterly fearless, wholly unpredictable, and devoid of any principles whatsoever.

"Your notion of a fair offer does not keep pace with mine," Philip said at length, "and in any event you are overlooking something which I told you a few moments since. The emerald is no longer in my possession."

Mr. Halliard laughed shortly, on a note of derision.

"You've had no time to sell it," he retorted, "and if you are asking me to believe that it has been lost or stolen, your memory of me is at fault. I am not one of these credulous villagers, who will swallow any traveller's tale. That stone has never left your person since the day it was given to you."

"It has not been lost, stolen or sold," Philip replied patiently. "It simply occurred to me that I was stretching my luck too far by continuing to carry it with me, and so I have found a safe hiding-place for it. Do you believe me, or would you like to search me to satisfy yourself that I am speaking the truth?"

"I might believe you, if I could perceive any reason for so sudden a change of habit."

"Oh, the reason exists, I assure you. Do not think that you are the first in the field, my friend. Ned Mullett was three days before you."

"Mullett?" Simon set down his glass to stare blankly at Philip. "By all the devils in hell! How did that damned scoundrel get ahead of me?"

Philip grinned.

"Best ask him, for I doubt if anyone else could tell you," he replied cheerfully. "Quite a reunion, is it not? I wonder how long we shall need to wait for Réné Leblanc to arrive to complete the party?"

Simon picked up his glass again and gazed reflectively at its contents.

"For ever," he replied succinctly. "Leblanc is dead."

There was an infinitesimal pause, and then Philip said lightly:

"He is, is he? Did you kill him, or did Mullett?"

"Neither of us. The need did not arise," Simon replied with disarming frankness. "The poor fellow died of a fever during the voyage. We were fellow passengers, you understand."

"Yes, I understand!" There was resignation in Philip's voice. "You wished to keep at least one of your rivals under observation. That fever must have saved you a deal of trouble."

"It certainly lessened the odds against me," Simon admitted, "and maybe saved your life into the bargain. Leblanc's plan was to take you unawares, slit your throat, and make off with the emerald. Poor Réné! He was always impetuous."

"In this instance, impetuosity would have gained him nothing." Philip was still lounging in the chair, eyes half-closed and a mocking smile on his lips. "I am the one man alive, my dear Simon, who knows where the star of death is hidden, and if I carry that secret to the grave, it may lie where it is until the crack of doom. At present my life is almost as precious to you as it is to me."

Halliard rubbed his forefinger reflectively against the bridge of his nose.

"You might be persuaded to share the secret," he suggested.

"I might," Philip agreed, "but not by any of the means which you are contemplating. It is possible, however, that I might strike a bargain with you—on my own terms."

He paused, looking inquiringly at his companion. Simon nodded.

"Go on," he said briefly.

"You have threatened to make certain disclosures concerning me," Philip continued, "and though you would gain nothing by doing so, I will admit that for the truth to become known would ruin all my plans. I have gone to a good deal of trouble to establish myself creditably in the neighbourhood, and I have no desire to see my schemes brought to a standstill by your unruly tongue."

"I can believe that," Simon said with a chuckle. "Mr. Philip Digby, lifelong friend of the new Earl of Varne! The gallant who has taken the whole district by storm!

Oh, I have been hearing a deal of talk about Mr. Digby in the past hour or two, I give you my word! The pretty creature who brought me my supper—Ellen, is it not?—was very willing to tell me all I wished to know."

"I'll wager she was!" Philip spoke between amusement and exasperation. "You did not, I trust, tell her anything in return?"

"Nothing concerning you, so set your mind at rest," Halliard retorted with a grin. "I know how to bide my time when I can see some chance of profit. Tell me more of the bargain you propose to make."

"Very well!" Philip sat upright and spoke briskly. "I have admitted that you are in a position to ruin my present plans, but do not forget that Mullett is able to do the same. He has not yet realized it because it is natural to him to gain his ends by force alone, but presently it will occur to him that he has a more potent weapon at his command than a pistol or a bludgeon. He does not know me as well as you do, certainly, but he knows enough to overset my schemes." He paused, and after a moment added softly, "Mullett must be silenced."

"That much is obvious!" Halliard stretched out a lazy arm for the bottle of wine, and filled his glass again. "I would be as happy as you would to know that we were rid of him. I suppose he was one of the so-called footpads who set upon you the other day?"

Philip nodded.

"That affair has already made too much noise in the village for my liking," he said shortly. "The Constable has been warned to keep watch for any suspicious characters, and so has every damned gamekeeper in the neighbourhood. It is imperative that I find Mullett and his crony before they do."

"And that is something which two may accomplish more speedily than one," Simon concluded for him, and Philip nodded again.

"I would rather have you with me than against me," he said frankly. "I am gambling for big stakes here, Simon, and if all goes as I hope, you shall have your fair share of the profits, I promise you. But the business is delicate, and I cannot spend all my time tracking down those two confounded rogues. Yet found they must be, and that without delay."

"It would seem that my arrival was happily timed," Halliard remarked with a laugh. "A delicate business, you say? Damn you, Philip, what deep game are you playing now?"

"A deep game, in truth," Philip replied. He was smiling, but with little mirth in eyes or lips. "It leads to murder, Simon."

"Murder?" Halliard's voice snapped; he set down his glass and stared at the other man with narrowed, suspicious eyes. "What tomfoolery is this?"

"None at all. I am serious. There is a gentleman in these parts who wishes another out of his way, but for various reasons dare not do the deed himself. I have offered myself as his deputy."

Halliard slowly straightened himself from his seat on the edge of the table and stood erect. His brown face had hardened, and his eyes were like sapphire ice. With the cloak of careless gaiety cast aside the dangerous mettle of the man was revealed, like the blade of a sword drawn from its sheath.

"So you have been making game of me, have you?" he said softly. "By God! do you think you can trifle with me? You—a hired assassin!" He gave a short, contemptuous laugh. "Did you expect me to believe that?"

"In exceptional circumstances all things are possible," Philip replied calmly. He had not moved, and seemed more amused than perturbed. "And these circumstances are very exceptional indeed. The intended victim is the new Earl of Varne."

"The new Earl?" Simon stared at him, and slowly understanding crept into his eyes, and a grim smile lifted the corners of his mouth. "Richard Colyton, of course! I should have guessed it."

"You should indeed," Philip agreed mockingly. "Now sit down, in God's name, and let me tell you a little concerning this noble family of Colyton. Believe me, I have unearthed a deal of unsavouriness about them since I reached England."

Simon obeyed him, and Philip recounted briefly the story of Bertram Colyton's persistent efforts to make himself Earl of Varne. Halliard listened in silence, and when the tale was told said merely in a tone of some amusement:

"You have certainly spared no pains to present our friend Richard in an unsavoury guise, but, of course, you had to make your story convincing."

"Precisely! Both Bertram Colyton and I are aware of the wisdom of plotting Richard's death, but we would not agree so happily if he suspected my real reason for offering him my aid."

"You say he has a son?"

"Yes, young Francis, but I doubt whether he has any part in his father's scheming. He is a dreamy-looking lad who would make a poor conspirator, I fancy, but there is another kinsman, Gregory Trayle by name, who it would not surprise me to learn is party to the plot. We have already fallen foul of each other, he and I, and I've small doubt it will come to a fight between us in the end."

Simon laughed.

"With one thing and another, time does not hang heavily upon your hands, does it?" he said whimsically. "I can see now why you are prepared to enlist my aid."

"You accept the bargain, then?"

"To be sure I do! I would not forego this adventure for a thousand pounds." He yawned and stretched. "Now tell me how you propose to track down Ned Mullett. You say there is another man with him?"

"Yes, a lad I have never seen before. I had another brush with them this evening and I believe one of them sustained some hurt, although they both made their escape. Tomorrow I will take you to the place where they waylaid me, and we will endeavour to trace the path they followed. I have taken the trouble to make myself familiar with the country and to get on friendly terms with the people, so we may meet with some success."

"God send we do!" Simon agreed heartily. "Much as it

will please me to put an end to Mullett's career, I can think of more pleasant diversions."

Since Mr. Halliard's notions of entertainment were well known to Philip, these words caused him to feel a twinge of uneasiness which proved justified as early as the following morning. They were about to set out for the Queen's Oak, and while Digby examined the priming of his pistol, Simon stood looking idly from the parlour window. Suddenly his gaze quickened and he gave a low, appreciative whistle. Philip looked up.

"What now?" he asked resignedly.

"There is a goddess riding down the street," Simon replied, without turning his head. "A brown-haired goddess on a bay horse. Tell me who she is, Philip! Devil take me if ever I saw a lovelier creature."

"The devil will take you in any event," Philip retorted, crossing to the window. "That, my friend, is Miss Julia Stonehurst, who, so it is said, is destined to be the next Countess of Varne."

"Is she, indeed?" Simon shot him a quick, inquiring glance. "Who says so?"

"Her father, for one. Also Bertram Colyton and his son. They might not agree upon the name of her future husband, but of his title they have no doubt whatsoever."

He turned away as he spoke and picked up his pistol again. Halliard made no reply, but continued to watch Miss Stonehurst with admiring eyes until she passed out of sight.

They left the inn some ten minutes later, and Philip led the way at a brisk pace along the road towards Greydon. Before they had ridden a mile they rounded a bend to see Miss Stonehurst and her attendant before them. Simon's eyes brightened and he urged his horse forward.

Julia glanced over her shoulder at the sound of their approach, and, recognizing Digby, drew rein and waited for them to come up with her. She greeted Philip with a smile, and looked curiously at his companion.

"Well met, Mr. Digby," she said. "It is a fair morning, is it not?"

"How could it be otherwise, when Miss Stonehurst

rides abroad?" he replied gallantly, concealing the mild
dismay he felt at the encounter. "Give me leave, madam,
to present my good friend Simon Halliard, of Jamaica."

Julia graciously inclined her head, and Simon swept off
his hat and bowed low over the withers of his horse. As
he came erect again he said audaciously, his eyes upon
her face:

"Madam, your most humble servant! Until this moment
I did not know why I had journeyed so far across the
sea."

She coloured furiously but did not seem displeased, and
Philip's heart sank. He bore Julia no ill-will, and did not
wish to see her fall victim to Halliard's scapegrace charm.
With a quelling glance at his friend, to which the only response was a flash of mockery in the clear blue eyes, he
inquired if Miss Stonehurst was bound for Greydon Park.

"Yes, I am the bearer of a message to Lady Selbourne
from my mother," she replied. "Do you go there also,
sir?"

"I regret to say that we do not," Philip replied firmly,
not looking at Simon. "Our way lies along the higher
road."

"Then let us ride together as far as we may," Julia suggested, and taking their assent for granted allowed her
horse to move forward again, adding after a moment: "I
am glad of this opportunity to speak with you, Mr. Digby.
I have no wish to revive memories of what is best forgotten, but I feel that no adequate apology was made for my
brother's behaviour at your last meeting with him. It was
quite inexcusable."

He made a gesture of dissent, casting a swift, sidelong
glance at Simon as he did so. Mr. Halliard was apparently
absorbed in contemplation of the pleasant scene about
him, but Philip felt quite certain that he was listening with
the liveliest curiosity.

"You speak truly, madam, when you say that the incident is best forgotten," he said repressively. "My own
conduct in arriving uninvited at your home was not above
reproach, but the situation which led to the visit was a
trifle difficult."

"Yes, Joanna told me about that," she replied reflectively, and turned upon him a glance which held a hint of mischief. "She also told Oliver in no uncertain terms what she thought of his conduct."

He smiled faintly.

"Then your brother has my sympathy. Miss Selbourne can be outspoken when she chooses."

Julia laughed and let the matter drop, turning with a civil remark to include Simon in the conversation. Before long the road forked, and there the two young men took leave of Miss Stonehurst, who rode on sedately towards the gates of Greydon Park while Philip led Simon up over the crest of the hill and down through the woods to the Broad Ride, coming at length to the mouth of the narrow, overgrown track along which he had walked the previous night.

Somewhat to his surprise, Simon had made no comment upon the meeting with Miss Stonehurst, and though Philip, who had expected to be questioned concerning the reason for Oliver Stonehurst's hostility, was thankful for this forbearance, he could not help reflecting that it was strangely foreign to Halliard's usual manner. He said nothing, however, as, having tethered their horses, they made their way in single file along the path. Not until they reached the hollow where the Queen's Oak stood did Simon betray any curiosity, and then he said in a tone of deep perplexity :

"What the devil were you doing in this place, anyway?"

"They brought me here on a fool's errand," Philip replied briefly, "but I had my suspicions from the first and since they know nothing of woodcraft it was not difficult to detect them. One was hiding in the tree, ready, I suppose, to drop upon me as I passed beneath, and the other crouched yonder, in the bushes."

"That was the one you shot?"

Philip nodded.

"The other joined him and they made off together. The trail was plain enough last night, but let us see what it can tell us now."

He went towards the tree and Simon followed him with

a tiny crease of perplexity between his brows, but as he passed beneath the oak he halted, staring at a scrap of white stuff caught among the brambles by the path. Philip had gone on, thrusting his way into the undergrowth, and did not see his companion stoop and pick up the thing which had attracted his attention.

It was a woman's handkerchief, a wisp of lace and cambric with an embroidered monogram in one corner. Simon looked at the dainty thing and his brow cleared.

"So you came here on a fool's errand, did you?" he said under his breath. "I think I know now what manner of folly it was." He spread the delicate stuff between his hands, looking at the embroidered letters. "A J and an S," he mused, "Julia Stonehurst or Joanna Selbourne—which?"

He shrugged and, thrusting the handkerchief into his pocket, followed Philip into the undergrowth.

X

The Opportunist

Through the woods the trail was not difficult to follow. It bore away from Greydon Park and swept in a wide half-circle up the hillside, crossing the Broad Ride and emerging at last on the treeless upper slopes where sheep grazed on the close-cropped turf. Here they received their first serious check, for there had been rain in the night, and not even Philip's experienced eyes could detect the path which Mullett and his crony had followed thereafter. The only alternative was to return to their horses and endeavour to pick up the trail by means of inquiries among the neighbouring farms and hamlets, for if one of the fugitives was wounded, it was unlikely that they could have gone far afield in search of shelter.

This course they set out to follow, but before long they were halted again, this time by a chance encounter with Sir Andrew Selbourne, who insisted jovially that they should ride back with him to Greydon Park. Since it was impossible to decline the invitation without disclosing the

nature of their present errand they were obliged to go
with him, a circumstance which pleased Simon better than
it pleased Philip.

He found even less cause for pleasure when the house
was reached, and they discovered Joanna entertaining not
only Miss Stonehurst but Gregory Trayle, for Mr. Trayle
was the last person Philip wished to encounter at that
time and place. Those hard grey eyes were a good deal
too perceptive for his comfort, and the sneering tongue
would be only too ready with some barbed comment calculated to arouse Sir Andrew's suspicions.

To his relief, however, Trayle's attention seemed to be
wholly occupied with Simon's arrival on the scene, and
his claim to an acquaintance with Richard Colyton. He
studied the newcomer with thoughtful, speculative eyes,
and while accepting his story with polite credulity, contrived to convey the impression that he did not believe a
word of it.

"Perhaps, Mr. Halliard," Julia said with her slow smile,
"since you, too, are a friend of Lord Varne, you will
gratify our curiosity concerning him. Mr. Digby's reti-
cence on that subject is the most provoking thing in the
world."

Simon laughed and shook his head.

"Ask anything else of me, Miss Stonehurst," he de-
clared, "and I will be happy to gratify your wishes, but on
this one subject I pray you to hold me absolved. If Digby,
whose acquaintance with Lord Varne is much longer and
more intimate than my own, keeps silent, it is not for me
to speak."

"This, of course, raises curiosity to fever-pitch," Gregory
remarked unpleasantly. "Upon my soul, the aura of mystery which you have cast about Varne is beginning to intrigue even me. What hideous secret does my kinsman harbour, that those who style themselves his friends will not
disclose?"

"A secret common to most men, sir," Philip replied
swiftly. "Merely that he is a very ordinary sort of fellow,
after all."

"Unlike Mr. Digby, to whom extraordinary adventures

happen." Gregory spoke quietly, but there was an edge to his voice. "I hear that you were set upon in the woods yonder a few days ago."

Philip shrugged, though his eyes had grown wary.

"If you perceive anything extraordinary, Mr. Trayle, in an attempt at robbery by a pair of footpads, I fear I cannot agree with you," he said shortly. "Such a mishap might befall anyone."

"True, but not in such a spot as that. What plunder could they hope for in those woods, where in the general way only a keeper or a labourer might fall into their hands?" He paused, regarding Philip mockingly. "It seems to me, Mr. Digby, that you were their chosen victim. Are you sure you have no enemies who might have instigated the attack?"

Philip's eyes met his squarely, hostility answering hostility in a brief, unspoken challenge.

"I have enemies, sir," he replied. "What man has not? But I do them the honour of supposing that they are not afraid to meet me face to face."

Simon laughed under his breath, but Sir Andrew frowned and said hurriedly:

"Stuff and nonsense, Trayle! Rogues of that sort will attack anyone who looks prosperous enough to offer a hope of plunder. I would to God we had been able to lay hands upon them. I'll wager they would rob no one else for many a day."

"Besides," put in Joanna, "it is not true to say that no one but keepers and labourers go through the woods. Why, I was there myself the very morning Mr. Digby was set upon! It is one of my favourite rides."

"A happy coincidence," Trayle said with a sneer, but if he hoped to provoke some retort from Joanna he was disappointed. Before she could reply, Philip said calmly:

"Happy indeed, for me. If Miss Selbourne and her servant had not come upon us, I might have fared ill at the hands of those ruffians. One sword is a poor match for a pair of cudgels."

Gregory looked sceptical but said no more, and the subject was allowed to drop. It was clear, however, that he had no intention of leaving Greydon Park in advance of his fellow-guests, and since Simon was obviously bent upon making a favourable impression on Miss Stonehurst and remained maddeningly impervious to all Digby's hints of departure, Philip was obliged to wait with impotent annoyance while valuable time slipped by. At last he succeeded in making an excuse to leave, but even then his temper was further exacerbated by the fact that for the rest of that day the search they pursued for Ned Mullett and his companion proved barren.

Meanwhile Gregory Trayle rode back to Brinkbury in a thoughtful frame of mind. Reaching his cousin's home, he was surprised to meet Dr. Towne coming along the avenue away from the house, and paused to bid him good-day and to inquire, more in jest than in earnest, whether the business which brought him there was of a serious nature.

"Serious enough, Mr. Trayle, to be treated with more respect than my patient is willing to accord it," the physician replied curtly. He was plainly put out by whatever had occurred during his visit. "I do not hesitate to tell you, sir, that unless my advice is followed, I will accept no responsibility, no responsibility whatever."

Gregory, knowing the doctor to be of an irascible disposition, was not greatly perturbed by this, and said casually:

"Do not tell me that your skill has been brought into question. Is it my cousin who is ailing?"

"Yes, Mr. Trayle, it is, and if you have any influence upon him I beg that you will persuade him to follow my instructions. He is a sick man indeed, though nothing I can say will make him believe it. You may recall that I was obliged to attend him at the time of Lord Varne's death?"

Trayle nodded, remembering how Bertram, striding in a black rage from his kinsman's death-bed and inveighing bitterly against Varne's scheming, had suffered a kind of collapse, and how Dr. Towne, summoned to his aid, had ordered him immediately to bed and kept him there for several days. Gregory had paid little heed at the time, thinking that the shock which Bertram had received was enough to prostrate any man no longer in his first youth, but now it seemed that the matter might have been more serious than he had supposed.

"You mean that the mischief was wrought then?"

The doctor shook his head.

"No, sir, it goes back farther than that, but that was its first grave manifestation. I have been visiting Mr. Colyton each week since, but today he informs me that this is no longer necessary." He made a helpless gesture. "I repeat, Mr. Trayle, that I refuse to accept any responsibility for what may follow."

Gregory was watching him with narrowed eyes.

"Just how grave is my cousin's condition, Dr. Towne? I think I have a right to know that."

"In the absence of the present Earl, sir, you have every right," the doctor agreed promptly. "I hesitate to speak of it to Mr. Francis, for I believe, if I may say so without offence, that his father would pay even less heed to his urgings than to mine. I trust that you will meet with greater success than either of us."

"I trust so also, sir," Gregory replied impatiently, "but you have not yet answered my question."

"Then I will do so now, sir. To be frank, another such shock as he received when his kinsman died would almost certainly prove fatal."

There was a moment's silence, and then Gregory said quietly:

"I see! My thanks to you for your frankness."

He nodded curtly and rode on up the avenue. The doctor watched him out of sight and shook his head in a baffled manner before going on his way. He had known Gregory Trayle for many years, but he had never been able to understand him, or to feel completely at ease in his presence.

Gregory found his kinsman in a fretful humour, but unwilling to disclose what had offended him. Trayle did not press him, nor did he make any mention of his meeting with Dr. Towne. There was another matter, of more urgent import, which was vexing him.

"Are you aware," he asked abruptly, "that your friend Digby has acquired a companion?"

Bertram stared.

"What do you mean?" he said blankly.

"I mean that there is another man lodged with him at the Colyton Arms. His name is Simon Halliard, and, like Digby, he claims friendship with Varne. What do you know of him?"

"Nothing!" Bertram was still frowning, and there was a set look about his mouth. "Digby made no mention of him."

"It seems to me that there is a good deal of which Digby has made no mention," Gregory replied curtly. He dropped his hat and riding-whip on to a chair and began to strip off his gloves. "This mysterious attack upon him, for one thing, which he would have us believe was no more than a chance attempt at robbery by a couple of footpads." He gave a short, scornful laugh. "And Selbourne supports that preposterous tale!"

"Selbourne?" Bertram repeated incredulously. "Why the devil should he care whether or not Digby's story is believed?"

"Because he desires no one to look more closely into the matter," Gregory said savagely. "Even if the attack were a chance one, do you suppose that Joanna's arrival on the scene was equally fortuitous? Sir Andrew is concerned lest his daughter's waywardness harm her reputation."

An expression of relief descended upon Mr. Colyton's face, and he leaned back in his chair as though his misgivings were at an end. There was even a glint of amusement in his eyes.

"So now we come back to that, do we?" he remarked. "Your suspicions spring from jealousy of Digby's success in that quarter."

"My jealousy, as you term it, did not conjure up Simon Hilliard," Gregory retorted. "I tell you, Bertram, there is something confoundedly suspicious about the whole affair. That Varne should have given one man such cause to hate him that he is ripe for murder I can believe. That there should be two of them is straining credulity too far."

"Have you any reason to suppose that Halliard's purpose is the same as Digby's?"

"Good God! would he be here if it were not? Digby says that though they both know Varne, they met each other for the first time when they chanced to choose the same vessel to bring them to England. Chance again, you perceive! It appears to play a large part in Mr. Digby's affairs."

"It is possible, I suppose," Bertram said reluctantly.

"Oh, it is possible! What is not possible is that Digby, with the purpose he has in mind, should have informed a chance acquaintance of Varne's inheritance and the locality of his estate. He must have known that Halliard would come seeking him here. No, Bertram, I would wager every penny I possess that Digby and Halliard are in league with each other. They are two of a kind!"

He paused, jerking the gloves between his hands with short, vicious movements; there was an ugly expression in his dark face. "I warn you, Bertram, if Varne does not come soon you will need to look elsewhere for a henchman. I'll not tolerate Digby's impudence for ever."

His cousin regarded him with interest.

"Upon my soul, this is a new part for you to be playing," he said. "I do not understand you, Gregory, stap me if I do! You have never lacked success with women, and I should have thought you would find it easy enough to persuade some young heiress or rich widow into marriage. Yet you must needs set your fancy on a wilful, headstrong child like Joanna, who does not even like you. Why, in God's name? Does she mean so much to you?"

Trayle did not reply for a moment. His expression had not altered; he looked above Bertram's head to the window and the garden beyond.

"So much," he said quietly at length, "that I swear I will wed her, or no one."

"As Gad's my life!" Mr. Colyton was decidedly taken aback. "I always supposed that expediency alone prompted your wooing. It never occurred to me that you were in love with her."

"In love?" Gregory's gaze came back to his kinsman's face. There was contempt in his eyes, and in the sneering lines of his mouth. "My dear Bertram, do not confuse me with that love-sick whelp of yours. I dangle at no woman's apron-strings! Joanna dislikes me, you say. True! She has spared no pains to show me that, but I will have her, cousin, in spite of it." His hand was clenched hard on the gloves he held; his voice was soft and very deliberate. "I will not be flouted."

Bertram's eyes rested upon those ruthless fingers and then, very slowly, lifted to his cousin's face. Some of the accustomed assured calm was missing from his expression.

"My God!" he said in a low voice. "You damned blackguard!"

Gregory laughed quietly. It was not a pleasant sound.

"This from you, cousin? What of Charles, cut off in the very flower of his youth, and of Richard, soon to go the same road? I do not think you are in a position to censure me."

The entry of Francis into the room at this point gave Bertram no chance to reply. The younger Mr. Colyton was obviously in an ill humour, for a heavy frown marred the perfection of his features, and after only the briefest of greetings he flung himself down in a chair and sat drumming his fingers on its arms and staring before him in morose silence. Trayle regarded him derisively.

"Behold a star-crossed lover," he gibed. "What ails you, cousin? Did the fair Julia prove elusive?"

Francis glared at him. He had been at great pains to manufacture a plausible excuse to visit Foxwood Grange, only to find on his arrival that Julia had been sent off on what he suspected to be a trumped-up errand to Greydon Park. Since Francis was certain that Gregory himself had been at the Park that day, his cousin's question touched him on the raw.

"Did you fare any better?" he snapped. "I would not begrudge Julia's visit to Greydon Park if I thought it had spared Joanna your importunities."

Gregory remained unmoved by the retort; he said sarcastically:

"Miss Julia had other matters to occupy her mind. I fancy you have not yet made the acquaintance of Simon Halliard?"

Francis eyed him resentfully.

"Who the devil is Simon Halliard?"

"He is a friend of Philip Digby's, and also, so he says, of Cousin Richard," Gregory explained briefly. "He, too, has come to Brinkbury to await Varne's arrival. Our kinsman appears to be an exceedingly popular young man."

"What has that to do with Julia?" Francis demanded, and Trayle laughed.

"Merely that Halliard and Digby were at the Park today, and Miss Julia seemed vastly taken with the newcomer," he said trenchantly. "I've no doubt that he is as big a rogue as Digby himself, but he seems to have a way with women. Precisely the sort of man to appeal to an inexperienced country girl like Julia Stonehurst. You have acquired a rival, Francis, and a formidable one at that."

"He'll need to be formidable if I find him trifling with Julia," Francis retorted with unaccustomed spirit. "I may not be able to compete with Varne in wealth or rank, but by Heaven! I'll match myself against any damned adventurer."

His father chuckled with indulgent mockery, but Trayle stood staring at his young relative with an arrested expression in his eyes, and for once refrained from taunting him. A sudden inspiration had been born in his mind, disclosing a vista of transplendent possibilities and giving rise to an excitement which needed all his gamester's experience to conceal. After a moment or two his glance slid round to Bertram, marking for the first time the unhealthy pallor and the oddly haggard appearance of his plump countenance, and then he turned and went quietly from the room, seeking privacy in which to perfect the plans which, in that instant of revelation, had unfolded in his mind.

XI
Another Bargain Is Made

A note from Bertram Colyton was waiting at the inn when Digby and Halliard returned that evening. Philip glanced through it and then tossed it across the table to Simon.

"Trayle has been talking, it seems," he said lightly. "We are bidden to Brinkbury House tomorrow."

"Are we indeed?" Simon read the note and looked up, grinning. "Has Mr. Colyton any pretty daughters?"

"No, he has not. He is a widower, and Francis is his only child. Nor do I advise you to praise Miss Stonehurst's charms too openly, in the boy's presence at least. It would not be well received."

"That would be unfortunate," Simon said softly. "I see that I must be careful not to offend this young buck."

Philip's face hardened, for he had heard that note in Halliard's voice before and knew that it betokened trouble. He said quietly:

"No good will come of making mischief for mischief's sake! Francis Colyton is, I believe, a man governed by his emotions, and capable of any foolhardiness under the spur of them. The purpose of our presence here is to plot against Richard Colyton, and not to enable you to engage in disputes, or flirtations with the village belles. Do I make myself clear?"

Simon's brows lifted.

"Damn you, Philip! Are you presuming to give me orders?"

"I am!" Digby retorted promptly. "In an affair such as this, one must lead and the others follow."

"Oh, lead where you will, my friend, but what guarantee have you that I will follow you?"

"A very potent one," Philip replied with a grin. "I know where the star of death is hidden. You do not."

For a moment or two longer the hazel eyes met the blue in a measuring glance. Then Simon's expression relaxed and he shrugged.

"Yes, you have me there," he admitted ruefully. "I had forgotten the emerald." His glance fell again upon the note from Colyton, and he nodded towards it, adding with a chuckle: "What of that gentleman? Does he also follow you?"

"He does!" Philip's voice was mocking, and ironic laughter glinted in his eyes. "He follows, but he thinks he leads. That, my dear Simon, is the difference between you."

Mr. Halliard remembered those words the following day, when he made the acquaintance of Bertram Colyton. There was some truth in them, he thought. This large, self-assured man must always believe himself the leader in any business in which he engaged, but Simon's acquaintance with Philip Digby's quicksilver wits and forceful ways was sufficiently close for him to be certain in whose hands the real leadership lay.

Gregory Trayle was not at Brinkbury House when the guests arrived, but Francis was there, doing his best to hide the hostility he felt towards Simon beneath a courteous manner, and succeeding tolerably well. Halliard refrained from provoking him, and the lengthy meal passed to the accompaniment of innocuous conversation. When it was over, Francis excused himself and left his father and the two guests to linger over their wine. Philip lost no time in coming to business; drawing his chair closer to Mr. Colyton's, and signing to Simon to do the same, he said briskly:

"No doubt you are wondering, sir, what part Halliard is to play in the business we have in hand. I must tell you that he is fully in my confidence."

"He is, is he?" Bertram spoke with some asperity. "Let me inform you, young man, that it would have been more becoming in you to seek my consent before admitting a third person to the secret."

Simon laughed.

"My dear sir, in that event it is my consent which should have been sought, not yours. I was admitted to the plot before we reached England."

"Why?" Colyton asked bluntly. "Do you also harbour a grudge against my kinsman?"

"No more than against any other puffed-up popinjay who thinks that his birth and his fortune give him the right to ride rough-shod over all who oppose him," Simon replied frankly. "I have been obliged to bear with a deal of impudence from Richard Colyton during the course of our acquaintance, have I not, Digby?"

"You say so," Philip agreed in a tone of some amusement, "though I'll warrant you returned it in good measure. You have some talent for impudence yourself."

Mr. Halliard grinned, apparently taking this as a compliment, but Bertram refused to be diverted. He looked from one to the other with some suspicion.

"A poor pretext for murder, Mr. Halliard," he said curtly. "If you have no deeper cause for resentment against Varne, why embroil yourself in so dangerous a gamble? You risk ending your days upon the gallows if anything should go amiss."

Philip looked at him. The amusement had faded from his face, and the hazel eyes were cold.

"You will remember, sir," he said quietly, "that I told you at our first meeting that the destruction of Richard Colyton is a task I will delegate to no one. When I ride to meet him, I ride alone. His life is mine, and I will yield it to no man."

"Well enough," Bertram agreed slowly. "He has given you good cause to hate him, God knows! But if that is your intention, what part does Halliard play? Why admit him to the affair at all?"

"To secure a line of retreat, of course!" It was Simon who spoke, his cheerful accents in striking contrast to Philip's deadly tone. "Do you suppose, sir, that that is a matter which can be left to chance? The hue and cry will be up before Digby has ridden half a mile. There must be a secure hiding-place and a fresh horse, and a craft ready to take him aboard when the coast is reached. It is the ordering of these things which has occupied me since we landed at Bristol, but now it is done. I will bring him off safely, never fear!"

"I am enchanted to hear it!" Colyton's voice was ironic. "It is a rare thing indeed to encounter a friendship so staunch and undemanding that it will risk so much with no hope of reward."

Simon grinned.

"As to that, sir, I have my own reasons for wanting Digby to win safely out of England. I have a project of my own in mind for when we reach America again, and it needs him in it if it is to have a hope of success. I put it to him before we left the Indies, and the only answer he would give me was that his quarrel with your kinsman must be settled first." He shrugged and spread out his hands. "What else could I do but come to England with him and do my best to see that he comes to no harm?"

For a brief space Mr. Colyton studied the two young men in silence. Some of the suspicion had died out of his expression, but after a little he said:

"Would it be indiscreet, Mr. Halliard, to inquire what manner of enterprise you have in mind?"

"Not in the least," Simon replied promptly. "Since you are unfamiliar with the country in question, I will not weary you with details, but, in brief, it entails an expedition into the wilderness, which, if we are successful, will bring us great profit."

"If we survive it," Philip put in laconically. "In my opinion the odds are against us."

Bertram's sleepy gaze transferred itself thoughtfully to him.

"Then why embark upon the venture, Mr. Digby?"

Philip shrugged.

"A man can die but once, sir," he said carelessly, "and as Halliard says, the prize justifies the risk. Besides, it is his venture, not mine. All I bring to the bargain is a slight familiarity with the country."

"Digby is too modest, Mr. Colyton," Simon retorted. "There are not half a dozen men alive with his knowledge of the trail we must follow." He grinned cheerfully at his host. "You perceive the cause of my anxiety to see him safely out of this other affair."

Bertram nodded. It seemed that his suspicions had

been finally set at rest, for he asked no further questions but merely said:

"All, then, is now in readiness, and we do but await Varne's arrival. I confess that I shall be glad when news of his coming reaches us. It seems to me that he is unaccountably tardy."

"I share your eagerness, Mr. Colyton," Philip replied grimly, "but I think you place too much importance upon the delay. There are so many things which can keep a ship at sea far beyond the expected span of a voyage."

"No doubt, no doubt!" Bertram agreed dubiously. "My knowledge of maritime matters is not extensive. However, you may be sure that word of Varne's arrival in England shall be sent to you immediately it reaches me."

"That is all I ask, sir," Philip replied. "The rest you may safely leave in my hands."

Little more was said on the subject of the conspiracy, but to terminate a social visit abruptly for no apparent cause would arouse suspicion, and it was not until late in the evening that they were able to leave Brinkbury House. As they rode back towards the village, Simon said reflectively:

"If our friend Trayle does know of his kinsman's schemes he is determined to keep his part in them secret. Consider how he absented himself today."

"A prudent gentleman," Philip agreed contemptuously. "He waits to see which way the cards fall before he reveals his own hand. If matters go awry, he will be the first to cry 'shame' at his kinsman, depend upon it!"

"What of Colyton himself?" Simon asked. "Do you think we convinced him of our good faith?"

"I believe so. Your tale was plausible enough to keep his suspicions in abeyance for the short time we are likely to need. No, it is the thought of Mullett, not Colyton, that plagues me now. If we do not find him soon, then either the authorities will be before us, or he will recover sufficiently to risk another attack upon me. That I cannot afford. It would arouse too much suspicion."

"Then find him we must!" Simon said decisively. "We had best separate tomorrow and cast about in different directions. That way we can cover twice as much ground."

In accordance with this suggestion they set out betimes next day, riding together out of the village but thereafter going their separate ways. Simon, saying nothing to Philip of his intentions, turned towards the nearest town, for it seemed to him extremely unlikely that Mullett would, unless driven by dire necessity, linger in any small hamlet or wayside inn where his presence was likely to provoke comment which might reach Digby's ears. In a town he would have far more hope of escaping notice, so to the town Simon went.

Remembering Digby's assertion that one of the fugitives was wounded, his first action there was to seek out the local apothecary, who, after some persuasion, admitted that he had tended a man answering to Mullett's description only the previous day. His patient was suffering from a bullet wound in the leg, and could be found at the sign of the Black Dog in Market Street.

Simon located the inn without difficulty, but the palpably nervous landlady at first denied the presence in her house of any injured man. Halliard, knowing Mullett to be an arrant bully, paid no heed to this, but set himself instead to calm her fears, succeeding so well that at length she protested no longer, and directed him to the second room on the left at the head of the stairs.

Simon smiled and thanked her, and went briskly up the steep, dark staircase. The passage above was narrow and low-pitched, and at the door of Mullett's room he paused to glance quickly to right and left before taking out his pistol and cocking it. Then he rapped sharply on the door.

There was a subdued murmur of voices within, then footsteps slowly crossed the room and the door opened a few inches to reveal a pallid, sharp-featured face. Simon levelled his pistol at it, then, as its owner involuntarily recoiled, thrust his way into the room and kicked the door shut behind him.

Ned Mullett was lying, half-dressed, upon the bed, but at that impetuous entrance he heaved himself up on to one elbow, his ugly, swarthy face a study in astonishment and dismay, while his accomplice backed away and stood staring at the intruder with dropped jaw and starting eyes.

Mullett's free hand was groping among the pillows and tumbled covers as though in search of a weapon. Simon moved his own pistol suggestively.

"Don't be a fool, Ned!" he advised him briskly. "I'd as lief not put the apothecary to the trouble of digging another bullet out of your ugly carcase."

The other man froze into stillness and lay staring at him, his eyes evilly narrowed. Simon nodded his approval.

"That's better," he said mockingly, "and it will be better still if we have no repetition of that folly. I have not come here to quarrel with you."

"Haven't you, by God?" Mullett sneered, eyeing the pistol in his visitor's hand. "Blast you, Halliard! How did you find me out?"

"By using my wits, Ned. I knew one of you was wounded, so it was reasonable to suppose that the apothecary could tell me where to find you."

"So you knew that, did you? How, in the devil's name?"

Simon grinned at him.

"Philip Digby told me."

"Digby!" Mullett made another convulsive movement, checked only by the unwavering barrel of Halliard's pistol. "What trickery is here?"

"I will tell you." Simon leaned back against the door, keeping the weapon levelled. "You are a fool, Ned, as I told you just now. You will never lay hands on the emerald by the means you have tried."

"I won't, eh?" Mullett said sullenly. "I've been mighty close to it a couple of times."

Simon shook his head.

"Once, perhaps," he replied, "but after that warning of your intentions, do you suppose that Digby was mad enough to go on carrying the jewel with him? He has it safely hidden away somewhere, and the three of us might search until doomsday with small hope of finding it." He watched dismay flood into the two unprepossessing faces confronting him, and laughed. "That possibility never entered your mind, did it? You would have murdered him, and then found, too late, that you had killed the only man who could tell you where the emerald is hidden."

"No need to kill him!" It was Mullett's companion who spoke, breaking his long silence. "If we can lay hands on him there's many a way of making him share his secret."

"Not Digby," Simon said scornfully. "You do not know him, my friend! He would send you on half a dozen false trails, and probably contrive to escape while you were following them." He glanced inquiringly at Mullett. "Do I speak truth, Ned?"

"Aye, more's the pity," Mullett growled. "That young devil's more tricky than a fox with the hounds at his tail." He stared at Simon, suspicion kindling in his eyes. "How came you by your knowledge?"

"From Digby himself," Simon answered frankly. "I used my wits, Ned, as you might have done had you possessed any. There is a deal that you and I could tell the good people of Brinkbury concerning Mr. Philip Digby. I went to him openly and demanded the emerald as the price of my silence."

The other continued to watch him, disbelief and grudging admiration struggling with the suspicion in his eyes.

"He never agreed?" he said slowly at last.

"No," Simon admitted ruefully, "but I did strike a bargain with him. You were becoming something of an embarrassment to him, Ned, and he was glad enough to enlist my aid in tracking you down. Oh, be easy!" For Mullett had made a sudden movement. "He'll not learn of your whereabouts from me. I told you I was not here to quarrel."

There was a pause. Mullett shifted himself into a more comfortable position on the bed, though without removing his sullen stare from Halliard's face, while the pale youth looked uncertainly from one to the other.

"Why, then?" Mullett asked at length.

Simon was in no haste to reply. As though in proof of his good faith, he uncocked the pistol and returned it to his pocket. Then, folding his arms, he said softly:

"To make a bargain in my turn. At present Digby is convinced of my good faith, and sooner or later I shall discover where he has bestowed the jewel. When that time comes, the three of us together should be able to get possession of it and to dispose of him. We make our escape to France or Holland and there sell the emerald, the price we get for it to be divided into two, one half going to me, the other being shared between you in whatever manner you choose. What do you say?"

Mullett shook his head.

"Three equal shares, or nothing," he said promptly. "Why in hell's name should your gains be twice as great as ours?"

"Because I bring more to the bargain than you do. Remember, my friend, though I might possibly contrive to get possession of the jewel without your help, without mine you have no chance at all. Digby would rather it lay hidden for ever than fell into your hands."

The silence which greeted these words was a tacit admission of their truth. After a few moments of baffled deliberation Mullett said sourly:

"You say Digby wants to track us down. What if he succeeds before you can discover what we need to know?"

"He will not, I give you my word. I shall tell him that I have found you, and that the wound he dealt you is grave enough to keep you out of mischief for many a day. That will content him. The authorities are seeking you also, and Digby has no wish for you to fall into the hands of the Law. You might disclose what you know, and that would spoil the game he is playing here."

"What is his game, Halliard?" Mullett demanded. "Plague take me if I can make a guess at it!"

Simon chuckled.

"It is subtle beyond your comprehension, Ned," he told him bluntly, "and he has far more at stake than a single jewel, no matter how costly. That, however, need not concern us, since we cannot hope to profit from it. What do you say? Are you with me in this?"

"Aye, we're with you," Mullett agreed grudgingly. "There's naught we can do till we know where the jewel is

hidden. But if you try to play me false, Halliard, by God,
I'll——"

"Spare me your threats!" Simon broke in contemptuously. "If I did have it in mind to betray you, do you suppose such blustering would alter my purpose? You know
me better than that, I'll wager! Now heed what I say. Lie
close here till I come again, and do not show yourselves in
the town. Digby has made powerful friends in these parts,
and half the county is on the watch for you." He nodded
towards Mullett's bandaged leg. "How grave is that injury?"

The other man shrugged.

"I've known worse," he said laconically. "A week will
see me on my feet again."

"Good!" Simon straightened up and set his hand on the
latch. "In a week's time I will come again, and God send I
have news of the emerald by then. Meanwhile, keep close,
as I warned you."

He nodded curtly in farewell, and went out of the room
and down the stairs, whistling merrily. He was well satisfied with his morning's work and not in the least concerned by the trick he had played on Ned Mullett, for he
knew that the other man would spend the next week considering ways and means of cheating him once the aptly-
named star of death had been secured. His mood of exhilaration survived the ride back to Brinkbury, and was still
upon him when, reaching the crossroads on the hill, he
recognized a solitary horseman approaching from the
direction of the village as Gregory Trayle. Simon hailed
him with his usual cheerful self-assurance, and drew rein
where the roads met to wait for the other man to come
up.

Mr. Trayle, it seemed, was in an unwontedly affable
mood, for he announced that he was on his way to
Foxwood Grange and pressed Halliard to accompany him.
Nothing loth, Simon agreed, though he wondered a little
that Trayle should be at such pains to oblige him.

He wondered more than ever when the Grange was
reached, and he found Trayle using every opportunity to
thrust him into the company of Miss Stonehurst. Perplex-

ity did not prevent him from making the most of the opportunities for gallantry thus offered, but he was conscious all the while of a faint uneasiness, for he was sure
that Gregory Trayle never exerted himself to oblige anyone unless he could see in the deed some benefit to himself. Deciding, however, that the simplest way to discover
his motive was to fall in with his obvious wishes, Simon
applied himself to the task with zest. As he told Digby on
the night of his arrival, there were more pleasant diversions than the pursuit of Ned Mullett.

XII

The Path Through the Wood

Simon reached the Colyton Arms again to find that Digby
had not yet returned, nor did he put in an appearance until supper was on the table. He came in then dusty and irritable, for a day of fruitless searching had terminated in
the further disappointment of a brief call at Greydon Park
which had failed to grant him even a glimpse of Joanna,
Sir Andrew remarking casually that Lady Selbourne and
her daughter were visiting the house of a relative some
miles distant and were not expected to return that night.

He entered the inn parlour to find Simon already at
table, and Halliard, after one glance at the set of his lips,
and the frown between his brows, decided against making
any mention of Gregory Trayle's remarkable affability, or
his own visit to Foxwood Grange. Neither piece of information was likely to be well received at present.

Philip greeted him briefly and took his seat at the table,
but Simon observed that he ate very little of the food
which was set before him. After a while, when Ellen had
left the room, Halliard said cheerfully:

"Well, what fortune had you?"

"None!" Phillip's voice was curt. "I tell you, Simon,
matters begin to look serious. Until Mullett is found, we
hover on the brink of disaster."

Simon grinned at him.

"Calm yourself, my friend," he replied. "Mullett is found, and silenced."

He described his visit to the Black Dog Inn, and as Philip listened some of the strain and weariness faded from his face. It was clear that Halliard had been able to deal far more effectively with Ned Mullett than he could possibly have done himself, for the only weapons at his disposal would have been threats or bribery, neither of which could have been depended upon. Now that Simon had offered himself as their only hope of finding the emerald, greed alone would hold them in check, at least until his next visit a week hence.

"And if our business is not concluded by then, we must find an excuse for further delay," Simon agreed when Digby remarked on this, and Philip nodded.

"Though I hope to God it is concluded by then," he said. "It promises already to drag on for longer than I expected."

Halliard cocked an inquiring eyebrow.

"Growing impatient?" he queried mockingly.

"Yes!" Philip spoke in a low voice, stifling a sigh. He stared at the candle-flames, seeing Joanna's face at the heart of their golden glow. "Yes, Simon, damnably impatient!"

For a moment or two Halliard watched him in thoughtful silence. At length he said, jerking his head in the general direction of Brinkbury House:

"But you are not yet satisfied yonder?"

"Colyton?" Philip shook his head. "Not entirely. I would like to know with more certainty what part Trayle means to play. That he is ignorant of the plot I do not believe."

"Nor I," Simon agreed emphatically. "What say you to letting me try to discover how far he is involved in Colyton's scheming? 'Tis plain he will disclose nothing to you, for I never saw two men so plainly destined to be enemies as you and Trayle.

Leave it to me, my friend! I will find out how far he is committed, and what he hopes to gain."

He did not consider it necessary to disclose his conviction that Julia Stonehurst was, in some obscure manner, involved in whatever plot Gregory Trayle was weaving, or that he intended to begin his inquiries at Foxwood Grange. Digby had made it very plain that his friend's interest in Miss Stonehurst did not meet with his approval.

Fortune favoured him next day, for Philip, relieved of the pressing anxiety of betrayal by Ned Mullett, and knowing that he had little hope of seeing Joanna that day, decided to ride into Bristol on business of his own. The double journey, which few inhabitants of Brinkbury would have attempted in one day, necessitated setting out soon after dawn, and could not be completed until after nightfall, so that Simon had the entire day to himself.

He spent the greater part of it at Foxwood Grange, where he exerted himself to please and was soon on the best of terms with the whole family, and Julia in particular. So great, in fact, was his success in that quarter that when, shortly before dinner, Francis arrived with Gregory Trayle, she bestowed upon her old playfellow no more than the most casual greeting.

Francis had already been wrought to a dangerous pitch of jealousy by his cousin's subtle hints, and this encounter added fresh fuel to the flames. Gregory watched him with secret satisfaction; he knew from experience what Philip Digby had guessed, that Francis was capable of any recklessness if his feelings were sufficiently aroused.

When Digby returned to Brinkbury that night, Simon said little of his own activities that day, and Philip, tired after his long ride, did not press him. He showed no greater curiosity at breakfast next morning, merely informing Halliard that he had a matter of importance to attend to, and did not know how long it would be before he returned.

The matter of importance took him, a short while later, towards Greydon Park, but before he reached his destination he found that his horse had cast a shoe. Leaving the animal at the forge in the little village of Greydon, he set off to walk to the manor-house, but he had barely left the last cottage behind him when he came face to face with Joanna herself.

She was alone, tripping along the lane in a cloak of sapphire blue, with a large basket on her arm. She was peeping anxiously beneath the white cloth which covered it, but when she looked up and found him confronting her, surprise and delight flooded into her face, and setting her burden down anyhow in the road, she went without hesitation into his arms and clasped her own about his neck.

"Philip!" she whispered. "Oh, my dearest, at last! How lucky that we should chance to meet like this."

He kissed her swift and hard upon the lips and then let her go, conscious of the folly of thus betraying their feelings in a spot where anyone might stumble upon them. Holding her hands lightly in his own, he looked down at her with laughing eyes.

"Lucky indeed," he replied. "I was coming to call upon you, though I scarcely dared to hope that I would see you alone." He released her hands and bent to retrieve the basket. "What have you here?"

"My mother told me to carry some comforts to old Mrs. Hedges," Joanna explained, "and though I was hoping that you would come today, I did not dare to make an excuse in case she guessed the truth."

"I will carry it for you the rest of the way," he said, "and then escort you home. I have been cursing myself for a fool these three days past that I had no means of communicating with you without your parents knowledge."

"I have been thinking about that, too," Joanna agreed, "and I believe I know just how we can arrange it. Nancy, my maid, is cousin to Ellen at the Colyton Arms, and they are close friends. They would both be willing to carry messages for us, I am quite sure."

"Willing, perhaps," Philip said with a frown, "but in such a matter discretion is needful also, and Ellen does not seem to me an ideal go-between."

"She is a trifle scatterbrained," Joanna admitted, "but Nancy is older and much more sensible. We could depend upon her without question."

"Very well, then, but we must make use of neither

unless there is a real need for it. Messages can too easily go astray." He broke off as Joanna halted at the gate of one of the outlying cottages. "Is this your destination?"

"Yes." She pushed open the gate and took the basket from him as she spoke. "I will be as quick as I can."

She hurried along the path and disappeared into the house, while Philip leaned against the gate-post and gazed idly at a plump black kitten which was playing among the fallen leaves at the foot of a nearby tree. After a short while Joanna rejoined him, saying, as they began to retrace their steps:

"We need not go by way of the road. There is a path through the Lower Wood and across the park. We are not likely to meet anyone that way."

The path was soon reached, and within a few minutes they were walking through the dying splendour of the autumn woods. Philip took Joanna's hand and drew it through the crook of his arm, and so for a space they walked in silence. At last she said:

"Is there no news yet of Lord Varne, Philip?"

"Not yet," he replied. "I was at Brinkbury House a few days ago and Mr. Colyton was in some concern at his tardiness."

"I do hope he will come soon," she said with a sigh. "I do not wish to be troublesome, but can you not speak to Father now, today? Why do we have to meet secretly like this? We have nothing of which to be ashamed."

He did not reply for a moment, but then he said in a low voice:

"You promised to trust me, Joanna."

"I do, Philip! You know I do, but I do not like to deceive my parents. Suppose someone else guessed our secret—someone like Gregory Trayle, for instance—and told them? They would be so hurt and angry. They might even forbid us to meet again."

He shook his head.

"We cannot tell them, Joanna. I am sorry, my love, but believe me, I have good reasons for refusing, reasons which I cannot disclose even to you. We must await Varne's coming. It cannot now be long delayed." He paused, looking at her with a curious expression. "Perhaps then you will be glad of this secrecy. Perhaps when Varne has come, you will regret the promise you have given to Philip Digby."

"You have no right to say that!" She pulled her hand from his arm and swung round to face him, her eyes bright with hurt and anger. "I am not interested in Lord Varne! I do not care if he is the richest, cleverest, handsomest man in the world, and if he begged me on his knees to marry him, I would refuse! Oh, you are cruel even to think such a thing of me!"

Her voice broke and she turned her head away, brushing one hand across her eyes. Philip, half laughing, half concerned, pulled her into his arms, ignoring her half-hearted attempt to thrust him away.

"What a little spitfire you are, to be sure," he said softly. "My dearest love, I did not mean to grieve you. It is merely that when Varne does come, you may find that you have been mistaken in your feelings for me. Only, whatever may befall, remember one thing." His voice was very serious now. He turned her face towards him, and the brilliant, green-flecked eyes looked deep into hers. "In my feelings for you I have always been completely honest. You are not my first love, Joanna, but you are the dearest and the last. No other woman has ever meant, or ever could mean, as much to me as you do. Always believe that."

She put up her hand to touch his cheek, smiling a little now although her eyes were wet.

"I would so much rather be the last than the first," she whispered, "and nothing could change my feelings for you. I know that, even though I do not understand why you should fear that it might. Lord Varne would not say anything against you, surely? You are his friend."

There was a pause, so brief as to be scarcely perceptible. Philip had laid his cheek against her hair and she could no longer see his face.

"We have known each other for many years," he said slowly, "but whether or not we are friends would be hard to say. One thing, however, I must in justice tell you.

Compared to the Earl of Varne, or even to plain Richard Colyton, Philip Digby is a person of no account. My father was Richard's tutor, and that is the reason for our close acquaintance. It is not likely to recommend me to yours, in the light of a suitor for your hand."

"I think you wrong him," Joanna said quietly. "It is his custom to judge a man, not by what he has, but by what he is."

"And you, Joanna?" he prompted gently as she paused. "Does it not trouble you that I have so little to offer?"

She shook her head.

"I think I am glad," she said softly. "If you were like your friend, Mr. Halliard, and owned a family estate in Jamaica, you would feel it your duty to go back there, would you not? I would go anywhere with you, Philip, but it would grieve me to be so far away. My parents are not young, and they would be so lonely without me."

The latter part of what she said was lost upon him, for he was considering, with astonishment and dismay, that reference to Simon's ancestral acres. He lifted his head, and looked at her with a faint frown.

"Who told you that Halliard owns an estate in the Indies?"

"Why, Julia did. She came to see me this morning, so early that I thought at first that something must be wrong." She gave a little laugh. "Lord Varne had best come soon, if Mr. Stonehurst's ambition is to be realized. Julia can think and talk of nothing but your friend. I have never seen her in such a fluster!"

The frown deepened in Philip's eyes.

"Have they met, then, since that first time at your home?"

"Yes, of course! Mr. Trayle took Mr. Halliard to Foxwood Grange two days ago, and he went there again yesterday.". She broke off, her wide eyes searching his face. "Philip, what is it? What is wrong?"

He was still frowning, but shook his head in quick denial.

"Nothing that cannot be set to rights, sweetheart," he said reassuringly, "though Miss Stonehurst would do well to beware of Simon Halliard. Encourage her to confide in you if you can, so that we may have warning of any folly she may be contemplating, for I would not put it beyond his power to persuade her into an elopement."

Joanna looked horrified.

"Phillip, you are not serious? Her father would never forgive her."

"Let us hope, then, that Halliard realizes it," Philip replied lightly, "for that would be her surest safeguard. Do not look so anxious, Joanna! I think I know how to prevent such a thing from happening."

"I hope you do," she said fervently, "for Julia's sake. Mr. Stonehurst is determined that she shall marry Lord Varne, and does not care what her feelings may be. Oh, thank heaven he is not my father!"

"Amen to that," Philip replied with a smile. "Sir Andrew I may succeed in winning over; Mr. Stonehurst, never!" He put his hand into his pocket and took out some small object which she could not see. "I have something for you, Joanna. Give me your hand—no, the left one."

Wonderingly she did so, and he slid a ring on to her finger, a dainty thing of sapphires and pearls. Joanna gave a gasp and stood staring at it, while Philip, still holding her hand imprisoned in his own, continued quietly:

"Will you wear it for me, Joanna? Whether or not your father gives his consent, will you promise to be my wife?"

Eyes as blue as the sapphires themselves were lifted to his. Without shyness and without hesitation she gave him her answer.

"Yes, Philip, I will. Whatever befall."

A little later, as they walked on along the path, Joanna stretched out her hand to admire the ring and said happily:

"It is the prettiest thing that ever I saw. Where did you get it, Philip? Not in Brinkbury, I know."

He shook his head.

"No, in Bristol. I rode there yesterday." He captured the extended hand again and bore it to his lips. "I fear you will need to keep it hidden, sweetheart, for a while at least. God send the time is not far distant when you may wear it openly."

"I will be very careful," she promised. "When we are together I will wear it, but for the rest of the time . . ." She broke off, conscious of the sudden tenseness of the man beside her. A questioning glance showed that he was no longer attending to her, but appeared to be listening intently to some sound which had escaped her ears.

"What is it?" she whispered. "What do you hear?"

He had neither halted nor hastened his lazy steps, and his arm around her shoulders drew her with him, but he said, so softly that she could scarcely catch the words:

"Someone is following us."

She caught her breath and her fingers tightened on his, but she forced herself to give no other sign. In the same tone as he had used, she asked:

"Do you think it is Ned Mullett?"

"No!" Philip bent his head so that his lips brushed the curls at her temple; he spoke crisply, just above his breath. "Do not let them guess we have discovered them. I must find out who it is."

She nodded, straining her ears to detect some betraying sound from the stealthy pursuer. She could hear nothing but the rustle of their own footsteps through the fallen leaves, and the small, habitual sounds of the woodland. The minutes crawled by on leaden feet, and then, at a spot where the path curved sharply to skirt a big tree, Philip halted and drew her into the shelter of the gnarled trunk.

"Stay here, my love," he said softly, "and do not be frightened. I shall not be far away."

He moved past her and into the undergrowth beyond the tree, and the thinning autumn foliage swallowed him up. Joanna stood where he had left her, pressing herself back against the trunk of the tree and fighting a growing desire to scream, to shatter the silence of the woodland which suddenly seemed charged with menace.

Philip moved cautiously among the trees and bushes, working back in the direction of the road, and after a few minutes emerged again on to the path only a short way

from the spot where he had left it. The tree was still
visible from where he stood, with the edge of Joanna's
hooped skirt and blue cloak peeping from behind it, and
between him and the tree a man was crouching in the
shelter of a clump of bushes, his back towards Digby. He
was powerfully built, and wearing a green riding-coat
which seemed vaguely familiar. Philip smiled grimly and
drew his pistol from his pocket.

"Behind you, my friend!" he said briskly. "You are
seeking me, I think?"

With a choking cry the man sprang up and around, revealing the dismayed countenance of Oliver Stonehurst. It
was clear that he had thought Digby to be still with
Joanna, and his chagrin on discovering his mistake was
ludicrous. Philip's smile grew a trifle broader, and even
more bleak.

"I have a profound dislike of being spied upon," he
continued, "so perhaps you will be good enough to explain what the devil you are about."

Oliver glared at him.

"Damn your insolence, Digby!" he stuttered. "Explain,
is it? I fancy you have a trifle of explaining to do yourself!"

"Not to you, Stonehurst," Philip retorted softly. "I am
not accountable to you for my actions."

"Oliver!" It was Joanna's voice, eloquent of anger and
astonishment. She had emerged abruptly from behind the
tree and was regarding him indignantly. "Of all the despicable, underhanded tricks! How dare you give me such a
fright?"

"If I frightened you, Joanna, I am sorry," he replied
stiffly. "That was not my intention."

"What was your intention?" Philip's voice was still
quiet, but in no way reassuring. "I should be interested to
hear it."

"So, too, should I," Joanna agreed, and added bod-
ingly: "Though I can think of nothing which could excuse
such ungentlemanly conduct."

"Of that you shall be the judge," Oliver told her. "As I
rode down the hill I saw you coming into the wood with

Digby. I knew how little this path was used, and so I dismounted and followed you, in case you should have need of me." His voice trembled; try as he would, he could not maintain his pose of lofty dignity. "I need not have troubled myself. I have seen more than enough to tell me that."

"You have said more than enough also," Philip broke in. He was calm enough on the surface, but an overwhelming anger throbbed in his voice. "Why, you impudent young cub, I am more than half minded to give you the thrashing you deserve!"

Oliver gave a snort of scornful laughter. He was a larger man than Digby and supremely confident of his own superior strength.

"Try it, then," he jeered. "You are ready enough with threats as long as you have a pistol in your hand."

Philip glanced down at the weapon, which in his anger he had forgotten, and thrust it impatiently into his pocket again. Then he looked at Joanna.

"Will you be good enough to walk on, my dear?" he said quietly. "I will join you again presently."

"No, I will not," she replied promptly, and brushed past Oliver to come to his side. Clasping both hands about his arm, she looked defiantly at Stonehurst. "I will not let you fight each other, because it is not at all necessary. Oliver has no right to come spying upon us, and whatever he may have seen is no concern of his."

"I have no wish to start brawling, God knows!" Oliver said furiously. "This is not a matter which can be settled with fists." He looked at Philip. "Name your seconds, Digby!"

"If it cannot be settled with fists, still less can it be settled with swords," Philip replied contemptuously. "You had best go home, and learn not to let your temper get the better of your wits."

"Yes, please go!" Joanna added coldly. "You have behaved abominably, and I do not wish to talk with you at all."

For a moment or two longer Oliver stood staring sullenly from one to the other, and then he thrust past them and strode furiously towards the road. When the sound of his footsteps had died away, Philip looked at Joanna.

"Will he go to your father?"

She looked troubled, but shook her head.

"No, I think not. Tale-bearing has never been Oliver's way. I am afraid he is more likely to try to force a quarrel on you under some pretext which does not involve me."

Philip's expression was grim.

"He may do that with my good will. That young man stands in need of a sharp lesson, and he will find me ready and willing to administer it."

Joanna looked at him, at the set lips and frowning brows, and the eyes from which laughter and tenderness alike had wholly vanished. For the first time she realized that this man to whom she had plighted herself, whose ring was even now upon her finger, was in many respects still a stranger to her. With that look in his face he seemed suddenly older, and somehow remote.

"Do not talk so," she said softly, "and do not look so, either. You must not fight with Oliver." She laid her hands on his shoulders, looking up anxiously into his face. "Promise me, Philip!"

His expression softened, and he smiled.

"Very well, I promise it, you little tyrant, and if I am branded a craven as a result of it, you will be well served. Now we had best go on our way, in case your belief in Stonehurst's forbearance is mistaken, and he is hurrying to betray us to your father."

XIII

The Challenge

This fear, however, proved groundless. There was no sign of young Mr. Stonehurst at Greydon Park, and Sir Andrew and his lady welcomed Philip with their customary kindness. They insisted that he should stay to dine, and since there were no other guests, dinner was very much a family affair. It was all very pleasant, but beneath his enjoyment of it, and his delight in Joanna's company, Philip was conscious of a growing restiveness induced by the falseness of his position.

He said farewell at last and, mounting the horse which Sir Andrew had sent one of his grooms to fetch from the smithy, rode back to Brinkbury at a pace which was in itself an indication of his mental unrest. Simon was at the inn, and Philip lost no time in coming to the point. Eyeing the other man in a measuring fashion, he said abruptly:

"Did you visit Foxwood Grange today?"

Halliard's glance flickered and grew wary, but when he spoke his tone was casual.

"I did. Have you any objection?"

"To the visit, none. To your pursuit of Julia Stonehurst, many. It will not do, Simon! She is not for you."

"No?" This time the voice was silky, dangerously so. "For you, perhaps? Yet I could have sworn that your interests lay elsewhere."

"No, not for me," Philip replied contemptuously. "I am not prompted by jealousy, if that is what you are thinking, but I am in some sort responsible for your presence here, and I will not stand aside and let you ruin that unfortunate girl."

"You have a high opinion of my morals, have you not?" Simon leaned back in his chair, watching Philip with half-shut, mocking eyes. "How do you know that I do not mean honestly by her?"

"Because where women are concerned you never had an honest intention in your life," Philip retorted frankly. "Unless, in this instance, you are attracted by the thought of her father's money."

"I'll not deny," Simon admitted with a grin, "that the chink of the old gentleman's gold sounds pleasantly in my ears, but you will not deny that Julia has charms of her own? If wealth were the only lure that draws me, I should not look beyond Miss Selbourne, who has no brother to claim a major share of the estate."

For all his seeming indifference he was watching Philip closely, and was rewarded by a further tightening of the

lips, and a gleam of anger in the hazel eyes. Digby refused to be side-tracked, however, and said scornfully:

"Do you think her father would let her marry you,
even if he believed that tale of an estate in the Indies?"

"Damn you, Philip! Are you calling me a liar?" Simon
demanded aggrievedly. "When I told them that my father
owns one of the largest plantations in Jamaica, I spoke no
more than the truth."

"No more, but a good deal less," Philip retorted. "I'll
wager you made no mention of your three elder brothers,
or of the fact that your father kicked you out of his house
more than ten years ago and told you to go to the devil at
your own expense, not his."

Simon grinned again, and rubbed a finger against the
bridge of his nose.

" 'Tis unbecoming to air family disputes in public," he
said brazenly, "and besides, you warned me when we
made our bargain that I must do nothing to injure your
credit in these parts. You should be grateful to me for
providing a background of such solid respectability."

Philip looked at him, and despite his genuine anger the
flicker of a smile touched his lips. Halliard looked anything but solidly respectable, lounging there in the chair
before the fire with a glass of wine in his hand and the
light of the flames flickering across his reckless, rakehell's
face. It was astonishing that Mr. Stonehurst, who appeared to be a man of some shrewdness, should make so
shameless an adventurer free of his house. Philip could
only suppose that he was blinded by ambition, and Simon's supposed friendship with the new Earl.

"Setting aside the question of my gratitude," he said, "I
will warn you again that you would never be permitted to
marry her; and if you are thinking of persuading her to
elope with you and so forcing her father's hand, I must
remind you again of your own father's example. Daughters can be disinherited as well as sons."

There was a moment of silence before Simon replied.
He was holding up his glass and watching the play of the
firelight through the wine it held, a contemplative smile
lingering about his lips. At last he said lazily:

"I am aware of that, my friend! 'Tis true that at first I did consider mending my fortunes with a marriage-ring, but, apart from the obstacles in my way, I don't doubt that I should find even golden bonds too irksome to be borne. If, however, the fair Julia were to elope with me, do you not think that her ambitious parent would be willing to pay handsomely for her return—and my silence?"

This time the pause was even longer, but at length Philip said in a tone of quiet disgust:

"I wonder if you realize just how despicable you are."

Simon laughed softly.

"Hard words, my friend, hard words!" he retorted. "Are you not playing precisely the same game at Greydon Park?"

He put his glass to his lips, but before he could taste the wine it was dashed aside to shatter into fragments on the hearth, and the point of Philip's sword was at his throat. He looked along its gleaming length into a face tight-lipped and narrow-eyed, white with anger.

"One word more in that strain," said a crisp, deadly voice, "and as God is my witness, it will be your last! Joanna Selbourne is my promised wife."

Simon blinked at him, more in astonishment than in alarm. Then he raised his hand and delicately set the sword aside.

"My felicitations!" he said calmly. "Had you not knocked the glass from my hand, I would have been happy to drink your health."

For a second or two longer Philip continued to glare at him, but when Simon continued to meet the look with complete self-possession, he shook his head resignedly and began to laugh. Slamming his sword back into the scabbard, he went across to the table and filled two glasses, one of which he handed to Simon. Mr. Halliard accepted it with a grin.

"Then do so now, confound your impudence!" Philip told him. "Only mark this! Unless you abandon your design against Miss Stonehurst, there is an end to our bargain, and to your hopes of ever seeing the emerald again.

I mean that, Simon! She is Joanna's friend, and I'll not let her come to any harm at your hands."

Mr. Halliard accepted the ultimatum philosophically, admitting that he would be more reluctant to relinquish his claim upon the emerald than upon Miss Stonehurst. When the promised toast had been drunk, however, he said reflectively:

"You are very anxious to foil my villainous designs upon the fair Julia, but others feel differently, it seems. I am more than a little curious to know why Gregory Trayle is so determined to thrust her into my arms."

"Trayle?" Philip said blankly. "What has he to do with it?"

Since further secrecy was pointless, Simon gave him a brief account of Trayle's activities, and concluded by saying:

"It may have escaped your memory that I undertook to discover the extent of Trayle's part in the plot. I am little wiser as yet, but our friendship ripens apace. Look at this!"

He pulled a piece of paper from his pocket and tossed it across to Digby. It was a note from Gregory Trayle, couched in the friendliest terms and inviting Mr. Halliard to Brinkbury House next day for a bout with the foils.

"Fencing?" Philip said blankly, raising his eyes from the note. "Why that, in the devil's name?"

Simon shrugged.

"We had some talk together yesterday on the subject of swordsmanship," he replied, "and Trayle made mention then of matching his skill against mine, though I thought no more of it until I received that." He laughed suddenly. "Perhaps he shares your belief that it will come to a meeting between you, and does not wish to rust for lack of practice."

Philip smiled grimly.

"Perhaps he does," he said, "and it is none so bad a notion at that. We'll have the foils out ourselves, Simon, before many hours have passed, for something tells me that we may have need of all our skill before this game is played."

Have them out they did, early on the following morning, on the frost-whitened bowling-green behind the inn. When the bout was over, they went indoors with prodigious appetites to breakfast, and then, towards mid-day, Simon set out for Brinkbury House and his engagement with Gregory Trayle.

That gentleman welcomed him with a friendliness which matched that of the invitation, coming to meet him in the square, spacious hall with its polished floor and vast, old-fashioned fireplace. This was the oldest part of the house, and no longer used as a living-room as in days gone by, but it was admirably suited to their present purpose. The big table which usually occupied the centre of the apartment had already been pushed to one side, and on it reposed a pair of fencing foils and a silver tray bearing bottles and glasses and a large jug of ale. Simon surveyed these preparations with some amusement.

"You mean to waste no time, Mr. Trayle," he remarked.

Gregory smiled.

"I'd not be guilty of the discourtesy of keeping you waiting," he replied. "In fact, my dear Halliard, I have to thank you for accepting my invitation. I like to keep my wrist in practice, but here in Brinkbury it is devilish hard to find an opponent."

Simon's brows lifted.

"I should have supposed that your cousin would be willing to accommodate you."

"Francis?" Gregory laughed gently. "I take a turn with him from time to time, naturally, but at risk of appearing conceited I must admit that my part is that of teacher more than anything else. Oh, the boy has some skill and in time will no doubt develop into a very tolerable swordsman, but as yet he lacks experience."

Halliard had taken up one of the foils and was balancing it thoughtfully in his hand, but he shot the other man a swift, humorous glance.

"You seem very certain, sir, that I am not similarly lacking."

"My dear Halliard," Gregory expostulated with a

laugh, "you are not, I trust, trying to convince me that you have never fought in earnest?"

"No," Simon admitted cheerfully. "I have enjoyed a fair share of fighting during the course of my life, but whether my skill is of a calibre to match yours remains to be seen. Rumour has it that you are known in London as a duellist of some note."

Gregory shrugged slightly.

"Such a reputation is not hard to acquire," he said with a hint of scorn in his voice, "and even easier to lose. However, we waste time in idle speculation. The question can soon be settled, can it not?"

Halliard agreed that it could, and without more ado they removed their coats and boots and took their places in the centre of the room. The bout began cautiously, each man seeking to judge the other's ability, and it soon became evident to Simon that Trayle's reputation was by no means undeserved. His mastery of the sword was considerable, for he had some cunning tricks of fence which needed all his opponent's skill to combat, and he fought with a kind of cold concentration which might well have unnerved a less experienced swordsman than Halliard.

When they finally desisted they were both breathing heavily, and the honours rested fairly equally between them. Trayle laid his foil once more upon the table and gave a little nod of satisfaction.

"I must thank you again, Halliard. An excellent morning's sport."

"No need for thanks," Simon replied with a grin. "My enjoyment has equalled yours. Permit me to congratulate you. I should have been hard put to it had we been fighting in earnest."

"You are too modest!" Gregory went to the other end of the table, where the tray had been placed. "Will you take ale, sir, or wine?"

"Ale, I thank you, and as for modesty, that has never been among my very few virtues. I was outmatched, and I know it." He paused, watching the other man without seeming to do so. "You should take a turn at the foils with Digby, Mr. Trayle."

"Indeed?" Gregory had filled two tankards, and now handed one to Simon. His voice expressed no more than a polite interest. "Is that to imply that he is a better swordsman than yourself?"

"At his best, I know of none to equal him," Simon replied readily, "and his powers of endurance are far beyond the ordinary. That is not to be wondered at, I suppose. The life he has led fosters such endurance."

"The life he has led!" Gregory repeated softly. "And what manner of life may that be? Mr. Digby himself chooses to shroud it in mystery."

"The devil he does!" Simon appeared surprised at this. "I thought he had made no secret of the fact that he has spent much time on the frontiers of the American colonies. The life there does not make for softness."

For a moment or two Trayle's glance rested coldly upon his companion's face. He suspected Mr. Halliard of trifling with him, and the possibility pleased him not at all. On the other hand, it would not suit his present purpose to quarrel with him.

"I should not have supposed," he said sarcastically, "that it made for swordsmanship, either."

"You are in the right of it there," Simon agreed promptly. "It was buckskins and a musket then, rather than a laced coat and a sword. But Digby is equally at home with either, I give you my word."

"A gentleman of parts!" Trayle was sneering openly now. "I am astonished that a man of such wide and varied interests should be content to rusticate in this quiet spot."

"There are certain, somewhat potent lures which hold him here, as you may perhaps have heard," Simon said casually, and waited hopefully to see whether Trayle would rise to the bait.

He was disappointed. Trayle's hard grey eyes met his squarely, with the faintest glimmer of mocking comprehension, but he made no reply, waiting instead for the other man to speak again.

Mr. Halliard was for the moment nonplussed, and to cover the awkward pause he turned away to take up his

coat, fumbling carelessly in the pocket for a handkerchief
with which to mop a brow heated by the exertion of the
past hour. He pulled it out, and something else besides, a
smaller, daintier wisp of lace and cambric which floated to
the floor at Trayle's feet. He bent to pick it up, and as his
gaze fell upon the initials embroidered upon it his brows
lifted a fraction.

"Not so potent, I fancy, as the lure which holds you,"
he said meaningly. "It is my turn to congratulate you, my
dear Halliard. The lady is charming."

He handed the handkerchief to Simon with a flourish,
and the other man accepted it in silence. He had completely forgotten its presence in his pocket, but it was
clear that Trayle, seeing the initials J.S. upon it, had leapt
to the conclusion that it belonged to Julia Stonehurst. For
several reasons, this was a mistake which must not be
corrected.

"I venture to think so," he said at length, replacing the
handkerchief in his pocket, "but it would be indiscreet to
mention her name."

"Indiscreet, indeed!" Gregory replied with a laugh, and
clapped him on the shoulder in friendly fashion. "May I
say, however, that I wish you every success?"

Simon made some suitable reply to this and endeavoured, without success, to lead the conversation back
to the subject of Philip Digby and his business in Brinkbury. Trayle evaded the issue, changing the subject with
an adroitness which Simon admired but could not emu-
late, and he was finally obliged to take his leave very little
wiser than before.

When he reached the inn again he found Digby in the
taproom, in quiet conversation with a soberly-dressed,
elderly man whom Simon had never seen before. Philip
nodded in greeting and said something to his companion,
who immediately made ready to depart, pausing to bow to
Halliard as he went past him on his way out of the room.
Simon eyed him with some surprise and strolled across to
join Digby.

"Who the devil was that?" he asked, jerking his head in
the direction of the door.

Philip grinned.

"His name is Forester, and he was valet to the late Earl," he replied. "I gather that he has a poor opinion of Bertram Colyton, and an even poorer one of your friend Trayle." He paused, looking questioningly at Simon. "Have you learned anything in that quarter yet?"

Simon shook his head.

"Only that Trayle is a devilish fine swordsman," he said ruefully. "I was hard put to it to hold my own against him. As for the other business, I'll swear he knows of it, but there's no making him admit it. He is as slippery as a confounded eel."

"Or as a snake!" Philip smiled, but his eyes were thoughtful. "He goes too secretly to work for my liking. Something he expects to gain, but what? I would be easier in my mind if I knew that."

He was to have some indication of it before the day was done. They lingered over their dinner, and afterwards pulled a small table close to the fire, intending to pass the evening at cards.

Their game was destined never to be finished. Before an hour had passed, hasty footsteps sounded in the passage and the door of the parlour was flung open, causing the candle-flames to leap and flicker wildly. Looking round in surprise and indignation, they beheld Francis Colyton standing on the threshold, one hand still grasping the handle of the door.

For the space of a few seconds he remained there, his tall, slender figure fitfully illuminated by the uncertain light, and then he slammed the door shut and strode forward to the table. Without a word, he lifted his hand and struck Simon hard across the mouth with the gloves he was clutching.

With a crashing oath Halliard started up, oversetting the table and scattering cards and coins across the floor, but before he could return the blow, or retaliate in any other way, Philip was on his feet and gripping him by the arm. Startled and dismayed, he tried to avert a disaster which was already inevitable.

"He's drunk!" he said urgently, and rounded upon

Francis. "You young fool, what in hell's name do you think you are about?"

"Drunk or sober, I take a blow from no man!" Simon shook off the restraining hand. He was white with anger, and there was the light of murder in his eyes. "Name your seconds, Colyton!"

"Wait, in God's name!" Philip struck in before Francis could reply. "If he is not drunk, he is surely mad. You cannot quarrel without a cause."

He swung again to face the younger man, who had not yet uttered a word. His appearance was enough to justify either of Philip's accusations, for he was hatless and di-shevelled, his dark eyes burning feverishly in his pallid, olive-skinned face. His mouth worked uncontrollably, and the hand which still clutched the gloves was trembling.

"There is cause enough," he said in a shaking voice, and rounded again upon Simon. "You'd deceive her, would you? Make her believe you honest in your inten-tions, yet boast behind her back that you'd no thought of marriage in your mind. Boast of it, damn you!" His voice broke on something very like a sob, compound of anger and grief. "It was a jest to you, you cur! Just another amusing incident to be recounted over a glass of wine! But this time you have gone too far! You shall never harm her while I live."

"No?" Simon's lazy drawl caressed the silence which followed this impassioned speech. "That, my friend, is not likely to hinder me for long."

"Be quiet, confound you!" Philip snapped. "Why make a bad business worse? Colyton, you do not know what you are saying! Miss Stonehurst is in no danger at Halli-ard's hands. I swear it!"

"You swear it?" The most bitter contempt rang now in Francis's voice. "How can you swear to anything on his behalf? Let him deny it if he can! Let him deny that he has the handkerchief she gave him, or that he has been flaunting it in public and boasting of his conquest."

"Damn it, you are mad! Stark, raving mad!" Philip ex-claimed helplessly. "My God! was there ever such a far-rago of nonsense? If Halliard has ever flaunted a love-to-ken, from Miss Stonehurst or anyone else, I will——"

"Don't make any rash promises, Philip," Simon interrupted softly. He put his hand into his pocket and drew out a scrap of delicate, lace-trimmed fabric and held it up between finger and thumb. "I've no wish to see you forsworn on my account."

With a careless gesture he let the handkerchief fall, and it fluttered down on top of the scattered playing-cards. Francis pounced on it, stared for an instant at the embroidered letters, and then with a groan crushed it between his hands.

"Now will you name your seconds, Colyton?" Simon repeated, and the boy raised his head. There were tears on his cheeks.

"Oliver Stonehurst will act for me," he said dully, in a voice oddly different from his previous impassioned tone. "No need for another."

Simon bowed in mocking acquiescence and cocked an eyebrow at Digby.

"Philip?" he said questioningly.

"Yes, of course," Philip replied curtly. "The fewer people to know of this the better." He glanced at Colyton. "I will wait upon Mr. Stonehurst in the morning."

Francis nodded and turned away, the handkerchief still clutched in his hand. Half-way to the door he seemed to become aware suddenly of what he held, and with a gesture of despair cast it from him. A moment later the door closed behind him and they heard his footsteps, slow and leaden now as though he were very weary, recede along the passage again.

"Poor young devil!" Philip spoke quietly but with deep feeling, and was silent for a few moments. Then he rounded upon Halliard and added bitterly, "I trust that you are satisfied!"

"Not entirely!" Simon had dropped again into the chair he had vacated. His anger seemed to have subsided, and there was a puzzled expression in his eyes. "I am still curious to know why Trayle goes to such trouble to force a quarrel between young Colyton and me."

Philip, who had bent to set the table on its legs again, looked up quickly.

"You think this was his doing?"

"I am sure of it. Only he knew I had that handkerchief. It dropped from my pocket this morning when I was at Brinkbury House."

Philip stooped and picked up the handkerchief, looking from it to Halliard with a frown.

"There is something here that does not ring true," he said slowly. "I have never known you to cherish sentimental keepsakes before."

"Nor do I cherish one now. That handkerchief should be carried against your heart, not mine, for to the best of my belief it belongs to Joanna Selbourne."

"Joanna?" Suspicion rang sharply in Philip's voice. "Then how the devil did you come by it?"

A smile flickered across Simon's face, and he shook his head.

"No need to take that tone," he remarked. "I am already embroiled with one jealous lover, and that is quite enough. I picked up that trifle at the foot of the Queen's Oak on the day we sought Mullett's trail there. I meant to tax you with it, but it slipped my memory." He leaned back in his chair, regarding Philip with grim amusement. "There is some irony in that, I think."

"There is some villainy in it also!" Philip sat down again, frowning at the handkerchief in his hand. "Trayle has been at great pains to further your pursuit of Julia Stonehurst and to make his cousin believe the worst, but why? What does he stand to gain from your quarrel?"

"Wait!" Simon leaned forward; his voice was urgent. "He told me that Francis is only a moderate swordsman, but after our bout this morning he knows that I have some skill in that direction. What if it is the boy's death he seeks?"

Philip's eyes narrowed.

"By God, I believe you are right!" he said slowly. "If Trayle knows that there is a plot afoot against Richard Colyton's life, he knows, too, that his cousin Bertram may look to be Earl of Varne ere long; and who, after Francis, is Bertram's heir?"

"Gregory Trayle!" Simon exclaimed, and laughed softly. "So he would be heir to the earldom, would he? And if he reached that goal successfully, what would Bertram's life be worth?"

"Less than nothing, I imagine!" Philip spoke drily. "But even with Bertram still alive, Trayle's gains would be great enough to justify the small risk he takes. The heir of the Earl of Varne could obtain almost unlimited credit."

"A pretty piece of roguery, by my faith!" Simon said indignantly. "So he would make me his tool, would he, and lay the blame for that lad's death on my shoulders? By heaven, Philip! Mr. Trayle must be taught that he has mistaken his man."

"I agree, but we must consider carefully how best to administer the lesson," Philip warned him. "You will have to meet Francis, of course, but there must be no killing. If he is as indifferent a swordsman as Trayle suggests, you should meet with no difficulty."

"And Trayle himself?"

Philip smiled coldly.

"You may leave Mr. Trayle to me, Simon," he said quietly. "When the time comes, I will deal with him. I give you my word on that!"

XIV

Miss Selbourne Is Indiscreet

Francis Colyton was not the only man in Brinkbury that day to be suffering the pangs of jealousy and unrequited love. Oliver Stonehurst, too, was smarting under the sting of these uncomfortable emotions, and he lacked even the meagre satisfaction of being able to strike a blow on his lady's behalf, since Digby had so firmly and, to Oliver's mind, so contemptuously refused to accept a challenge.

After his disastrous attempt at spying in the Lower Wood, Oliver had ridden home in a mood of black and bitter rage, and spent the rest of the day, as Joanna had predicted, in considering a number of pretexts which might be used to force the interloper into an open quarrel. Though none of these met with his entire approval, he hit upon one or two which might serve, and was only deterred from going immediately to the inn by the certainty that Digby would not yet have returned from Greydon Park.

The enforced delay gave him time to consider other aspects of the situation, and the longer he thought of them, the more uneasy he became. Joanna, it was clear, had completely lost her head over this adventurer, and it was his clear duty to point out to her the nature of the trap into which she was so blithely hastening.

This conviction took him, late on the following afternoon, to Greydon Park. With the familiarity of long acquaintance he left his horse at the stables and walked through the gardens towards the house, but before he reached it he had the good fortune to encounter Joanna herself. The gardens of Greydon Park were old-fashioned in design, with the elaborately shaped flower-beds, clipped yew hedges and pleached alleys which had been popular during the previous century, and it was into one of these last that Miss Selbourne was disappearing when Oliver caught sight of her. He quickened his steps, congratulating himself on his luck in finding her in a place so admirably suited to private conversation, for even now that the leaves were falling, the interlaced branches of the trees forming the alley would screen those within from curious eyes.

He reached the entrance through which she had passed, and halted there for an instant. The long, straight walk stretched before him, streaked with sunshine and shadow, and a short way along it Joanna was walking slowly away from him. A blue cloak covered her gown, but her fair curls were bare save for a tiny cap of lace and ribbon, and gleamed as the sunlight touched them. She looked very much as she had looked in the woods the day before, and in memory he once again saw Digby at her side, his arm about her and his red head bent close to hers. A fresh wave of jealous rage swept over him, and he strode forward along the alley.

She swung round with a frightened gasp at the sound of his footsteps, thrusting her left hand out of sight beneath her cloak, but when she saw who it was, the alarm in her face was replaced by anger. Her chin lifted and she said coldly:

"What are you doing here?"

"I want to talk to you," he said abruptly. "I must talk to you, Joanna."

There was no sign of relenting in the wilful, heart-shaped face. The blue eyes considered him disdainfully.

"I told you yesterday that I did not wish to speak to you," she said, "And I meant every word of it. I have no patience with spies."

He flushed at that, and at the contempt in her voice, but said defensively:

"If I behaved unworthily I was prompted by concern for you. At least do me the justice of believing that."

She raised her eyebrows and gave a little shrug to indicate her complete indifference to his motives, and turned to walk on. In an instant he was at her side and gripping her arm to detain her. She turned on him then like a small fury, dignity perishing in anger as she struck ineffectually at him.

"How dare you!" she panted. "Take your hands off me!"

"Not until you promise to hear what I have to say," he retorted. "By God, Joanna, you shall hear me, if I have to keep you here by force."

"If you do not take your hands off me this instant," she said with dangerous calm, "I shall scream for help. Now will you let me go?"

He shook his head.

"I'm damned if I will—and if you do scream, Joanna, I shall be obliged to tell your father what I saw in the Lower Wood yesterday! That would interest him, I fancy, and so would this pretty trinket."

He transferred his grip to her left wrist as he spoke, pulling her hand out from beneath the concealing cloak.

On the third finger gleamed the pearl and sapphire ring.

"You—you traitor, Oliver!" she exclaimed furiously. "Oh, to think that I told Philip you were no tale-bearer! I wish he had fought with you! I wish he had killed you!"

"It may come to that yet, but as God sees me, you shall hear me first! Which is it to be? Will you stay here quietly, or must I continue to hold you?"

Joanna stared up into the angry brown eyes, her own blazing with scorn and futile resentment, for she had known Oliver long enough to be certain that he meant what he said. To defy him would mean the betrayal of the precious secret, and she had promised Philip that it would not be betrayed.

"I will stay," she said sulkily, "but only because you give me no choice. Now let me go, you bully!"

He released his grip on her wrist and she stepped back, pressing her left hand against her breast and covering it with her right, cherishing the ring with a gesture which twisted the knife of jealousy in his heart. Rage and misery rose choking in his throat, and for a moment he could not trust himself to speak.

"Well?" Joanna asked impatiently. "Say what you have to say, for pity's sake, and then go."

"You have plighted troth with Digby, have you not?" he said thickly.

"Would I be wearing his ring if I had not?" she retorted. "Yes, I am going to marry him."

"Without your father's consent?"

"If need be, but I do not think the need will arise. When Philip speaks to him——"

"Aye, when!" he sneered. "Good God, Joanna! If his intentions were honest he would have sought your father's leave before now. Did I come creeping like a thief to woo you in secret?"

She flushed at that, partly with anger, partly because of her inability to confound him with a denial of all that the words implied. She said proudly:

"There are reasons for the delay."

"Oh, to be sure, but has he told you what they are? If he has, I'll warrant 'twas not the truth! Did he tell you that he dare not approach your father lest Sir Andrew discover him for the adventurer he is? That he has lured you into this secret betrothal because you are the Selbourne heiress and he no more than a penniless fortune-hunter?" Oliver's feelings were getting beyond his control, overwhelming his determination to be calm and dispassionate. Heedless of the stormy anger darkening Joanna's eyes, and of the fury with which she was literally trembling, he rushed on in a shaking voice: "He comes here and boasts of his friendship with the Earl of Varne, but what proof has he ever given of his claim? He will not even talk of Varne because he is afraid of betraying his ignorance. He lies and tricks his way into all our homes, he and that damned crony of his, and because they know how to fawn and flatter they are accepted without question, and you and Julia vie with each other to fall into their arms. . . ."

He broke off abruptly. With a sob of anger Joanna had started forward and dealt him a stinging slap across the cheek, so that he fell back a pace in astonishment and dismay.

"And if Philip were all of these things, and more," she panted furiously, "I should still love him! Yes, and I should still think him more honourable than you, who come here and force me into listening to you slander him when he is not here to defend himself. But he is none of these things. No, be silent!" For Oliver had tried to interrupt. "I have listened to you, and answered your impertinent questions, and now you shall listen to me. Philip is neither penniless nor a fortune-hunter, and he has not spoken to Father because until Lord Varne comes there is no one here to vouch for him. And until Lord Varne comes he cannot sell the emerald, either, because no one would buy so costly a jewel from a man they did not know, but when——"

"What did you say, Joanna?" Oliver asked incredulously. "He cannot sell what?"

Halted thus in the full flight of her denunciation, she stared blankly at him for a moment. Then she turned pale and a hand crept to her mouth, covering her lips while above it her eyes grew enormous with dismay.

"Oh!" she exclaimed in a small, guilty whisper. "Oh, I should not have spoken of it! I promised!"

She sounded so much like the Joanna he had always known, the headstrong child betrayed by her uncontrollable temper into an indiscretion, that he involuntarily answered her as he would have answered her in the past, before Philip Digby intruded into their lives.

"The harm is done now," he said authoritatively, "so you may as well tell me the rest. What is this nonsense about an emerald?"

"It is not nonsense," she retorted, firing up again, and plunged headlong into a breathless history of the star of death, of Digby's possession of the jewel and the attempts which had been made to steal it from him. Oliver listened to the artless tale with astonishment and growing disbelief, but when he scornfully expressed these feelings Joanna confounded him by disclosing her father's knowledge of the jewel and the fact that it was at present in his care, awaiting the coming of Lord Varne.

"Are you telling me that Sir Andrew accepted Digby's story?" Oliver demanded incredulously.

"Of course he accepted it!" she replied impatiently. "Do I not keep telling you that Philip left the emerald with him? How could he not believe it, when the jewel was there in front of him?"

"Very well, I will believe that the emerald exists. What I do not believe is that Digby came by it honestly."

"Oh, you are intolerable!" Joanna exclaimed angrily. "First you make wicked accusations against Philip, and when I prove to you that you are mistaken you invent others. I wish that you will go away, Oliver, and leave me in peace. I love Philip and I am going to marry him, and nothing that you or anyone else can say will make me change my mind."

With that she turned sharp on her heel and walked away from him along the alley, and this time he made no effort to prevent her. He stood staring after her until she passed out of sight, and then he went slowly back to the stables, fetched his horse and rode away in a mood which was very close to despair.

He felt curiously uncertain of the course he should follow now. His attempt to convince Joanna of her lover's unworthiness had most dismally failed, and though he was as ready as ever to force a challenge upon Digby, he felt vaguely that this was not the complete solution. Reaching Greydon village, he drew rein before the door of the inn and shouted for an ostler to take charge of his horse. The problem must be thrashed out thoroughly before he took any further action.

His deliberations occupied him until darkness was falling, and as an aid to thought he resorted to brandy, but the spirit was more successful in deadening his wretchedness than in clarifying his mind. This, in fact, was decidedly fuddled when at length he arrived at his first definite conclusion, which was no more than a resolve to seek the advice of his friend Francis. He might find some help there he thought hazily, or, failing that, he could at least be certain of sympathy. Francis, poor devil, knew what it was to lose the woman he loved to an adventurer, for Julia's enslavement by Simon Halliard had been even swifter and more shameless than Joanna's by Philip Digby.

"Damn Digby, and damn Halliard, too," Oliver said aloud, reeling to his feet in the little parlour to which the landlord of the inn had conducted him some two hours before, "and damn all women who let themselves be deceived by a flattering tongue! To the devil with the whole pack of 'em!"

He tossed off the remaining brandy in his glass as a toast to this sentiment and staggered out of the room, calling in slurred accents for his horse.

Oliver rode back to Brinkbury in a kind of drunken nightmare, kept in the saddle by force of habit alone, and some instinct, or flicker of a half-forgotten resolve, checked him at the gates of Brinkbury House. These were open, and after staring owlishly at them for a full minute, he urged his mount between them and along the avenue.

There were lights in several of the windows, and Oliver, sliding out of the saddle and leaving his horse to wander as it willed, stumbled up the steps and pounded on the door. When it was opened he thrust past the staring servant and lurched into the centre of the hall, demanding Francis in a thickened voice.

On the other side of the room a door was flung sharply open, drowning whatever reply the lackey made, and Gregory Trayle appeared on the threshold. Oliver, resting both hands on the table, leaned forward to peer hazily at him and then, having identified the newcomer, shook his head regretfully.

"Francis!" he stated with drunken solemnity. " 'Twas Francis I wanted to see."

"Francis is not here at present." Trayle advanced into the hall, dismissing the servant with a gesture and regarding Oliver with slightly contemptuous amusement. "A pretty state you are in to be paying social calls!"

Oliver shook his head.

"Not a social call," he said thickly. "Want his advice. Not sure what to do next. Ought to call Digby out. What d'you think?"

"I should not advise it." Gregory spoke casually, though his eyes had grown alert. "I have it on excellent authority that he is an exceptionally fine swordsman."

Oliver nodded gloomily, as though this confirmed his own opinion.

"That he might be," he admitted, "but damn it, must do something! Can't let her marry the rogue." He lifted his head and focussed a bleary gaze on Gregory's face. "Why don't you call him out? You're a duellist."

"My dear Stonehurst, why should I call Digby out?" Trayle asked patiently. "Go home and sleep it off, my boy! You will feel differently in the morning."

"I'll feel like the very devil in the morning," Oliver replied with morbid relish, "but one of us must do it, y'know. Fellow's a cursed scoundrel! Can't let him marry her."

"If you are referring to Miss Selbourne, let me assure you that Digby will not marry her. Now for God's sake, go home!"

"But he will," Oliver insisted, ignoring the latter command. He leaned closer to Trayle and took a confiding hold on the front of his coat. "They're betrothed, y'know. Saw him put the ring on her finger. And what's more," he added, gratified by the sudden riveting of Trayle's attention upon him, "he means to marry her as soon as he's sold this damned jewel Sir Andrew's keeping for him. Worth a fortune, Joanna says."

For perhaps ten seconds Gregory stood utterly still, staring at him with eyes like stone, while Oliver nodded drunken affirmation of the statement he had just made. Then with sudden decision he grasped the younger man by the arm and led him across the hall to the room from which he had emerged, saying in a kindly tone made horrible by the expression in his eyes:

"You are raving, my dear boy, and that's the truth! Sit down in here for a few minutes, and tell me just what it is that is troubling you."

Oliver allowed himself to be guided to a chair and lowered into it. Gregory drew another seat close to his and began, quietly and with infinite patience, to draw out the story of the previous day's happenings in the Lower Wood, and the interview that afternoon with Miss Selbourne. It was no easy task to sift the truth from Oliver's drunken meanderings, but at last he had it all, from Joanna's secret betrothal to the existence of the star of death, and had even drawn from the recesses of Oliver's drink-befuddled memory the name of Ned Mullet.

When at length he was satisfied that nothing remained to be told, Gregory got up and went to a table where bottles and glasses stood on a silver tray. Returning with a glass in each hand, he put one of them into Oliver's lax grip.

"You must be thirsty after so much talking," he said pleasantly. "Your very good health, Stonehurst."

Oliver made an uncertain answer and swallowed half the contents of his glass at a gulp. A satisfied smile touched Trayle's thin lips, but he made no comment as he resumed his seat.

For a while there was silence in the room. Gregory

Trayle's thoughts moved swiftly, reviewing with deepening satisfaction the progress of his plans. Francis, goaded to a frenzy, had gone to fling his challenge in Simon Halliard's face, and now fortune had brought this drunken lout with tidings which not only proved how sure had been the instinct which warned Trayle not to trust Philip Digby, but sowed in his mind the first small seeds of a plan whereby Joanna might be coerced into becoming his wife.

A loud snore suddenly intruded upon his thoughts, causing him to look sharply at his companion. Oliver was slumped in his seat, one arm trailing over the arm of the chair so that the glass drooping from his fingers emptied its dregs upon the floor; his chin was buried in his neck-cloth and from his half-open mouth issued the stertorous snores which had attracted Trayle's attention. Gregory bent forward to remove the glass from his hand, and then got up and summoned his own servant.

He came promptly, a thin, discreet individual in sober black, pale-faced and deferential. He had been in Trayle's service for a number of years, and enjoyed his master's confidence to a degree suspected by few.

"Lister," Gregory said softly, "Mr. Stonehurst has fallen asleep. Have my coach fetched out, and carry him home in it." He paused, considering Oliver's huddled figure with his faint, sneering smile. "No doubt he has a horse somewhere which should be found and stabled. See to it."

"At once, sir," Lister replied promptly. "Do you wish me to accompany the young gentleman myself?"

Gregory leaned against the edge of the table and took snuff from an elegantly enamelled box. The smile deepened a fraction on his lips, and Lister, studying that dark face with its frame of powdered hair, decided that his master was in an unwontedly pleasant mood.

"Of course, Lister!" Gregory said gently. "Mr. Stonehurst must have every possible attention. He has just placed me very deeply in his debt."

XV
The Decision

Francis rode home from the Colyton Arms in a mood very different from that in which he had approached it. He had been carried there on a wave of anger so intense that nothing less than Simon Halliard's death could, it seemed, appease it, but now the inevitable reaction had set in, bringing with it a cold despondency, and realization of the futility of what he had done.

At the gates of Brinkbury House he encountered his cousin's coach and reined in to let it pass, thinking without curiosity that this was an odd hour to be driving out, but the incident had passed from his mind before he reached the house. Leaving his horse at the stables, he went in by way of a side door and straight to his room, encountering no one and so remaining in ignorance of Oliver's visit.

He flung himself down in a chair and remained for a while lost in despondent thought. He did not regret what he had done, but he wished with all his heart that the period of waiting was over. Francis was one of those unfortunates who, intensely imaginative, suffer a thousand times more in anticipation of some dreaded event than in the event itself. He knew that when the time came he would acquit himself creditably, but to spend an unknown period of time under what amounted to a death-sentence was an ordeal which he doubted his ability to endure.

At last, in desperation, he resolved to seek counsel of his father. He had little hope of being received with anything but mockery or anger, for he knew that he failed in almost every way to measure up to Bertram's standard of what a man should be, but to share the burden might be to make it more endurable. He got up, and having restored some order to his appearance went slowly out of the room and down the stairs.

At the door of Mr. Colyton's study he paused to summon up his fast ebbing courage, for he stood a good deal in awe of his father and there was little affection or understanding between them. As he stood there, he became aware for the first time of voices within the room, and a moment later recognized his cousin's sardonic tones.

His first reaction was surprise, for he had supposed Gregory to be in the coach which had passed him at the gates, and, following surprise, a curious mingling of vexation and relief. In Gregory's presence, he had no intention of betraying the uneasiness he felt. He was about to turn away when Trayle spoke again, and this time the words came clearly to Francis's ears, to freeze him where he stood with astonishment and a sickening dismay.

"So you see, my dear Bertram," Gregory was saying mockingly, "Digby has deceived you with regard to his resources. Is it not likely, therefore, that he has also deceived you with regard to the proposed murder of Cousin Richard?"

There was a pause, and then Bertram said calmly:

"I do not see that one fact must necessarily follow upon the other. If Digby has kept secret his possession of this jewel, it is merely in order to extract as much money from me as he can in exchange for the service he proposes. I do not begrudge it. If he will remove Richard from my path, I shall be repaid a thousand times over."

"You can still believe him honest in that?"

"Certainly. He hates young Richard most bitterly, and will go to any lengths to gratify that hatred."

"He gives no sign of it."

"Because he knows how to dissemble his feelings. You did not see him, as I did, when he first told me of the wrong our kinsman did him. No, Gregory, in what you have told me tonight I find nothing to arouse distrust of Digby's good faith. Quite the reverse, in fact! The existence of the jewel explains Halliard's presence. They were probably accomplices in its theft and he fears to lose his share of the loot."

"That is most likely!" The sneering note was more pronounced than ever in Gregory's voice. "As I have said before, he and Digby are two of a kind. Well, I have warned you, Bertram, and there the matter ends. My share in your schemes remains a secret between us, and so I have nothing to fear."

"No more have I," Bertram replied confidently. "When I send word to Digby that Richard is on his way to Brinkbury, it will be our kinsman's death-warrant. Digby will ride out to meet him, and"—there was a pause, as though a descriptive gesture had been made—"there will be a new Earl of Varne."

"And I will be the first to congratulate you, cousin," Gregory replied sardonically. "Until then, I reserve my judgment."

Francis, who since the first words reached him had been standing with his ear pressed to the crack of the door, straightened himself slowly and retreated a cautious pace. His heart was thumping wildly and a sickness almost physical clawed at his vitals. His own troubles forgotten in the horror of this chance discovery, he turned and stole back the way he had come, nor did he pause until the door of his bedchamber was once more closed behind him. Then he sank trembling into a chair and tried to collect his scattered wits.

Ever since the day of the old Earl's death he had striven to put out of his mind the knowledge of his father's villainy, since it was beyond his power to right the wrong, but now a man's life was at stake. He groaned aloud and buried his face in his hands. Had he not troubles enough without having this fresh burden thrust upon him, this cruel temptation to regain all he had lost? If by some miracle he survived the duel, he had only to remain silent to be restored to the position of heir to the earldom. Yet, if he did not speak, would he ever know peace of mind again?

The question was still unresolved when he rose next morning, pale and heavy-eyed, and made ready to go to Foxwood Grange. Oliver must be warned of the impending duel, but the meeting which had loomed so large in Francis's thoughts the night before had now acquired an odd unreality, as though it concerned someone other than himself, and there was room in his mind for nothing except the decision which must somehow be made.

Oliver, roused from the heavy sleep induced by his po-
tations the night before, was inclined to be irritable until
the gravity of his friend's errand was made clear to him.
He listened to the story in appalled silence, sitting up in
bed with his throbbing head clasped between his hands,
and when Francis paused, he said gloomily:

"Plague take me if I know what ails those two girls!
Losing their heads over a pair of damned upstart adven-
turers! Oh yes!" This in answer to Colyton's inquiring
glance. "Joanna is as bad as Julia, or worse. She says she
will marry Digby whether her father gives his consent or
not!"

"Marry him!" There was consternation in Francis's
voice. "Oliver, she cannot! She must not!"

"Try to stop her, then, and see what sort of reception
you get," Oliver retorted grimly. "The only thing I can
think of is to tell Sir Andrew, and even then it's as likely
as not she would win him over. You know how he dotes
on her."

Francis got up and went across to the window, pulling
the curtain aside and staring out, though he saw nothing
of what lay beyond. So Joanna's future was at stake as
well as his own, for it seemed only too probable that
Digby meant to take her with him when he left Brinkbury. While Oliver shaved and dressed, he fought the
battle over again, and had still not reached a decision
when a servant came to inform them that Mr. Digby was
below. Oliver, fastening his neck-cloth about his throat,
said curtly:

"Ask Mr. Digby to wait. I will be with him directly."

He finished dressing and hurried away, bidding his
friend await his return. He was gone for some twenty
minutes, but Francis, absorbed in troubled thought, took
no heed of the time. At last Oliver returned, and closing
the door carefully behind him, said in a low voice:

"It is all settled. The meadow behind the Long Spinney, tomorrow morning at seven."

Francis nodded, and then suddenly the full implications
of those words dawned upon him. Tomorrow at seven! It
meant that he had less than twenty-four hours to live.

The realization had a curious effect upon him. The problem with which he had been wrestling all night, the conflict between right and wrong, self-interest and duty, ceased suddenly to exist, and he knew that there was only one course open to him. He drew a long breath, feeling as though a tremendous weight had been lifted from his shoulders.

Oliver was regarding him with troubled eyes, and after a moment or two said diffidently:

"Can I do anything for you, Francis? Would you care to have the foils out?"

Francis smiled faintly and shook his head.

"Would it be of any avail, do you think?" he said quietly. "An hour's practice, when I am to meet a man like Halliard? No, Oliver, I thank you for the thought, but I'll not waste the time. I doubt I have a great deal left."

Oliver made a protesting gesture.

"No need to talk like that," he said with forced cheerfulness. "You can only guess at the extent of Halliard's skill."

"It is great enough for Gregory to consider him a worthy opponent," Francis replied tranquilly. "They fenced together yesterday, I believe." He went across and picked up his hat and gloves from the bed. "I will go now. There is something I have to do."

Oliver went with him to the front door, and they stood there in the pale autumn sunshine and waited for Francis's horse to be brought. Oliver, profoundly disturbed, covertly studied his friend's face while perplexity deepened within him, for there was something here he did not understand. In his heart he had as little hope as Francis had concerning the outcome of the duel, and this calm indifference troubled him. It was so alien to the other man's nature that he found himself wishing that something would occur to shatter it.

His wish was to be granted before many minutes had passed. The horse had been brought, and Francis was already in the saddle, when a light step sounded within the house and Julia appeared in the doorway. She wore a gown of primrose-coloured silk over a petticoat of green,

and a little lace cap trimmed with green and yellow rib-
bons.

"Why, Francis!" she exclaimed, and came forward,
smiling. "I did not know that you were here. We see you
too seldom of late."

He made no reply, but stared at her for a moment with
eyes which seemed to burn in a face as pale as death.
Then with an incoherent exclamation in which grief and
anger and despair seemed strangely mingled, he wrenched
his horse savagely around. Gravel spurted beneath the
plunging hoofs, some of it spattering against her silken
skirts, and then he was gone, thundering away from them
along the avenue of beech-trees towards the road. Julia,
who had started back with a little cry, turned a hurt and
startled gaze upon her brother.

"What ails him?" she questioned in dismay. "What did
I say?"

"What did you say?" Oliver repeated wrathfully, his
own anger and anxiety breaking forth. "My God! Do you
need to ask? 'We see you too seldom', i'faith! Do you
suppose the poor devil is likely to come here, if he is
obliged to watch you fawning and doting upon that rogue
Halliard?"

Julia gave a little exclamation of anger, but at the same
time a bright flood of colour stained her throat and face.
Oliver watched that betraying blush with grim satisfaction.

"That touches you, does it?" he said bitterly. "You are
not yet so lost to modesty that you cannot blush for your
shame."

"How dare you speak to me like that!" Julia was on
the verge of tears. "I will not listen to such insults from
my own brother."

"Oh yes, you will!" he retorted, and grabbed her wrist
as she turned away. " 'Tis only a brother who may talk to
you in this fashion, my girl, and you are going to listen!
Come you within!"

Ignoring her struggles, and the furious words with
which she lashed him, he dragged her with him into the
house and across the hall to the library on its farther side.

Once within the room, and with the door closed behind them, he thrust her roughly into a chair and folded his arms, looking down at her with scorn and anger.

"Now," he said grimly, "we will have some plain speaking, if you please. It is time you learned whither your folly has led."

Bluntly, almost brutally, for he was in no mood to spare her, he described the quarrel between Francis and Halliard, and disclosed his own conviction that Francis had no hope of surviving the duel. As he spoke, all Julia's righteous indignation faded, and pure horror looked at him out of her white face and stricken eyes; by the time he had done she was huddled in the chair, her face hidden in her hands and her whole body shaken by the violence of her weeping. Her brother paused, and stood watching her with sombre eyes.

"You may well weep," he said heavily, "but no matter how many tears you shed, they cannot undo the harm that has been done. Upon my soul, I believe I pity you!"

He turned and went out, leaving her alone, and after a little while she raised her head, pressing a hand against her lips to stifle her sobs. Oliver's parting words still echoed in her ears, and she knew that he had spoken the truth. Tears would not mend matters, but somehow the threatened tragedy must be averted, and the hideous mistake which had provoked the quarrel set to rights. Her heedlessness had wrought the mischief; it was her duty to make amends.

Within an hour, very pale but outwardly composed, she was riding down the hill towards the village. She was alone, having told the groom who usually accompanied her that she was not going beyond the park and so would have no need of an attendant. Reaching the inn, she tethered her mount to a ring in the wall beside the door and stepped boldly into the house, for she was beyond caring for the monstrous impropriety of her present errand. All that mattered was to save Francis Colyton's life.

Outside the parlour she hesitated for a moment, and then, taking a deep breath, went quickly in and closed the door behind her. Simon was standing by the table, squinting down the long barrel of a pistol which he was apparently engaged in cleaning, and he glanced up casually at the sound of her entrance. Then his eyes widened with astonishment and he laid the weapon down, saying in a surprised tone:

"My dear Miss Stonehurst! This is an unexpected honour."

"I had to talk to you, sir! It is a matter of the utmost urgency." Julia spoke breathlessly, and advanced a few steps into the room. "Of some delicacy, also. Are we likely to be disturbed?"

He shook his head. He had conquered his surprise and was regarding her with a curious and faintly amused expression.

"I think not," he replied. "Digby has ridden out, and no one else is likely to intrude upon us. However, to make quite certain . . ." He left the sentence unfinished, and stepped past her to turn the key in the lock. Then, taking her hand, he led her to a chair near the fire. "Pray be seated, madam, and tell me how I am to have the pleasure of serving you."

Julia had watched rather dubiously the locking of the door, and now made haste to withdraw her hand from a clasp which showed no sign of freeing it voluntarily. She felt a little frightened, and less certain now of success than she had done when the idea of appealing to Halliard first occurred to her, but she made a determined effort to hide her nervousness and said quietly:

"I have come to ask a favour of you, Mr. Halliard."

"It will be a privilege to grant it, madam. May I know what it is?"

Julia looked down at the gloves which she was twisting between her hands. The matter was more difficult to put into words than she had anticipated.

"I believe, sir," she said at last, "that you have in your possession a handkerchief which is thought to belong to me."

"I did have such a handkerchief," Simon replied promptly, understanding beginning to creep into his eyes, "but unhappily I have it no longer. I found it by chance, but it was seen by someone else who leapt to the conclusion that it was yours."

"And that I had bestowed it upon you as a gift," she concluded for him, meeting his eyes squarely although the colour had deepened in her cheeks. "A mistake which you, sir, did not correct."

He made a deprecatory gesture but said nothing, waiting instead for her to speak again.

"As a result of that," she went on, "you are engaged to meet Francis Colyton tomorrow. That is true, is it not?" He nodded, and Julia, twisting again at the gloves, added in a stifled voice, "It is said that you are a far better swordsman than Francis, and that you mean to kill him."

"And you have come to beg me to spare his life," Simon concluded. "That is the favour you seek, is it not?"

"Yes, it is!" She leaned forward to lay a hand on his sleeve as he stood before her, and raised her eyes beseechingly to his face. "Mr. Halliard, I entreat you, do not do this dreadful thing!"

Simon laid his hand over hers to prevent its withdrawal, and stood looking down at her without speaking. The most profound satisfaction was stirring within him, for though he had fully intended to abide by the promise he had made to Digby concerning Miss Stonehurst, his good intentions were never proof against temptation, and the temptation confronting him now was irresistible. It was one thing to refrain from pursuing her; quite another to be equally forbearing when she came to him of her own free will.

"I have no choice," he replied, deliberately misunderstanding her. "Colyton forced this quarrel upon me, offering me insults which I cannot and will not take from any man. Honour demands that I should meet him."

"But not that you should kill him," she protested. "Surely, if you hold him at your mercy, it were nobler to spare his life than to take it. Can honour not be satisfied with that?"

He made no direct answer to this, but said instead:

"You seem very certain that the issue rests entirely with me."

Julia tried to draw her fingers from beneath his. Failing in this, she made an impatient gesture with her free hand.

"How can anyone doubt it? My brother says that Mr. Trayle considers you worthy of his sword, and he has killed men in duels before now. Francis can never hope to match such skill."

"Very well!" Simon continued to look down at her and now there was a smile on his lips which Julia did not find reassuring. "We will agree that young Colyton's life rests in my hands, and that he has given me reason enough to kill him. Can you give me a reason why I should not?"

"Generosity, sir, and mercy," she said earnestly. "Are these not reason enough?"

He shook his head.

"Fine-sounding words, my dear, but words, no more! Try again."

She bit her lip and cast a hunted glance to left and right. Instinct told her what answer he sought, but at the same time warned her against giving it. The silence seemed to drag on interminably, and at last she said with the utmost reluctance:

"Because I ask it of you?"

His smile broadened a little.

"That is a consideration more likely to persuade me than the first. To be frank, my dear, such lofty ideals are not for me, but the hope of winning your gratitude might well prompt me to spare young Colyton's life."

"Then spare it, sir," she replied eagerly, "and know that I shall be in your debt for ever."

Still smiling, he shook his head, and her eagerness perished in growing alarm. That sudden rush of uneasiness brought her to her feet, and again she tried to free her hand from his, and again failed.

"Not for ever," he said softly. "Debts, my dear, must be paid."

He pulled her closer to him and his other arm went about her shoulders, holding her with a strength against which all her efforts to break free spent themselves in vain. Terrified now, she struggled unavailingly, gasping protests and entreaties as she searched the bronzed face and bold, merciless eyes for some hint of pity.

"Debts must be paid," he said again, and there was a wealth of meaning in his lazy voice. "Since the boy's life means so much to you, I will spare him. At a price!"

XVI

Dismal Failure of a Plot

The morning of the duel dawned crisp and chill, with a thick mist shrouding a countryside white with frost. Oliver, dressing by candlelight, found himself shivering, though more from apprehension than the cold. He had slept hardly at all, for not daring to rouse the curiosity of the servants by demanding to be called at so unseasonable an hour, he had been in dread of oversleeping and so failing his friend at this most critical time.

He and Francis had arranged to meet in a small grove of trees at the edge of the grounds of Brinkbury House, but when the time fixed for their rendezvous came and went, and a further fifteen minutes had dragged by, Oliver's uneasiness could be endured no longer. He made his way to the house, and, taking a high-handed tone with the astonished servant who admitted him, succeeded in gaining access to his friend's bedchamber.

The heavy curtains were closely drawn, so that he could barely discern the outlines of the furniture, and going across to the window he drew them apart. Then he turned, and stood staring in astonishment and growing dismay at the bed, which was not only empty, but had obviously not been slept in the previous night.

It was several moments before the real meaning of the discovery dawned upon him, but when it did, surprise was succeeded by a feeling of sick disgust. Only one possible inference could be drawn from the deserted room and empty bed. Francis's courage had failed him, and he had sought refuge in flight.

For perhaps five minutes Oliver stood there in wretched indecision, wondering what to do next. He was completely at a loss, and the prospect of informing Halliard and Digby that his principal had fled rather than fulfil the demands of honour was one which he felt he could not face. At last he went slowly out of the room and down the stairs to the hall, where the servant who had admitted him was still lingering in the hope of gratifying his curiosity. Oliver summoned him with a jerk of the head.

"When did you last see Mr. Francis?" he asked abruptly.

"Why, when he went out about mid-day yesterday, sir," the man replied, staring. "He said he was likely to be returning very late, and not to wait up for him."

Oliver's heart sank. He had been trying to convince himself that Francis, unable to sleep, had left the house early and ridden to meet him by another route, but this was obviously not the case. After staring unseeingly at the servant for a moment or two, he decided that there was only one thing to be done.

"Go and tell Mr. Trayle that I wish to see him," he said.

The servant looked horrified.

"I dare not, sir," he replied. "Not even Mr. Trayle's own man would disturb him at this hour without he was ordered to."

"I can't help that!" Oliver's temper was beginning to give way under the strain of the situation. "Carry that message to him at once, and tell him that it is of vital importance."

Very reluctantly the man began to mount the stairs, and Oliver walked across to the table in the middle of the hall and stood drumming his fingers upon it. After about five minutes a brisk step on the stairs brought him swinging round to confront Gregory Trayle.

He was clad in a magnificent brocaded dressing-gown, and his dark, unshaven face contrasted absurdly with the curled and powdered wig on his head, but no one, looking at that face, could have felt any desire to laugh. He said curtly:

"Well?"

Oliver went forward to meet him.

"Send that damned fellow away," he replied, indicating the servant who had followed Mr. Trayle down the stairs, "and I will tell you."

Trayle turned his head slightly.

"Go," he said briefly, "and keep a still tongue in your head. Any gossiping, and I promise that you will regret it."

The man withdrew in some disorder. No servant, his own or anyone else's, ever dared to disobey Gregory Trayle. Gregory looked again at Oliver.

"I take it that your presence here is due to Francis's meeting with Simon Halliard?"

"Then you do know about it!" Oliver exclaimed in relief. "Thank God for that! It's a damnable business, Trayle. Francis has gone."

For a moment Trayle continued to regard him, his face expressionless, and then he said curtly:

"What do you mean—gone?"

"I mean that he has fled, run away! I was supposed to meet him in that beech-grove by the road, but when he didn't arrive I came seeking him. He is not here."

Gregory's eyes widened a fraction and Oliver took an involuntary pace backwards, for the most murderous anger was looking at him out of the other man's face. It was gone in an instant, but the memory of it was to linger unpleasantly in his mind.

"Are you telling me," Trayle asked in a hard, controlled voice, "that the meeting has not yet taken place?"

"No. It is fixed for seven o'clock." Oliver cast a distracted glance at the clock, and saw that its hands pointed to twenty minutes before the hour. "I have been to his room, but the bed's not been slept in and the servant says Francis rode out yesterday at noon and said he would be returning very late."

"The despicable little cur!" Gregory exclaimed in a voice of molten rage. "The cowardly, faint-hearted young cub! My God, to think that he is a kinsman of mine!"

"Yes, yes, I know, but what the devil am I to do?" Oliver demanded anxiously. "Halliard and Digby will be waiting. Must I go and tell them that Francis has fled? Hell and the devil, Trayle, I'll not do it!"

"Someone will have to do it, and you are Francis's second," Gregory retorted. "Believe me, I am sorry for you! It has put you in an infernal position." He glanced swiftly at the clock and appeared to reach a sudden decision. "If you like, I will come with you. Some apology must be made to Halliard."

Relief flooded into Oliver's face.

"I'll be confoundedly grateful if you will come," he exclaimed. "To tell truth, I have no experience in these matters."

"I am not exactly in the habit of offering apologies on behalf of cowards," Gregory replied caustically, turning toward the stairs. "I will make what haste I can, and meanwhile it will save time if you go to the stables and see that a horse is saddled for me."

They parted, and Oliver, having carried out Gregory's commands, hurried to fetch his own mount from the beech-grove. He expected to be kept waiting for a considerable time, but to his surprise the hour had not yet struck when Trayle came out of the house to join him. Oliver eyed him respectfully, wondering how he had achieved such elegance in so short a space of time.

Meanwhile, in the meadow behind the Long Spinney, Halliard and Digby were already waiting, accompanied by Dr. Towne. They had arrived there at about ten minutes to seven, the doctor some minutes later, and all three had since been engaged in desultory conversation. The doctor heartily disapproved of the whole affair, and said so bluntly at the outset.

"I do not approve of the practice of duelling," he announced, "and I do not scruple to tell you, gentlemen, that I have patients whose need is greater by far than that of two healthy young men who can find nothing better to do than attempt to spit each other upon a sword."

Simon made a comical grimace behind the doctor's back and strolled away to inspect the ground. Philip said soothingly that it still wanted two minutes to the hour, and began to talk of other matters, doing his best to calm the physician's ill-humour, which he judged to spring largely from anxiety on behalf of a lad whom he had known all his life.

Another five minutes slipped away. The doctor looked at his watch; a faint frown gathered in Philip's eyes; Simon rejoined them and said lazily:

"Our young friend is tardy. Can it be that he has had second thoughts?"

"Unlikely, I should think," Philip replied rather curtly, and Dr. Towne added indignantly:

"If you are accusing Mr. Francis of cowardice, sir, give me leave to tell you that you are talking nonsense. I have never known him to lack courage."

Simon shrugged, and leaning his shoulders against the trunk of the tree beneath which they were standing, folded his arms.

"Courage or cowardice," he said with a grin, "I do not mean to wait upon his pleasure for ever. If he does not come within five minutes, I am going back to the inn. This is a confoundedly unpleasant morning for standing about in a field."

Dr. Towne, who had been rubbing his hands and stamping his feet for some minutes, regarded him for the first time with a hint of sympathy, but before he could speak again the sound of approaching horses reached their ears, and a moment later two riders came into view along the path leading through the spinney from the road. Simon straightened up with an exclamation of satisfaction and then paused, his brows drawing together in a frown, while Philip and the doctor stared with equal perplexity. One of the newcomers was certainly Oliver Stonehurst, but the other was Gregory Trayle.

They halted close by and Trayle dismounted, tossing the reins to Oliver, who remained in the saddle and was apparently content to leave everything to his companion. Gregory confronted the little group beneath the tree, and they observed that there was a set look about his mouth and a decidedly grim expression in his eyes.

"Servant, gentlemen!" he said curtly, and then addressed himself to Simon. "Halliard, I have come merely to offer you an explanation, for an apology would be an impertinence. Your meeting with my cousin cannot take place. He has fled."

Dr. Towne uttered a shocked exclamation, but Philip was silent, watching Trayle with narrowed eyes. Somewhere the plot had gone awry—that much was certain. Trayle had himself well in hand, but a hell of baffled fury must be seething beneath the surface.

Simon's brows had lifted; he said mildly:

"You are sure of that?"

"Quite sure! By this time he is no doubt many miles away."

Philip scarcely heeded Simon's reply. He had lifted his head and was listening intently, for his ears, keen beyond the ordinary, had caught a sound which as yet none of the others had noticed, the sound of galloping hoofs which drew nearer at headlong speed. A premonition of who this reckless rider might be brought with it a feeling of relief; he had not liked the thought of young Francis proving a coward.

The sound grew until all became aware of it, and silence fell over the little group. The hoofbeats sounded a more sober rhythm as they approached along the winding path between the trees, and then at last the rider came into view. Philip laughed under his breath.

"Your mistake, Mr. Trayle," he said softly, and Gregory flashed him a glance of mingled dislike and relief.

"I am happy to discover it," he replied, and went forward to meet his cousin.

Francis slid wearily out of the saddle. He had obviously ridden fast and far, for his horse was in a lather of sweat and stood now with drooping head and heaving flanks. Gregory cast a swift glance over it before he addressed its rider, his voice clearly audible in the still air.

"Where the devil have you been?" he demanded angrily. "A fine pair of fools you have made us look!"

"Where I have been is my concern, Gregory, not yours." Francis spoke calmly, the words reaching with equal clarity to the men beneath the tree. "I did not ask you to busy yourself in my affairs." He turned to speak to

Stonehurst, who had dismounted and come to his side. "I am sorry, Oliver! There was something I had to do, and it took longer than I had foreseen. Will you convey my apologies to Mr. Halliard, and tell him that if he is willing to overlook the lateness of my arrival, I am at his disposal?"

After a moment's hesitation Oliver obeyed. Philip, who had been looking thoughtfully at Colyton, said quietly:

"That boy is in no case to fight. He can scarcely stand for weariness. The meeting should be postponed until he has had time to recover his strength."

Simon was already stripping off his coat. He grinned at his friend.

"Would that make any difference to the ending?" he asked carelessly. "I have already been kept waiting longer than I have the patience to endure. We fight now."

Philip shrugged, knowing that Francis was in no serious danger, but Oliver naturally assumed these words to confirm his worst fears. His heart sank, and he returned to his principal more firmly convinced than ever that a very few minutes would see his friend dead at his feet.

Francis was equally certain that he had no chance of survival, for even at his best he could not hope to match Halliard's skill, and now, as Digby had observed, he was utterly exhausted. Yet, strangely enough, he felt no fear, but only the tranquil knowledge that his last hours had been well spent. He removed his coat and rolled up the sleeves of his shirt, and then sat down on a convenient tree stump to pull off his boots.

Oliver and Digby had gone to the centre of the ground and were comparing the two swords; Gregory and the doctor withdrew a little distance to the spot where the horses were tethered; Halliard was still standing beneath the tree, his hands resting lightly on his hips and his gaze fixed indifferently upon the two seconds. Francis looked at him and tried to revive something of the anger and hatred which had possessed him when he issued the challenge, but a curious feeling of detachment had settled upon him, as though he were already divorced from earthly rancours.

He got up as Oliver came back to him, and took the

proffered sword in a steady hand. Oliver looked at him, at the handsome young face livid with fatigue, and the heavy shadows beneath the dark eyes, and his own face quivered uncontrollably.

"Francis!" he said in a stifled voice. "Oh, my God! what can I say?"

Francis looked at him for a moment in silence. Then he transferred the sword to his left hand and took Oliver's in a hard grip.

"Nothing, Oliver," he replied tranquilly, "but tell Julia——" He broke off, and a faint smile touched his lips for an instant. "Oh well, no matter!"

He released his friend's hand and walked calmly out to the centre of the ground to confront Halliard. The mist was lifting now, and had taken on a pearly tint which told of the sun trying to break through. Francis knew a fleeting regret that he would not feel its warmth again, and then Philip Digby's crisp, pleasant voice recalled his wandering thoughts.

"Ready, gentlemen?" it said. "On guard!"

The two slim blades flashed to the salute, and thereafter Francis had no room left in his mind for any thoughts not immediately concerned with swordplay. He was determined to give a good account of himself and met Simon's attack with every ounce of skill he could muster, though he knew that to attack on his own account was impossible and that in his present exhausted state even defence could not be long maintained. The sword felt incredibly heavy, the misty meadow appeared to be wavering about him, and when something which seemed compounded equally of ice and flame pierced his left shoulder, the only thought that flashed through his mind was relief that the end had come so soon.

The seconds' swords struck the blades upwards, and Francis reeled back and fell to the ground with a bright red stain spreading across his shirt. Oliver dropped to one knee beside him and raised him in his arms, saying in a dazed, unsteady voice:

"Francis! Oh, my God! Is he dying?"

Philip was already kneeling at Colyton's other side,

baring the wound with swift, competent hands, staunching the flow of blood as best he might with a folded handkerchief. He shook his head.

"It is a clean thrust, high in the shoulder. I should imagine he has collapsed from sheer exhaustion."

Dr. Towne came hurrying up and Philip rose to his feet to give place to him. Looking past the little group, he saw that Gregory Trayle was coming slowly forward, and he stepped past Francis and his attendants to meet him.

"A happy conclusion, Mr. Trayle," he said with a hint of malice. "Your cousin has taken no serious hurt."

For a moment Trayle's eyes looked with cold fury into his, and then without speaking he brushed past Philip and stood looking down at the prostrate form of his kinsman. Philip smiled somewhat grimly and went to join Simon, who had already pulled on his boots and was now unrolling his sleeves. He grinned cheerfully at Digby as he came up.

"Is all well yonder?" he asked, jerking his head towards the group in the meadow. Philip nodded.

" 'Twas skilfully done," he replied. "He has lost some blood, and will be devilish sore for a day or two, but that's the extent of the harm."

"I'll confess I am glad of it." Simon picked up his coat and shrugged himself into it. "That lad has more courage than one would guess from his looks." He glanced again towards the centre of the meadow, and chuckled. "I take it there is one man present who does not share the general satisfaction?"

"Not in the smallest degree," Philip replied, smiling. "He is in the devil's own temper and dare not show it, which must set the seal upon an extremely trying morning. To see one's hopes first dashed, then raised again, and finally shattered beyond repair, would tax the patience of a saint."

"Which our friend Trayle most certainly is not," Simon remarked with a laugh. "Well, I have no wish to stay for him if he is in that kind of humour. What say you to breakfast?"

"An excellent suggestion," Philip agreed, adding as

they walked towards the horses: "I believe we have come well out this business, Simon. It could have led us into trouble had we not perceived whose was the hand behind it. As it is, Trayle has given us undeniable proof that he is aware of his cousin's plan to secure the title and estate of Varne, for if he had not known of it there would have been no profit to him in plotting young Francis's death. As matters have fallen out, we have gained all, and lost nothing."

"I am inclined to agree with you." Simon spoke in his usual lazy drawl, and since his back was towards Philip as he untethered his horse, the other man could not see the secret, mocking laughter in his face. "The gains, undoubtedly, are all upon our side."

XVII

A Promise and a Parting

Miss Joanna Selbourne, all unaware of the stirring events taking place so close at hand and involving so many of her friends, was delighted, on the afternoon of the day of Francis's meeting with Simon, to receive a visit from Julia. She was alone when Miss Stonehurst arrived, for her mother had gone to visit an old servant who was gravely ill and whose affliction was, she thought, a trifle too harrowing for her daughter to encounter.

Joanna, bored and lonely, was thankful for any diversion to relieve the tedium of the afternoon. She greeted Julia eagerly and bore her off to her own pleasant, sunny bedchamber, for one glance at her friend's face had informed her that this was no casual visit. Miss Stonehurst was obviously in the grip of a profound agitation. Joanna made her sit down before the fire and then seated herself close by, waiting hopefully to be taken into her confidence.

Julia began, calmly enough, by describing the quarrel between Francis and Hilliard, and the duel which had followed it. She paused there, and Joanna, regarding her with faint perplexity, said in a matter-of-fact voice:

"It seems to me that you are in a great fluster over nothing. Of course, I am sorry that Francis has been hurt, but it was quite his own fault, for he should have known better than to believe that stupid story about the handkerchief. If it is true that Mr. Halliard could have killed him, then he is lucky to have escaped so lightly."

"Luck had nothing to do with it!" Julia spoke vehemently, almost shrilly. "Mr. Halliard could have killed him, and would have done so, had I not begged him to spare his life."

She gave a shattering sob and buried her face in her hands. Joanna stared at her in the blankest stupefaction, and then, a nameless dread seizing upon her, jumped up and went to kneel beside her.

"Julia!" she said urgently. "What is the matter? What are you trying to tell me?"

"Oh, Joanna, can you not guess?" Julia raised a despairing, tear-stained face. "Mr. Halliard would only agree to spare Francis if—if I would promise to go away with him tonight."

Joanna gave a gasp of dismay and sat back on her heels. After a moment or two of stunned silence, she said bluntly:

"Does he mean to marry you?"

Julia shook her head, covering her face once more with her hands, and after another appalled silence Joanna got up and began to walk up and down the room, her brow furrowed with concentration. At length, halting again by the chair, she said in a tone of great decision:

"Julia, you must not go with him!"

"But I gave my word," Julia replied hopelessly, "and he has kept his part of the bargain. Oliver said he could have killed Francis without any difficulty at all. If I break my promise, he might make him fight again."

"I do not think that is possible," Joanna said doubtfully. "To fight the same man twice, I mean. Still, he might try to make mischief in some other way. We must think of something else."

"There is nothing to think of," Julia said forlornly. "No

one can help me, Joanna. That is not why I have told you of it."

"Why, then?"

Julia moved her hands in a vague, pathetic gesture.

"So that you may tell Francis the truth—afterwards. Oh, do you not see? When he hears that I have eloped with Mr. Halliard, he will think that we were planning it all the time, that I did not care whether he lived or died." She caught Joanna's hands in hers, clinging tightly to them. "Will you do that for me? I cannot bear to think he will never know the truth!"

"You love him, do you not?" Joanna asked quietly, and Julia nodded wretchedly.

"Oh, so much!" she said in a breaking voice. "If only I had realized it sooner! It was not until Oliver told me he would be killed, and that through my heedlessness . . ." the rest of the sentence was lost in a fresh bout of weeping.

"And he loves you," Joanna said relentlessly. "Do you think he would ever be able to forgive himself if he knew that you had done such a thing to save him?"

"You think he should not be told?" Julia asked disconsolately, and Joanna dropped once more to her knees beside her, still clasping her hands.

"I think you should forget this wicked bargain," she said earnestly, her eyes anxiously searching the other girl's ravaged face. "Only think for one moment, my dear! Even if Halliard meant to marry you, your father would never forgive either of you, for you know how determined he is that you shall be Countess of Varne. He would cast you off, and then what would become of you, for I do not believe one word of all Halliard's grand talk of his estate in the Indies? And if he does not marry you, you will be ruined. Oh, Julia, think what you mean to do!"

"Do you suppose I have not thought?" Julia pulled her hands free and started to her feet; there was an edge of hysteria to her voice: "All day and all night, until I can bear it no longer? Do you think I am not sick with shame and dread? But I have given my word, Joanna, and I must keep it!"

From this conviction she refused to be persuaded, and Joanna, finding all her efforts vain, was wise enough not to persist in them too long. Instead she set herself to discover what arrangements had been made for the actual flight, and once these were in her possession she said no more. Julia appeared to derive some comfort from unburdening herself to her friend, and when she finally took her leave she had recovered at least an outward composure. Before mounting her horse to return home, she clasped Joanna in her arms and kissed her, saying wistfully under her breath:

"You will tell Francis, will you not? You will do that for me?"

"He shall have no cause to think badly of you," Joanna replied firmly in the same tone. "I promise that, Julia."

She stood at the door to watch Miss Stonehurst out of sight, dwelling with some satisfaction upon the ambiguity of those parting words, and then hurried back to her bed chamber. She was profoundly disturbed, for in spite of Digby's warning she had never seriously considered the possibility of Julia eloping with Simon Halliard, but the shock seemed to have sharpened rather than dulled her wits.

She scribbled a hasty note to Philip, begging him most urgently to meet her that evening at the orchard gate, and sent Nancy off post-haste with it to Brinkbury. She had toyed with the idea of disclosing the whole matter in her letter, but decided against it. If such a letter were to go astray, the consequences would be disastrous.

Nancy, returning at last, brought the disquieting news that she had not found Mr. Digby at the inn. Ellen had assured her, however, that he was certain to return before long, and that the moment he did so she would deliver the note into his hands.

With this Joanna had to be content, but it was with some trepidation that she slipped out of the house some hours later and hastened in the direction of the orchard. What if Philip did not come? Ellen might have forgotten to give him the note, or his return to the inn might have been delayed. If he did not arrive in time to help her,

Joanna could see no alternative but to tell her father of the ingenious Mr. Halliard's intentions. One way or another, Julia must be saved.

She reached the gate, drew the bolt with trembling hands, and pulled it open. In the pallid light of a waning moon the strip of meadowland lay deserted, and beyond it the woods rose like a solid black wall against the sky. Joanna shivered and pulled her cloak more closely about her, and then turned with an exclamation of relief as Philip materialized out of the shadows at the foot of the orchard wall.

He took her in his arms and kissed her, and she clung to him in the reaction from her recent anxiety, breathlessly pouring out the tale of Julia's visit and the errand which had brought her. He listened in silence and with growing anger, and when she had done, said bitterly:

"So this is how he keeps his word! I should have known better than to trust him, particularly where both money and a pretty girl are concerned."

He paused, looking down at her, and then added abruptly, "Do you know when and where they are to meet?"

"Yes, I made her tell me, for I felt certain you would need to know. Julia is to make believe that she is unwell and will go to bed early. Then she will slip out and meet Mr. Halliard a little way from the main gates of the Grange. The wall of the park swings away from the road there, close to a clump of trees. Do you know where I mean? You have to pass the place on the way from the village."

"Yes, I know it. Set your mind at rest, my love. There will be no elopement tonight."

"I had better tell you," Joanna said dubiously, "that Julia feels obliged to keep her side of the bargain because Mr. Halliard kept his, and did not kill Francis this morning."

"She need not trouble herself on that account," Philip said grimly. "There was never any danger to his life. I cannot explain it all now, sweetheart, for it is an infernally tortuous piece of villainy, but I give you my word that there was no need for Miss Julia to strike a bargain of any kind. By going to plead with Simon she played straight into his hands, and he was quick to take advantage of her fears."

"What a despicable thing to do!" Joanna exclaimed hotly. "I do not wish to speak ill of any friend of yours, Philip, but I think Mr. Halliard is thoroughly dishonest."

"He is," Philip agreed calmly, "but he has his virtues as well as his vices. He has his uses, too, so do not expect me to call him out on Miss Julia's account. Just at present I happen to stand in need of him."

"That," Joanna pointed out somewhat tartly, "does not seem to weigh with him, since he is planning to elope with Julia."

"True, my love, true! I must have a word with him on that score when next we meet."

A tiny pang of doubt stirred in Joanna's mind. He did not seem to be treating the matter with the gravity it deserved, and it flashed through her thoughts that his anger at the news of Halliard's treachery might be due more to the use he had for the other man than to concern for Julia. She said anxiously:

"You will prevent their flight, will you not? I have placed all my dependence upon you."

"I will prevent it," he promised her, in a tone which admitted no doubt of his sincerity. "I warned him three days ago that Miss Julia is your friend and that I would not suffer him to harm her." His arms tightened about her, and his next words were spoken in a murmur against her lips. "He may give thanks that it is your friend, and not yourself, whom he has deceived. If this plot had been directed against you, I would have had his life for it!"

Her momentary doubts were banished, and remorse for that fleeting disloyalty lent an added warmth to her kisses, but at last she said with a sigh:

"You must go, Philip. There is not very much time."

"Yes!" He looked down at her, his eyes searching her face in the pallid moonlight. "I must go, but before I do, Joanna, tell me one thing. Miss Julia means to elope tonight with Simon. Would you come away with me, if I asked it of you?"

"If need be," she replied at once. "If that were the only way we could be together."

"You would not hesitate to trust me, even though I have told you how Simon intends to betray your friend?"

"What are his intentions to do with me? It is you I have promised to marry, not Simon Halliard. I love my parents, and my home, and the people and places I have known all my life. But I would leave them all to go with you. Do I need to tell you that?"

"Joanna!" he said unsteadily. "Oh, my dearest love!"

A sudden, furious exclamation close at hand jerked them apart, and brought them swinging guiltily around in the direction from which it had come. The moonlight showed them, framed in the open gateway leading to the orchard, the figure of Sir Andrew Selbourne.

Joanna gave a gasp of dismay, and with a movement which was purely involuntary shrank against Philip again and laid her hand on his arm. The gesture, so completely that of a woman seeking the support of her natural protector, ranging her as it did in opposition to her father, fanned Sir Andrew's mood to a white heat of pain and anger. Lifting the cane he held in one shaking hand, he pointed it accusingly at Philip.

"So this is what goes on behind my back!" he said in a voice trembling with fury. "This is the manner in which you repay my hospitality! Why, you young scoundrel, you deserve to be horse-whipped!"

Philip had not moved again, save to place his hand reassuringly over Joanna's. His face was very pale, but otherwise he appeared to be quite composed.

"You have every right to be angry, Sir Andrew," he said quietly, "but, however it may appear to you, pray believe that my intentions towards your daughter have never been anything but honest. It is my most earnest desire to marry her."

"I'll wager it is, and my fortune with her!" Sir Andrew retorted implacably. "I have met your kind before, my lad! A good appearance and a flattering tongue to enable him to bewitch some silly girl—these are the adventurer's stock-in-trade, but this time you have chosen the wrong

prey. Consent to your marriage with my daughter?" He
gave a short bark of angry, mirthless laughter, and then
as swiftly was grim again, to add deliberately, "I would
sooner see her dead!"

Joanna gave a choking cry of protest, and so drew her
father's attention upon her. For a moment he regarded
her in baleful silence, and then he stepped aside and
waved his cane imperatively towards the house.

"I will deal with you presently, my girl," he informed
her menacingly, "when I have sent your upstart suitor
about his business. In with you!"

"No! I will not!" Joanna clung more tightly to Philip's
arm; her voice was trembling but defiant. "Is this how you
keep your word? You promised me that I should be free
to wed where I chose."

"You will be free to feel my stick across your back if
you defy me in that fashion!" Selbourne's violent temper,
usually kept within rigid bounds, was now completely beyond his control. His face was congested and his whole
body trembling with the violence of his rage. "You impudent jade, do as I bid you!"

"Sir Andrew, I protest!" Philip broke in angrily. "Say
what you will to me, for I have merited your displeasure,
but in the name of mercy, spare your daughter any further reproaches."

"Protest and be damned to you!" Sir Andrew retorted,
and striding forward he seized Joanna by the arm and
dragged her by main force from Digby's side. "I will
chastise my daughter as I see fit. Now I will give you a
warning, young man! If you are not off my land within
five minutes, then, by heaven! I will summon my servants
to flog you off it for the rogue you are!"

"Philip!" Joanna was struggling to break free of her father's grip. "Philip, take me with you!"

He took a step towards her, but Sir Andrew, with an
agility marvellous in a man of his years, thrust her through
the gateway into the orchard and blocked the narrow arch
with his own substantial person. Tossing aside his cane,
he wrenched his sword from its sheath. Philip halted in
baffled dismay, and the elder man mocked him furiously.

"Why do you hesitate, Digby? You are something of a swordsman, I am told! Here's to prove your mettle!"

Philip shook his head.

"You tie my hands, sir," he said bitterly. "I could not cross swords with a man of your years, even if you were not Joanna's father. I will go now, but that does not mean that I relinquish my claim to your daughter's hand. That I will never do!" He paused and looked at Joanna, just visible to him behind her father's broad shoulder. When he spoke again it was to her, in a voice wondrously different from that in which he had addressed Sir Andrew. "Good night, my love! You know what I go to do."

"Yes, I know!" Joanna's voice came clearly in reply. She stood on tiptoe to peer over Sir Andrew's shoulder, and defiantly wafted a kiss from her fingertips. "Dear Philip, come back soon! I shall be waiting for you."

With an incoherent exclamation Selbourne thrust her back and slammed the gate in Digby's face, shooting the bolt with a grinding sound. For a full minute Philip stood staring at the blank, barred door, his lean face rigidly set, and then he turned and walked swiftly across the meadow to vanish into the sombre woods.

XVIII

The Death-Warrant

For perhaps another five minutes the strip of grassland lay silent and deserted in the moonlight, and then a clump of bushes at the foot of the wall close by the gate shook and parted, and a man's figure rose from the midst of them. Thrusting his way out on to the grass he flung back the dark cloak in which he was wrapped, and stretched his cramped limbs, and then fell to brushing dust and dead leaves from his clothes. The pale light, falling across his face, revealed the harsh, cynical features of Gregory Trayle.

He was laughing softly to himself as he stood there. It had been as undignified as it was uncomfortable to crouch skulking in a bramble thicket, but it had been worth it.

Yes, by God, it had been worth it! He had learned all that he desired to know, and been highly entertained into the bargain.

Sheer luck had given him knowledge of the assignation. After seeing his plans for the removal of Bertram and Francis thwarted by Halliard's forbearance—a forbearance which Gregory had been at a loss to understand—he had returned to Brinkbury House in a mood of suppressed fury, but when he grew calmer it occurred to him that it might be wise to discover why so promising a quarrel had ended so tamely. If Halliard, knowing of the plot against Varne, had guessed any part of the truth, then either his suspicions must be allayed or his help enlisted without delay.

Gregory reached the inn late on that fine October afternoon, and finding the parlour deserted desired the landlord to find out whether Mr. Halliard was in the house. Awaiting the man's return, he glanced idly about the room and so perceived a letter addressed to Digby set in a prominent position on the mantelpiece. It was, in fact, Joanna's appeal for help which Nancy had left in her cousin Ellen's charge: the younger girl had been sent on an errand by her mother and, having been thoroughly impressed with the urgency of the note, had left it where it would catch Mr. Digby's eye as soon as he entered the room. That it would be equally conspicuous to anyone else had not occurred to her.

Trayle was naturally not familiar with Miss Selbourne's writing, but the fact that the letter was addressed in an unmistakably feminine hand was enough. He lingered in the parlour on the pretext of awaiting Halliard's return, and before he left the inn had succeeded in acquainting himself with the contents of the note.

By the time he reached Brinkbury House again his plans were made, and all that remained was to write to Sir Andrew Selbourne, informing him of Digby's clandestine courtship of his daughter. Gregory prided himself on his ability to plant rankling seeds of suspicion with a few well-chosen words, and the letter which he presently despatched by the hand of the faithful Lister was a mas-

terpiece of subtle innuendo, calculated to make Selbourne's temper break all bounds.

Nor had it failed of its objective, he reflected now, re-
calling the scene he had just witnessed. Sir Andrew, for
all his talk of allowing Joanna freedom to choose her own
husband, had proved himself as arbitrary as any other
parent when put to the test, and Digby could have little
hope now of reconciling him to the match. That he would
attempt it before resorting to an elopement, Gregory felt
sure, for the Selbourne fortune was not to be lightly cast
away.

He allowed Digby ample time to get well out of earshot
and then followed the same path across the meadow and
into the woods. He spared a thought as he went for what
he had heard Joanna say concerning Julia Stonehurst, and
laughed under his breath at Halliard's ingenious dou-
bledealing. That was the sort of villainy which Gregory
Trayle could appreciate, even though it had played havoc
with his own plans.

Mr. Halliard himself was equally satisfied with his own
ingenuity, and troubled not at all by any considerations of
loyalty towards Digby or fear of reprisals from him. He
arrived in good time at the appointed rendezvous, and tethered the horses in the dense shadows beneath the trees.
Then he took up a position on that side of the little copse
nearest to the Grange, where he stood leaning one hand
against the trunk of a tree and looking along the moonlit
road towards the gates. There was no thought of betrayal
in his mind, no suspicion that the secret of his rascally
bargain was known to anyone save himself and Julia, and
when a shadow moved silently among the shadows behind
him, and a pistol-butt descended hard and accurately
upon the back of his head, his knees buckled and he
dropped to the ground without a sound.

It might have been hours later, or merely minutes,
when he struggled back to consciousness. At first he was
aware only of a painfully throbbing head, and of the almost leafless branches of a tree which appeared to be
spinning dizzily against a luminous sky somewhere far
above him, but as his senses cleared he realized that he

was not alone. Philip Digby was leaning with folded arms against the tree where Halliard himself had stood to wait for Julia. Simon dragged himself into a sitting position and glared furiously up at him.

"So it was you, confound it!" he said thickly. "I might have known it!"

"You might, indeed!" Philip's voice was cold. "I do not take kindly to treachery, Simon."

"Treachery be damned!" Halliard retorted. "You did not want the girl." He looked about him, though without much hope. "Where is she?"

"Safe in her own home by now, and aware of the damnable trick you played on her," Philip informed him curtly, "and when I spoke of treachery, my friend, I was thinking rather of the bargain you made with me. Did it never occur to you that my business here might come to a head while you were dallying with Julia Stonehurst, and that I might have need of you?"

"You would have contrived without my aid." Simon staggered to his feet, leaning against the tree-trunk for support and gingerly feeling the back of his head. "You are damnably heavy-handed, are you not?"

"Give thanks I came in time to thwart your schemes, or you would have suffered worse than a broken head," Philip said unfeelingly. "I warned you that I would not stand by while you harmed that girl, and you, as I remember, assured me that you would not attempt it."

"Aye, so I did, but when the silly wench all but threw herself into my arms, 'twas more than flesh and blood could stand. Devil take it, Philip! she's a lovely creature, and there were her father's money-bags to be considered also. Oh, a plague on your damned meddling!" He appeared to brood for a moment or two over opportunities lost, and then sighed and straightened his shoulders as though deciding that regret was a waste of time. "Well, what now? Is it to be swords at dawn, or do we go on as before?"

Philip was silent for a moment, struggling with reluctant laughter. At length mirth triumphed over exasperation and he said resignedly:

"If your effrontery were not so amusing it would be intolerable. We go on as before, curse you! I am too close to the climax of my plans to do aught else."

"That is what I depended upon," Simon replied, unabashed. He groped around on the ground for his hat, and, having found it, set it cautiously on his head. "I would still like to know, though, how you discovered my intentions. Never tell me that Julia appealed to you for aid?"

"No, she confided in Joanna, who had the wisdom to pass the information on to me. I may add, in passing, that she considers you to be thoroughly dishonest."

Simon gave a snort of laughter, but checked it at sight of his companion's face.

"What is it?" he said sharply. "Surely she does not couple you with me in that judgment?"

Philip shook his head.

"Sir Andrew came upon us while we were together," he replied curtly, and turned away without offering any further explanation. Simon made a grimace of dismay but said nothing, for he knew Digby well enough to guess the dangerous mood which must be simmering beneath that outward calm.

Philip fetched his own horse from the place where he had concealed it, and they rode back to Brinkbury in silence, each occupied with his own thoughts. At the door of the inn the landlord met them, looking flustered, and informed them that Sir Andrew Selbourne was in the parlour, awaiting Mr. Digby's return.

Halliard's brows shot up and he pursed his lips in a soundless whistle, glancing sidelong at Philip's face. It told him nothing; Digby said curtly:

"I will go to him at once. See to it that we are not disturbed."

He did not wait for a reply, but went past the man towards the parlour door. Simon looked thoughtfully after him and then strolled into the tap-room, speculating idly on the reason for this unexpected visit.

Sir Andrew was standing before the fire in the parlour with his back to the door, but he turned as Philip came in. Looking at him, Digby could see that he was still greatly angered, but it was a controlled anger now, vastly different from the violent rage which had ended their previous meeting.

"Your servant, Sir Andrew," he said briefly. "My apologies for keeping you waiting."

"It is no matter!" Selbourne's voice was curt. He took something from his pocket and moved forward to place it on the table. "I came merely to return the property which you left in my charge."

Philip found himself looking down at the little leather bag which held the star of death. For a second or two he regarded it, and then raised his eyes to the other man's face.

"I had forgotten it," he said simply. "I must thank you, sir, for your care of it."

He picked up the bag and was about to put it into his pocket then with an imperative gesture Sir Andrew restrained him.

"That jewel is of great value," he said coldly. "I would prefer you to assure yourself of its safety before I leave you."

Philip made a gesture of distaste.

"That is not necessary."

"Perhaps not! Nevertheless, be good enough to do as I ask."

Philip looked at him rather hard, and then with a shrug unfastened the bag and shook its contents out into his palm. The great emerald was there, and something else besides, a woman's ring of sapphires and pearls. He stood staring at it while the relentless voice continued:

"All your property, Mr. Digby, as you see. No doubt you will be glad of that trinket next time you go seeking a wealthy bride." Sir Andrew paused to take up his gloves and riding-whip from the table. Placing the whip under his arm, he began to draw on the gloves, saying as he did so: "Now, young man, I will give you a piece of advice. When that time comes, do not go so secretly about your wooing. If you had dealt honestly with me, if you had sought my leave to wed Joanna, I might well have given it. I am not one of those who believe wealth and rank to be the most important attributes of a man. But, as God is my witness, I will never give my daughter to a coward who comes creeping to woo her when my back is turned!"

He paused, and only then did Philip raise his head. His face was white and his eyes blazing.

"And if I tell you, sir, that I will marry her in spite of you?"

"Then not a penny shall she have of me, now or at any time!"

"To hell with your money!" Philip took a pace forward, his hand clenching hard on the jewels he held. "Do you think I care for that?"

Selbourne did not move, but regarded him dispassionately and with a hint of contempt.

"I wish I could believe you," he said coldly. "Unfortunately the protestation comes too late to be convincing." He walked past Philip to the door, but there paused and turned again to face him. "Whether or not you remain in Brinkbury is not for me to say, but I must ask you not to approach my house nor any member of my family again. If you do, I shall be obliged to take measures which you will find to be as painful as they are humiliating."

He went out, shutting the door firmly behind him. Philip took a step towards it as though to recall him, and then halted and turned back to the table. He returned the emerald to its bag and dropped it into his pocket, but the betrothal ring was still in his hand when Simon came into the room a minute or two later.

He entered briskly, carrying a letter, and came to Philip's side where he still stood by the table, looking down at the ring he held. Simon glanced curiously at it, and then raised his eyes to his friend's face.

"The ring you gave her?" he questioned laconically.

"Yes!" Philip looked up at last. He was still very pale, and a muscle quivered beside his mouth. "But no matter. She will wear it again!" He put the ring into his pocket, and nodded towards the paper in Simon's hand. "What have you there?"

Halliard held it out to him.

"For you," he replied briefly. "From Brinkbury House."

"So?" Philip took the letter and, breaking the seal, glanced quickly through the brief message. When he looked up again, Simon beheld him quite transformed, a grim smile curving his lips and a blaze of satisfaction in his eyes.

"The waiting is over, Simon," he said in a low, triumphant voice. "Varne arrives in Brinkbury tomorrow!"

XIX

Departure of Mr. Philip Digby

Next morning saw them early at Brinkbury House, Philip riding the great grey horse, El Diablo. With the news of or rather, that tremendous vitality which was part of his nature seemed deepened and intensified. His crisp, forceful speech, his decisive gestures, hinted at an energy barely controlled, as though the long weeks of waiting had tried his patience to the uttermost and the present demand for action sounded to him like a trumpet-call. Here was a man who would accomplish all he set out to do, sweeping difficulties and dangers aside with a forcefulness which was irresistible.

Bertram Colyton, receiving them in his study, regarded him with a tinge of envy. He felt very tired. The waiting game which he had been obliged to play had proved a greater strain than he had foreseen, and even now, when the prize he had coveted and schemed for was almost within his grasp, it was the anxieties of the next few hours which loomed larger in his thoughts than the triumph which would follow them if all went well. Looking at Varne's coming a change seemed to have come over him, Philip Digby, he wished profoundly that he had even a small part of his confederate's youth and vigour and undoubted confidence.

"Well, gentlemen," he greeted them, with as much cheerfulness as he could muster, "the time for action draws near. Varne left Bristol yesterday and looks to ar-

rive in Brinkbury this afternoon. I, with my son and Mr.
Trayle, are summoned to his house to welcome him."

Simon had seated himself astride a chair, resting his
arms along its back. He said with a grin:

"Two days to journey from Bristol? He is in no haste
to get here, it seems."

"I imagine that he travels in some state," Bertram replied drily, taking up a paper from the table before him.
"The tone of his letter suggests that Digby is right in saying that the inheritance of a title has gone to my young
kinsman's head. This is not an invitation to meet him. It
is a command."

"You will comply with his wishes, sir, of course?"
Philip asked briskly, and Colyton nodded.

"Of course. To refuse would invite suspicion."

"And Mr. Trayle and your son?"

"They, too. Francis insists upon being present, though
in my opinion he would do better to remain in his bed."

Bertram opened a drawer of his desk and took out a
heavy purse, which he handed to Philip. "There is the
sum we agreed upon, Mr. Digby," he remarked, "and let
me suggest that you waste no time in taking it, and yourself, out of the country. It would cause me profound regret
if you were captured."

"I am sure it would, sir," Philip agreed mockingly.
"The consequences could prove so embarrassing, could
they not? However, do not trouble yourself on my account. My plans are made down to the last, small detail. I
do not think they will go awry."

"Perhaps," Simon put in, grinning, "Mr. Colyton would
care to hear them? He might be reassured."

"Not in the least," Bertram replied hastily. "As far as I
am concerned, you are two young men riding out to meet
an old friend, and I desire to know no more. You do ride
together, I presume?"

"For a time!" Philip had pocketed the purse and was
pulling on his gloves again. "Then we part, and trust to
meet again later." He picked up his whip and glanced
at Halliard. "It is time we were away."

"Aye, to be sure!" Simon agreed, getting lazily to his

feet. "There is a deal to be done. Good day to you, Mr. Colyton."

He nodded amiably and sauntered out, and Philip and Bertram were left confronting each other. In the minds of both the memory of their first meeting was vivid, of the bargain they had made and the weeks of patient waiting which had passed since then. Colyton was the first to speak.

"My part is played, Mr. Digby," he said quietly. "Yours is yet to do."

"Yes!" There was a curious expression in the brilliant hazel eyes with their flecks of green. "I trust, sir, that you are troubled by no regrets?"

"None whatsoever!" Bertram assured him unhesitatingly. "Some anxiety concerning the outcome of the affair, but no regrets. Are you?"

"No!" The answer came swiftly, in a tone almost disdainful. "No, Mr. Colyton, I regret nothing."

He turned sharp on his heel, and with no other farewell strode briskly from the room, with a faint, musical jingle of spurs. Bertram remained in his chair, staring straight before him, while in an adjoining room, where he had listened to every word of the conversation with his own presence unsuspected, Gregory Trayle stood similarly lost in thought.

The news of Varne's coming had taken him by surprise, destroying some of the satisfaction he had felt the previous evening. The Earl's arrival meant that Philip Digby would be leaving Brinkbury for good, and it was certain that he would make some attempt to take Joanna with him. Gregory's own plans were laid, the plans which had been born of Oliver Stonehurst's drunken confidences three nights ago, but if they were to succeed he must know something of Digby's intentions, and it was in the hope of discovering these that he had eavesdropped upon the other man's conversation with Bertram. It had told him less than he had hoped.

One thing at least was certain. Digby could not take Joanna with him to waylay Varne. Did he then mean to take the appalling risk of returning to Greydon Park after he had killed the Earl? Trayle stood pondering the question, and then the answer to it flashed into his mind in the memory of something which Digby himself had said to Joanna the previous night. "He has his uses ... I have need of him at present."

Halliard, of course! They had set out together this morning, but on Digby's own confession they were to part, and meet again. While Digby went to settle his score with Varne, what was more likely than that Simon would be escorting Joanna to some prearranged rendezvous, probably in Bristol, or even aboard ship? If that were so, there was no time to be lost.

He summoned Lister and despatched him to the Colyton Arms with a message, purporting to come from Philip Digby, for Ellen to carry to Greydon Park. He had no doubt that she would do so without question, for Lister was well known to her and it was common knowledge that Digby was a frequent visitor at Brinkbury House. The man returned presently with an account of success, and Gregory listened with satisfaction, his faint, sneering smile on his lips.

"Excellent, Lister," he said softly. "Now unless Sir Andrew has seen fit to put his daughter under lock and key, all should go smoothly. You know what you have to do."

"I know, sir," the man assured him. "You may depend on me."

"I do, Lister, I do," Gregory replied sardonically. "You had best go now. I will join you—and your fair charge—as soon as may be."

In the village, excitement was running high. From the great house the news had filtered out that the long-awaited Earl was coming at last to claim his inheritance. Curiosity ran riot, and work was neglected as neighbours met to gossip over the news, and to speculate upon his lordship's character and whether his arrival would have any new and drastic effect upon their lives. The old Earl they had liked and respected; Bertram Colyton was as familiar to them as his kinsman had been, and commanded respect also, if not liking; the new young Earl from across the sea was an unknown quantity, who might use his great influence in the district for good or ill.

Into this ferment of excitement, early in the afternoon, came riding Sir Andrew Selbourne, a frown like a thundercloud upon his brow. He drew rein at the Colyton Arms, where the landlord was standing at the door in earnest conversation with a group of village worthies, and summoned him with a shout. Mine host came hurriedly.

"What time did Mr. Digby leave your house?" Sir Andrew demanded, in a tone which caused the landlord a twinge of alarm.

"Why, early this morning, your honour," he stammered. "He and Mr. Halliard have rode out to meet his lordship."

Sir Andrew stared.

"You mean that you expect him to return?"

"Yes, your honour, to be sure! There's his gear still in his room and his good roan horse in the stable. 'Tis likely he'll be staying at the great house now, I don't doubt, but——" he broke off, staring in bewilderment as Selbourne wrenched his horse around and rode back the way he had come.

Sir Andrew scarcely knew what to think. When his wife first raised the alarm he had stoutly refused to believe in Joanna's flight, but when a prolonged and exhaustive search finally convinced him that she had gone, he had leapt to the natural conclusion that Digby was to blame. The information he had received at the Colyton Arms shook that belief for a short while, but presently he decided that Digby's supposed intention to return was a bold attempt to throw him off the scent. A few minutes more sufficed to show him that it had succeeded. There was nothing for it but to return to Greydon Park and endeavour to take up the trail from there.

While Sir Andrew, in a mood of mingled anger and dismay, was riding back again towards his home, a coach bearing Bertram Colyton and his son and Gregory Trayle was lumbering up the long avenue towards the great house of Varne. It was a silent journey. Gregory's thoughts were occupied with the secret plans which were to give him not only Joanna herself, but in the course of time her father's handsome fortune, for it was not to be supposed that Sir Andrew would cut himself off altogether from his beloved daughter. Anger might prompt him to do so at first, but Gregory was confident that eventually the old gentleman would be won over by the entreaties of his wife and daughter, and accept the marriage with good grace since nothing could be done to alter it.

Bertram was equally preoccupied. Gazing from the window at the noble park through which they were passing, he reflected triumphantly that soon all this would be his, and felt a gnawing impatience to be done with waiting. How soon would the news come? Had Digby acted yet, and claimed his vengeance? Was he, Bertram, already Earl of Varne?

Francis, white-faced and haggard, his left arm supported in a sling, tried to brace himself against the lurching of the coach and to ignore the pain of his injured shoulder. For him the journey had a nightmare quality. He would have given all he possessed not to have made it, and yet some inner compulsion had forced him to disregard the excuse so ready to hand and to insist upon accompanying his father and cousin. Sick with apprehension, still a trifle feverish as a result of his wound, he sat with bowed head and wished miserably that Simon Halliard had shown him less mercy.

The coach halted at last, and the three occupants alighted. Behind them and upon either hand stretched the beautiful gardens, and before them rose the great grey pile of the house, warmed to mellow gold by the autumn sun. A liveried servant flung open the door, and with varying emotions they passed through it into the hall.

The servant, Forester, came forward to greet them, but this occasioned them no surprise. During the late Earl's lifetime, Forester had held a unique position in his household, for they had been boys together and to his master he was as much a friend as a servant. Bertram nodded to him and forced himself to speak naturally.

"Well, Forester, this is a sad day for you, I have no doubt, with a stranger coming as master to this house.

But I was forgetting, you have been here long enough to remember his father, have you not?"

"Yes, sir, I remember him well," Forester replied quietly, "and Mr. Richard's son can never be wholly a stranger at Varne." He paused to indicate a door on the far side of the hall. "Mr. Coleford is waiting, gentlemen. Will it please you to join him?"

"Coleford?" Gregory said softly as they followed Forester across the hall. "Why the devil is he here?"

Bertram shrugged.

"Our kinsman's idea, no doubt. Yet another way of adding to his own importance."

Francis heard this exchange as though from a great distance, and put his free hand to his head. How far it seemed to the library; he had forgotten that the hall at Varne was so wide.

"Pray take my arm, Mr. Francis," Forester's quiet voice said at his side. "I fear you are unwell."

"It is nothing. It will soon pass," Francis said faintly, but he grasped the proffered arm gratefully. His father and Gregory had walked on ahead and he hoped that they had not noticed his weakness.

In the library John Coleford rose to greet them. He had been seated by the long, polished table with papers before him, and though he bowed he remained standing beside his chair. There were other chairs grouped about the table, and into one of these Francis sank with a sigh of relief. Forester moved away, but was back in a moment or two with a glass which he put into the boy's hand.

Francis swallowed a little of the brandy it contained, and the mists cleared from before his eyes. He saw the lawyer still standing with one hand on the back of his chair, and Bertram seated at the head of the table, a large, assured man whose pose of calm was belied only by the restlessness of his heavy-lidded eyes. Gregory had gone to stand before the fire, and was taking snuff from his delicately enamelled box. He was the first to speak.

"Your presence here is unexpected, Coleford," he said sardonically. "Were you sent on ahead to prepare a greet-

ing of sufficient splendour to satisfy the vanity of my lord-
ly cousin?"

"No, Mr. Trayle, I was not." The lawyer's voice was
very grave, and Francis, clenching his fingers tightly on
the glass, braced himself for the blow about to fall. "I am
here because of a plot against his lordship's life."

There was a moment of utter silence, a silence so intense that the faint sounds from the logs glowing on the
wide hearth could be clearly heard, and the ticking of the
tall clock in a far corner seemed unnaturally loud. Then
Gregory spoke again, in a voice which had hardly
changed.

"A plot against his life? My dear Coleford, you must
be raving!"

"You have good cause, Mr. Trayle, to know that I am
not," Coleford replied grimly, and took up a paper from
the table. "I have here a signed statement which accuses
you and Mr. Colyton of conspiring with two other men,
Philip Digby and Simon Halliard, against the life of the
fifth Earl of Varne. Furthermore, it declares that five
years ago Mr. Colyton employed a man named Trevor to
kill his cousin, Viscount Ashmore, under the pretext of a
duel."

"Who says so?" It was Bertram's voice, harsh and ugly
with anger and with fear. "Who set his name to those
damnable lies?"

"I did, Father!" Francis's face was grey now, but his
voice came steadily. "Three nights ago I came down to
your study to speak to you. You and Gregory were
talking and I overheard what you said. I rode into Bristol
next day." He glanced briefly at Trayle. "That is what
made me late for my meeting with Halliard."

"You—you——!" Bertram struggled to find words
with which to lash his son, and before he succeeded Gregory had intervened again. Thinking and acting with a
swiftness admirable under the circumstances, he came forward to the foot of the table and said in a tone of indulgent amusement:

"Coleford, you disappoint me! Do you really propose
to take seriously a declaration of that sort? The hysterical

accusation of a lad probably in his cups, who has twisted an idle jest into a serious threat against a man's life? To the best of my recollection, Francis was in no state that night to know jest from earnest."

"It was no jest, you liar!" Francis cried wildly. "You may have taken no active part in the plot, but you were willing to stand by and let Richard be murdered, just as you stood by five years ago when Charles was killed. You are as guilty as the rest of them!"

He had half risen from his chair as he spoke, but now slumped back again, staring at Trayle with eyes which burned feverishly against the livid pallor of his face. Gregory regarded him with unshaken calm.

"So this is our accuser," he said mockingly. "Not a very convincing one, Coleford! You will need to do better than this."

"Perhaps I can, Mr. Trayle," the lawyer replied coldly. "Mr. Francis brought me warning of the plot, but it was not necessary. I already knew of it from another source."

"Another source?" Gregory spoke sharply this time, while both Francis and Bertram stared blankly. "What the devil do you mean?"

"He learned of it from me, gentlemen," a crisp, familiar voice replied, and the sound of it jerked their heads round in the direction from which it came. On the far side of the room a door had swung open, and on the threshold was standing a slim young man in riding-dress, with red hair like a flame above a bronzed, expressive face.

Francis uttered a strangled exclamation and his father leaned forward, staring at the newcomer as though unwilling to believe the evidence of his eyes, while Gregory stood as though petrified, his hard grey eyes narrowed to the merest slits. Digby strolled forward, and Simon Halliard followed him into the room and closed the door.

"So my instinct was not at fault," Trayle said softly, his voice breaking a silence tense with astonishment and dismay. "You were not to be trusted, as I suspected from the first. I hope that Cousin Richard paid you well for your treachery."

"You have not fully grasped the situation, Mr. Trayle,"

John Coleford remarked drily. "This gentleman is the Earl of Varne."

Gregory went white, and his hand closed convulsively on the snuff-box he still held, while Bertram caught his breath in a sound which was almost a groan. After a moment, Gregory said deliberately:

"You are Richard Colyton?"

"Richard Philip Digby Colyton, to give you the full sum of it," Philip replied calmly, and walked past him to where Francis sat, and held out his hand. "I have to thank you, cousin! It is good to know that not all my kinsmen desired my death."

As though scarcely aware of what he was doing, Francis grasped the proffered hand, looking up at the Earl with a dazed expression in his eyes.

"I do not understand," he said in a bewildered way. "In God's name, why did you do it?"

"It is very simple!" Philip turned so that he could face both Gregory and Bertram; his voice was cold. "When I arrived in England, Mr. Coleford gave me a letter which my uncle had written before he died. You are all aware of the suspicions he harboured concerning his son's death, and so you may guess at the contents of the letter, which was to warn me that I might find myself in mortal danger at your hands. I consulted with Mr. Coleford and found that he agreed in all respects with my uncle, although it was impossible to offer me any proof. So I resolved to obtain that proof myself."

He paused, looking from Gregory at the table's foot to Bertram at its head. Mr. Colyton's face was a ghastly colour and his eyes seemed to protrude as he stared in a mesmerized fashion at the speaker. Philip continued quietly:

"I came to Brinkbury House under an assumed name, with a tale of hatred and vengeance, and soon discovered how well-founded my uncle's suspicions were. My proposed bargain was accepted with unseemly eagerness." He put his hand into his pocket and pulled out a heavy purse and dropped it on to the table. "Blood-money, cousin! I am glad to be rid of it."

For a moment or two he waited, but then, as Bertram made no reply, Philip's gaze returned again to Gregory's face. Trayle returned the look sardonically.

"Ingenious, my lord," he sneered. "Allow me to compliment you. No doubt it was your hope to involve me also in this make-believe plot?"

"I desired to know which way you would choose to jump," Philip replied quietly, "and whether or not you were in your cousin's confidence. It became obvious that you were when you goaded Francis into challenging Simon Halliard. You were so sure that Bertram would soon be Earl of Varne that you planned his son's death in order to become his heir."

Francis's eyes widened and he opened his lips to speak, but before he could do so all attention was claimed by his father. Bertram had half risen, flinging out an accusing hand towards Trayle. Then, uttering a strangled gasp, he clutched at this side as though in pain and before anyone could go to him, pitched forward across the table.

Francis was the first to reach him, trying in vain to lift him from his huddled position and failing because of his injured arm. Philip put him gently aside and heaved the elder man up, supporting the lolling head against his shoulder. Bertram's face was livid, with an ominous, bluish tinge about the mouth, and the sound of his laboured breathing filled the room. Philip glanced at Forester, who had come forward from his post by the door.

"A doctor, quickly!" he said urgently, and took the glass of brandy which Simon was holding out to him. With difficulty they contrived to force a little of the spirit between Colyton's lips, though most of it trickled down his chin and on to his neckcloth, and in spite of all their efforts he showed no sign of returning consciousness.

When Forester came back into the room with the news that a servant had been sent in search of the doctor, Philip relinquished his place by Bertram's chair and drew him aside.

"Have them carry him to a bedchamber, and do everything possible for his comfort," he said in a low voice.

"For his son's sake I have said nothing, but I fear the doctor is likely to have a wasted journey."

Forester gave him a swift, searching glance, but said merely, "I will see to it, my lord," before turning away. Within a few minutes Mr. Colyton had been borne away by four stalwart lackeys, his son and Forester accompanying him, and Philip was left confronting his remaining kinsman across the width of the room, while Simon and the lawyer waited curiously to see what would follow.

Gregory had retired again to the fireplace and remained there throughout the commotion resulting from Bertram's collapse, eyeing the scene before him with complete indifference, but now at length he moved, strolling forward to where Philip was standing by the table.

"The most noble Earl of Varne," he said softly, "and not one of us suspected it. But you are not very like the Colytons, are you, cousin?" He looked down at the younger man from his superior height. "You lack their inches, their dark colouring, their——"

"Their villainy?" Philip struck in swiftly, and Trayle laughed.

"That is not an unfailing family trait," he replied. "Young Francis, for example, is obviously a most upright character, while Ashmore was a paragon of all the virtues—in short, a very tedious fellow. It was really quite a relief when Trevor killed him." He saw the blaze of anger and contempt in Philip's eyes, and laughed again. "Precisely!" he said softly. "There is only one way to settle our differences of opinion, is there not? Halliard told me that you are a remarkable swordsman."

"He said the same of you!" Philip was smiling, but with his lips alone. "Unhappily, this is neither the time nor the place to put his judgment to the test. No one regrets that more than I."

"Except myself," Gregory responded promptly. "However, I feel sure that we shall continue this most interesting discussion at some more appropriate moment. Until then, cousin, I will take leave to bid you good-day. My presence here is, I feel, not only unnecessary, but unwelcome."

He bowed with exaggerated courtesy, first to Philip and then to Simon and the lawyer. Then he turned and with his usual leisurely, arrogant gait crossed the room to the door giving on to the hall. There he paused, and turned, and bowed again.

"My lord," he said mockingly, "your very humble servant. I look forward to our next meeting with more than common eagerness."

A moment later the door had closed behind him.

XX
Demand for Ransom

For some twenty minutes after Gregory's departure no one else entered the library. Philip sat at the table in low-voiced conversation with the lawyer, while Simon wandered about the room or stood looking from one of the windows. At the end of that time the door opened and Forester came in from the hall. Philip looked up quickly.

"Mr. Colyton?" he asked, and the valet shook his head.

"He is dead, my lord," he replied gravely. "He died without regaining consciousness."

There was a brief silence, and then Philip said:

"And his son?"

"He is coming now, my lord," Forester replied in a low voice, and stepped aside to hold open the door. Francis came slowly into the library and halted there, as though still dazed by the shocks which had befallen him. Philip got up and went across to him, laying a hand on his shoulder.

"I am sorry, cousin," he said quietly. "More sorry than I can say. I never intended this."

The dark, heavily-shadowed eyes were lifted to meet his; Francis said in a low voice:

"Perhaps it is better so. He is spared the consequences of his crimes." His lips quivered suddenly and he bowed his head again. "I wish I could have asked his forgiveness before he died."

Philip led him across to the table and made him sit

down there, seating himself beside him, for Mr. Coleford had gone discreetly to join Simon at the farthest window. Francis rested his elbow on the table and covered his eyes with his hand.

"It was a hard decision which was forced upon you, Francis," Philip said after a moment. "No one could fail to honour you for the choice you made."

"I deserve no credit," Francis replied in a muffled voice. "You do not know how sorely I was tempted, how long it was before I could bring myself to betray the plot." He raised his head, and there was the weary glimmer of a smile in his eyes. "Do you know what finally resolved my mind? Oliver told me that Joanna had promised to marry you, and I felt I had no right to let her make so disastrous a match while it was in my power to prevent it. Yet at the same time I was sorry, for I had always liked you." He paused, his hand moving aimlessly among the papers which still littered the table, his eyes following its erratic course. "Will you tell me something, Varne? You said just now that Gregory provoked the quarrel between Halliard and me."

"It is quite true," Philip replied quietly. "The handkerchief belonged to Joanna, and Simon picked it up by chance. When Trayle saw it, he leapt to the conclusion that it was Miss Stonehurst's, and used it to goad you into issuing a challenge."

"My God, what a fool I have been!" Francis said wretchedly. "If Halliard had run me through, it would have been no more than I deserved for believing Gregory's cursed lies."

"Lies they most certainly were," Philip agreed. "No one save we four ever saw that handkerchief, much less supposed that Miss Stonehurst had given it to Simon."

Francis was silent for a space, still fidgeting restlessly with the papers before him. Finally, lifting his eyes to his cousin's face, he said in a tone which seemed to plead for contradiction:

"Nevertheless, she does care for him."

Philip's brows lifted.

"I cannot claim to be in Miss Stonehurst's confidence,"

he replied, "but Joanna declares that her interest in Simon was no more than a passing fancy, and is already forgotten."

"If I could believe that!" There was a sudden radiance in Francis's face, which faded as swiftly as it had come as he added dejectedly: "But even if it were so, what hope have I of winning her? Her father's ambitions are set too high."

"Perhaps when he knows that there is no hope of her becoming the Countess of Varne, he will look more kindly upon you," Philip suggested. "If he does not—well, nothing was ever achieved without boldness! Marry her out of hand, and trust to your friends to make your peace with her father. Harm enough has already been wrought by our cousin's villainy."

Of the extent of that villainy they were presently offered further proof. When Dr. Towne arrived, Mr. Coleford went out, at Philip's request, to meet him, and to explain to him the circumstances leading up to Bertram Colyton's death. When the lawyer came back into the library he was looking very grave, and drawing Philip and Simon aside, disclosed to them Trayle's knowledge of Mr. Colyton's precarious health. The inferences to be drawn from this were obvious.

"Trayle's a damned scoundrel," Simon remarked dispassionately, "and unless I am much mistaken, he will still have his eye on this earldom of yours. I tell you, Philip, the sooner you rid yourself of him for good, the better."

"I am inclined to agree with you!" Philip broke off, staring, for a sudden commotion had arisen in the hall, a babel of voices in which predominated the unmistakable tones of Sir Andrew Selbourne. Conscious of a sudden, inexplicable misgiving, Philip strode across the room and flung open the door.

A surprising scene met his eyes. Forester and two lesser servants were engaged in spirited altercation with Selbourne and Oliver Stonehurst, while Julia hovered agitatedly in the background. Then suddenly Sir Andrew caught sight of Philip standing in the doorway, and surged past the servants towards him.

"Digby!" he exclaimed, relief and anger struggling for mastery in his voice. "Thank God I have run you to earth at last!"

"I am sorry, my lord!" Forester hurried after Selbourne, his usual imperturbable calm a trifle ruffled. "I informed Sir Andrew that your lordship was engaged——"

"My lord?" Sir Andrew broke in, astonishment overwhelming all other emotions for an instant. "What tomfoolery is this?"

Philip's lips twitched.

"I fear I have been deceiving you, Sir Andrew," he replied. "I am Richard Colyton." He turned to offer his arm to Julia, who, with her brother, had followed Selbourne across the hall. "This is a charming surprise, Miss Stonehurst. Will you not come within?"

She was staring at him with the utmost stupefaction, but these words seemed to recall her to herself. Instead of merely laying her fingers on the proffered arm, she clutched it with both hands and said urgently:

"Sir, the most dreadful thing has happened. Joanna——"

"Joanna!" The faintly mocking amusement was wiped from Philip's face; his voice snapped. "What ails her?" He became aware of the staring footman, and without pausing for a reply added swiftly: "In here, all three of you! Now, what's amiss?"

Julia did not reply. A flood of colour had swept into her face and she was gazing at Francis, who had risen from his seat by the table to stare at her as though he could not believe his eyes. Sir Andrew put her impatiently aside and thrust a grubby scrap of paper into Philip's hand.

"That is what is amiss," he said in a shaking voice. "Those unspeakable rogues have dared to lay hands on my daughter. Read it, my lord! Read their damnable demands!"

Philip glanced rapidly through the note. It was written in a laboured scrawl, ill-spelt and almost indecipherable, and it announced that the writer held Miss Selbourne prisoner. If her father wished to see her again, alive and unharmed, the star of death must be given as her ransom. There followed instructions concerning the handing over of the jewel, and the letter was signed "Ned Mullett".

"For God's sake, Digby, give me that accursed jewel!" Sir Andrew said in an anguished voice. "You shall have its full value, I promise you, only give it to me, and let me fetch the child home."

"Do not talk to me of its value!" Philip exclaimed furiously. "Do you think you could not have it for the asking, if it would be of the least avail?" He crushed the paper in his hand; his face was white as death, and made terrible by the expression in his eyes. "This demand is no more than dust flung in our eyes. Ned Mullett and his accomplice were arrested two days ago!"

There was a stunned silence, and then Sir Andrew said blankly:

"Arrested? Then who——?"

"Aye, who?" Philip repeated. "Who save we two, and Joanna herself, knew that the emerald lay hidden at Greydon Park, or that Mullett was the name of the rogue who sought it?" He ground his clenched fist into the palm of the other hand, and after an instant's pause looked up to add, "How long has she been gone?"

"Since some time this morning," Sir Andrew replied hopelessly. "We do not know the exact hour."

"This morning?" Philip's voice was like the crack of a whip. "In hell's name, why delay your search until now?"

"I felt certain that she had fled with you. They told me at the inn that you had gone to meet Lord Varne and would be returning later, but I supposed that to be a tale to disarm suspicion. When I returned to Greydon, hoping to find some clue there, the lodge-keeper brought me that message. He had found it fastened to the gates of my house."

There was a pause. After a little, Julia diffidently took up the tale.

"Oliver and I were on our way to Greydon Park when we met Sir Andrew," she explained. "He told us what had happened and that he hoped to find you here, and we came with him to lend whatever aid we could." She laid her hand timidly on Philip's arm, her eyes anxiously searching his face. "My lord, what can we do? What has happened to her?"

"Those questions both wait upon another, Miss Stonehurst," he replied, "and that is not 'what', but 'who'?" He put her hand aside and began to pace the room as though he could no longer bear to be still. "Who knew of that damned emerald, and where it was hidden? Who?"

"Gregory!" It was Francis who had spoken. He took a pace forward, a flush of excitement rising in his cheeks. "I heard him speak of it to my father, the night I discovered all the rest. Varne, it must be he! He has been mad for Joanna this year past."

Philip had halted, staring at his cousin. He said abruptly: "Did he know of Ned Mullett?"

"Yes, he did!" Oliver spoke for the first time, in a strangled voice of misery. "My God, I have only just remembered! Joanna told me of the emerald, and the man Mullett, and the rest of it. I had made her angry and she spoke without thinking—you know her way! That night I went to Brinkbury House to see Francis. He was not there, but Trayle was. I—I was drunk. I remember him asking me question after question. He must have had the whole story out of me before he sent me home."

"So our question is answered!" Philip tossed the crumpled note on to the table; his voice was very grim. "It is Trayle who has made off with Joanna, and covered his tracks with this false demand for ransom. Had Mullett not been arrested, the ruse would undoubtedly have succeeded."

"But, my lord," Mr. Coleford protested, "Gregory Trayle was in this room less than an hour ago."

"Yes, he was here!" The most profound bitterness invested Philip's voice. "He was here, and I let him go. By God! had I but known the truth!" He swung round again to Francis. "Where will he take her, cousin? In what safe hiding-place will his hirelings wait for their master to join them?"

"There is only one place," Francis replied promptly. "Gregory's own house at Marwood. There, no one would dare to question his actions."

Philip nodded.

"How far?" he asked sharply.

"Twelve miles, maybe a little more. Marwood lies almost due south of Brinkbury."

Another nod.

"It is very well," Philip replied softly. "Forester!"

"My lord?"

"My horse to the door, at once!"

Simon strolled forward.

"Mine also, Forester." He glanced at Philip, amusement in his blue eyes. "I ride with you, my friend. I've a fancy to see your sword matched against Trayle's."

"Varne!" Francis took a step forward, gripping his cousin's arm. "Let me come with you, too!"

"With that hole in your shoulder?" Philip shook his head, but his voice was kindly. "No, Francis, though I am grateful for the thought. You must remain here." He turned to Selbourne. "Sir Andrew, I suggest that you return home. I will bring your daughter to you there."

Sir Andrew shook his head.

"I doubt neither your ability nor your honesty, my lord," he said decisively, "but it is my intention to ride with you."

Philip's brows lifted.

"We must ride hard, sir," he said with a faint note of doubt in his voice, "and spare neither our horses nor ourselves."

"Hell and the devil, boy, do you think me in my dotage?" Sir Andrew demanded wrathfully. "Have the goodness to lend me a fresh horse, and I'll warrant you will not need to curb your pace on my account. Do you suppose I can be still until I am certain that Joanna is safe?"

"I ask your pardon, Sir Andrew!" There was a gleam of appreciative amusement behind the strain in Philip's eyes. "I will give order for it at once."

He was turning to summon a servant when he found

Oliver at his side. He looked both determined and acutely uncomfortable.

"I have no right to ask it, I know," he said abruptly, "but I beg that you will let me accompany you. This whole damnable business is largely my fault, and I must do something."

Philip opened his lips to utter a curt refusal, and then thought better of it. Instead of the rebuff he had intended to deal the speaker, he said curtly:

"You may come if you wish. Is your horse fresh enough?"

"Yes, my lord, and thank you!" There was real gratitude in Oliver's voice. "It is more than I deserve."

"The Earl of Varne!" Sir Andrew remarked in a thoughtful tone, looking very hard at Philip. "I wonder if I am right in thinking that I can guess what is behind this very odd affair?"

Philip beckoned to the lawyer to come forward.

"Mr. Coleford will be happy to answer that question for you, sir, while we wait for the horses," he replied. "There will be many garbled versions of the story abroad before long, and it is best that you and Stonehurst should know the truth at once." He turned away, and said in a low voice to Halliard: "See to it that a horse is saddled for the old gentleman, Simon, and tell them to make haste. Trayle has an hour's start of us already."

Simon nodded and went out of the room. Sir Andrew and Oliver were both absorbed in what Mr. Coleford was saying. Francis, leaning against the edge of the table, was gazing fixedly at Julia, who sat nearby, her eyes downcast and her hands fidgeting with the gloves which lay in her lap. Philip went forward.

"I think, Miss Stonehurst," he said quietly, "that Lady Selbourne should be told what has happened, and be reassured as far as possible. If I place a coach and servants at your disposal, will you undertake that kind office? I am depriving you of your brother's escort, but"—he smiled faintly—"I believe my cousin will be willing to take his place."

Julia looked up, the colour coming and going in her cheeks, her eyes wide and panic-stricken.

"He is unwell," she said faintly. "His shoulder——"

"Prevents him from riding, that is all," Philip broke in relentlessly, and looked at Francis. "What say you, cousin? Will you go with Miss Stonehurst to Greydon Park?"

Francis came slowly forward until he stood by Julia's chair.

"Very gladly," he said in a low voice, "if she will accept my escort. Will you, Julia?"

She lifted her eyes to meet his, and nodded wordlessly. Philip laid a hand on his cousin's shoulder.

"Matters here can safely be left to Coleford and to Forester, Francis," he said, "and I will send word to Greydon Park as soon as may be. You had best tell Lady Selbourne the whole story. She has a right to know." He looked down at Julia and added with some meaning, "There are times when complete frankness is the only way to dispel misunderstandings."

Her eyes lifted quickly to meet his, and he saw comprehension in them. She coloured painfully, and said in a tone so low that it scarcely reached his ears:

"I understand you, my lord, I think. Folly must be atoned for, must it not?" She broke off, for the door had opened and Simon put his head into the room to announce that the horses were ready. Julia put out her hand to Philip. "Good fortune, my lord. I pray God that you will bring Joanna safely home."

He took the hand, and kissed it, and turned away. Simon had disappeared again; Sir Andrew and Oliver were moving towards the door, and John Coleford went with them. Philip followed them out of the room, but paused and glanced back before closing the door behind him. Francis was still standing by Julia's chair. Her hand was in his, and neither appeared to have noticed the departure of the rest of the company.

Philip smiled to himself as he went swiftly across the hall and out into the cold, autumn dusk. Francis had placed him very deeply in his debt, but he felt that during the past few minutes he had done his best to repay him.

XXI
Lady in Distress

Gregory Trayle's house at Marwood was a picturesque, rambling building standing remote from any neighbours in a fold of the hills. The estate had been prosperous enough in the days when its previous master married Lady Mary Colyton, but they had both been dead for many years, and the comfortable competence which Marwood brought its owner had been unable to keep pace with their son's expensive tastes and passion for gaming. What was left of the land was heavily mortgaged, and the house falling into disrepair in the charge of servants who saw their master only at rare intervals. Gregory himself disliked the place and spent as little time there as he could, preferring whenever possible to enjoy the hospitality of his more prosperous relatives at Brinkbury.

In one of the low-pitched rooms on the ground floor of the house, with its dark, old-fashioned panelling, Miss Joanna Selbourne sat before the fire and watched the autumn dusk falling over the unkempt garden. Escape, she knew, was out of the question. The door was locked, and one of the men who had captured her on guard beyond the window through which she was staring.

She was still faintly astonished at the ease with which she had been carried off. When Nancy brought her the message that morning, she had never for one moment doubted that it came from Philip. Her father had proved impervious to temper and tears alike, had wrested her betrothal ring from her and forbidden her ever to see Philip Digby again, and had no doubt gone to Brinkbury to issue a similar command to Philip himself. She had been more than half prepared for flight, and when the summons came she obeyed it unhesitatingly.

Pausing only to warn Nancy to use the utmost secrecy, she had slipped out unobserved through the gardens to the orchard, and thence by way of the gate to the meadow beyond. Philip was nowhere in sight, and, fearful of discovery, she had hastened across the grass to the shelter of the woods. Hardly had she set foot in their shadow when strong arms seized her from behind, a hand was clapped across her mouth, and she was dragged from the path into the thickets which bordered it.

Her assailants were two men whom she had never seen before. They tied her hands behind her back, thrust a gag into her mouth, and as a final precaution flung a dark cloak over her head. Then she was lifted to a burly shoulder and carried off she knew not whither.

She was very frightened. The shock of the attack, and the stifling folds of the cloth covering her head, combined to bring her close to swooning, and for a time she had only a very confused impression of what was happening. She thought that she was carried for some distance on horseback, but not until she was set down on the seat of a coach, and the covering removed from her head, was she able to collect her scattered wits.

Her first suspicion had been that the villainous Ned Mullett had carried her off so that he could bargain with Philip or her father for the emerald, but the sight which now met her eyes dispelled it. The coach, which was already lurching forward along the road, was unquestionably a gentleman's equipage, and the thin, pale-faced man in sober black who was seated beside her had all the appearance of an upper servant. What was more, his face seemed vaguely familiar. She shook the tumbled hair out of her eyes and stared at him in mingled indignation and alarm.

"Pray do not be afraid, Miss Selbourne," he said in answer to that look. "You are in no danger. I regret most deeply that it is not possible for me to make you more comfortable, but if I were to release you, and you contrived to summon aid or make your escape, I should be obliged to answer for it to my master."

The resentment deepened in the big blue eyes gazing at him above the kerchief which gagged her, and she jerked fruitlessly at the cord confining her wrists. Her companion shook his head.

"Madam, it will not break," he informed her placidly,

"and you will hurt yourself to no purpose. We have some miles to go, and it will be best if you resign yourself to your bonds. Mr. Trayle charged me to express to you his most profound apologies for the violence with which you have been handled, but to point out that circumstances left him no choice in the matter."

The tone in which these words were uttered was respectful, even obsequious, but with a note of finality in it which told her more surely than any threats that she was completely helpless. For a moment or two longer she continued to regard him, and then with assumed indifference turned her head away.

The knowledge that she was Gregory Trayle's prisoner provoked in her a tremendous anger, but no fear. She was certain to be rescued before very long, for although when her flight was discovered her father was bound to suppose that she had gone to Philip, it would not take him long to discover his mistake; and once Philip knew of her plight, he would come immediately to her rescue. As for Mr. Trayle when he deigned to appear on the scene she would make some comments upon his character and his conduct which should do a good deal to lessen his appalling conceit.

The journey was an exceedingly uncomfortable one for her, but this served only to increase her rage. At last the coach left the road and bumped along an ill-kept drive bordered with trees and shrubberies, and Lister, as though deciding that any danger of escape was now past, leaned forward to untie the gag. The kerchief fell away, and Joanna passed her tongue over her parched lips while the servant produced a knife and severed the cord binding her hands. Her arms were stiff and cramped and the bonds had left bright red weals about her wrists, but she forced herself to pretend that the discomfort did not exist. When the coach came to a halt and Lister jumped down to help her to alight, she allowed him to hand her down from the vehicle without making any protest.

The door of the house already stood open, and after one disparaging glance about her Miss Selbourne suffered herself to be conducted within, and into a room on the right of the entrance hall. A bright fire was burning there, and she walked across to it and held out her hands to the blaze, saying coldly over her shoulder:

"I am extremely thirsty. Please bring me something to drink."

"At once, madam," Lister replied deferentially, and she heard the door close behind him. Only when she was certain that she was alone did she turn to look searchingly about the room, rubbing her maltreated wrists as she did so.

The servant returned after a short while carrying a tray on which both food and drink was set out. Placing it on the table, he filled a glass and carried it across to her, saying respectfully:

"I have taken the liberty of bringing you some refreshment, Miss Selbourne. Will it please you to be seated?"

"I am not hungry!" Joanna raised the glass to her lips and drank gratefully. "I would prefer to be told how long it is intended to keep me here."

"No doubt Mr. Trayle will inform you of that, madam, when he arrives," Lister replied smoothly. "He hopes to join you later this afternoon."

"Very well. You may leave me," Joanna said frigidly, and remained where she was until the door had closed behind the man, and the sound of a key turning in the lock informed her that no precaution had been overlooked. Then she ran to the window and looked out. From a seat built about the trunk of a tree a short way from the house, a burly individual stolidly returned her regard.

Joanna went back to the fire and sat down. There was obviously nothing to be done but to wait with as much patience as she could muster for her rescuers to arrive. She wondered why Trayle had not been waiting at Marwood for the arrival of his prisoner, and decided that he had probably lingered in Brinkbury to disarm suspicion.

The long hours dragged slowly past. She ate some of the food, more for the sake of something to do than because she was hungry, and twice Lister came into the room to mend the fire and to inquire if there was anything she desired. Each time she replied with a curt refusal, and he withdrew again.

The sun went down and dusk began to fall over the countryside, a chill, autumn dusk with a white mist gathering in the hollows and between the trees, giving a promise of frost to come. Joanna's anger, deprived of an opportunity to express itself, began to fade, and with it faded also some of her confidence. She found herself sitting tensely on the edge of her chair, straining her ears for the sound of hoofs or wheels, for any sound to break the heavy silence which seemed to cut off this lonely house from the rest of the world.

Yet when at last the regular rhythm of approaching hoofbeats reached her ears, it brought her to her feet with quickened breath and wildly thumping heart. Once again she ran to the window and peered out into the gathering shadows, and so saw the tall, cloaked figure of Gregory Trayle swing out of the saddle and toss the reins to a youth who had come running from the rear of the house.

For a moment Joanna remained by the window, a knuckle caught between her teeth, and then she ran lightly across to the door and pressed her ear to its panels. She heard Lister say something she could not catch, and then came Trayle's voice in reply.

"See that supper is served immediately, and warn them in the stables that I want the coach at the door as soon as the moon is up."

"You are leaving tonight, sir?" Lister asked in a tone of profound astonishment.

"Unhappily, I have no choice. There is less time at my disposal than I had hoped. Where is Miss Selbourne?"

Footsteps approached the door, and Joanna darted back to her seat by the fire. The key grated, the door swung open, and Trayle's figure appeared in silhouette against the lights in the hall behind him.

"What, all in darkness, my dear?" he said sardonically, and added sharply: "Lights, Lister, at once! What the devil are you about, to leave my guest sitting here in the dark?"

With a murmured apology the servant bore a branch of

candles into the room, and began to kindle others from them. Gregory strolled across to the fireplace and stood looking down at Joanna.

She returned his regard defiantly. The scrap of conversation which she had overheard had restored her ebbing courage, for it could mean only that rescue was on its way, but she did not wish him to guess that she knew it.

"Why mince words, Mr. Trayle?" she asked scornfully. "We both know that I am not a guest here, but a prisoner."

He shook his head.

"If one of us is in bondage, Joanna, it is I. You have held me captive for a long while now."

She looked at him doubtfully. The words were loverlike, but the ironic tone, and the sneering half-smile which accompanied them, made a mockery of the declaration. She said vehemently:

"That, sir, was neither my intention nor my desire. Nor have I given you leave to use my name."

His smile broadened a fraction.

"To the best of my recollection, Joanna, I have never asked it."

"No!" Her voice was indignant. "You do not deal in courtesy, do you, Mr. Trayle? Today's events have made that amply clear. Will you be good enough to tell me why I have been brought here?"

"Certainly, my dear, but not just at present. As you see, supper is being brought in, and I am sure you do not wish to discuss such a matter before the servants. I will explain to you presently, when we are alone."

A qualm of uneasiness assailed her, but she stifled it resolutely and shrugged as though the matter was one of complete indifference to her. If he were prepared to sit down to supper, then the pursuit could not be so very close upon his heels, and it behoved her to use every opportunity for delay. Philip would come, but he must find her at Marwood when he reached it. The order she had heard Trayle give regarding the coach was lingering ominously in her memory.

With that thought in mind she allowed herself to be led

to the table, and forced herself to eat the food set before her, taking as long over it as she could and listening all the while for a sound which did not come, the sound of approaching deliverance. At length Gregory made a gesture of dismissal, and Lister and the other man who had waited upon them withdrew. Looking beneath her lashes, Joanna watched the door close behind them, and, assuming an indifference she was far from feeling, stretched out her hand to take a sweetmeat from the dish before her.

"Now, sir," she said, "perhaps you will be good enough to explain your extraordinary conduct."

Leaning back in his chair, his fingers crooked loosely about the stem of his glass, he studied her for a moment or two before he replied. There was an expression of amused approval in the grey eyes.

"First permit me to compliment you on your self-possession," he said lightly. "It would do credit to a woman twice your age. I confess that it surprises me. I expected tears and tantrums."

She ate the sweetmeat with great deliberation.

"Had you come earlier, sir, you would certainly have had a taste of my temper, for I was very angry then. But tears? No!"

He laughed softly.

"No, I believe not!" he agreed. "I wronged you in my thoughts, and I ask your pardon."

Joanna sighed.

"I might give it, sir, if you would come to the point. Why did you have me carried off and brought to this place?"

"With the most honourable intentions, I assure you," he replied. "I am going to marry you."

"Indeed?" She looked at him, opening her eyes very wide. "Is that a proposal, Mr. Trayle?"

"No, Joanna, it is a statement of fact. A proposal you would refuse."

"Perhaps you are not aware that I am already betrothed?"

"To Digby?" Gregory laughed and shook his head. "It makes no difference. You will marry me."

"I will not. You cannot force me to marry you. No parson would perform the ceremony."

"Not here in Gloucestershire, perhaps, but in London there are numerous places where marriages are performed whether the bride be willing or no. The Mayfair chapel is one; the chapel of the Fleet prison is another."

"In London?" Sheer astonishment rang in her voice. "Do you really suppose that you can carry me all the way to London without someone coming to my aid? Such a journey would take days!"

"That thought had occurred to me," he replied sarcastically, "and I fancy that I have solved the difficulty very ingeniously. We shall not take the London road. When we leave here we shall travel due south, and we shall not halt until the coast is reached. There we shall take ship as far as Dover. The journey from Dover to London can also be accomplished in one day, and once we reach London it will be only a matter of hours before you are my wife."

Joanna sat staring at him, while the little knot of fear which had been lurking somewhere deep inside her ever since his arrival began to spread and darken, overshadowing the assurance of rescue. Even if Philip guessed the identity of her captor, he would not dream of seeking her towards the south.

"I do not believe it," she said defiantly. "It is not possible to travel from here to the coast without stopping."

"We shall halt to change horses, of course. I have arranged for a fresh team to be available wherever necessary, but I shall be with you in the coach and I do not think you will be able to attract attention."

"I shall not need to," she flashed. "Philip will know your coach when he sees it."

Gregory lifted his glass and studied the wine in it reflectively. There was unmistakable amusement in his dark face, but it was not a pleasant expression.

"You delude yourself, my dear," he said lazily. "Brinkbury has seen the last of Philip Digby."

She achieved a scornful little laugh.

"You expect me to believe that?"

"Whether or not you believe it, it is the truth! Philip Digby rode out of the village this morning on his way to meet the Earl of Varne. He did not, nor will he ever, return."

"You waste breath telling me that, Mr. Trayle," she replied contemptuously, "but even if it were true, I need not despair of rescue. Have you forgotten my father?"

"By no means. My respect for Sir Andrew's wit and determination has prompted me to go to a good deal of trouble to throw him off the scent. At this moment, I have no doubt, he is endeavouring frantically to comply with the demand for ransom which reached him this afternoon, ostensibly from a man named Mullett." He laughed softly. "I wonder if he has yet succeeded? After that dispute last night I very much doubt whether Digby's emerald is still in his possession."

Joanna had unthinkingly stretched out her hand for another sweetmeat, but now she let it fall back into the dish as her eyes lifted in horrified disbelief to meet his. She felt as though an abyss had opened suddenly at her feet.

"How do you know about the emerald?" she asked in a shaken whisper.

"Because, my dear Joanna, you talk too much. You told Oliver Stonehurst, and Oliver told me. Do not blame him too greatly, however. He was exceedingly drunk at the time."

Joanna pushed back her chair and rose to her feet. Fear possessed her completely now, and she felt cold and rather sick. There was no need to question Gregory's story, for in a few brief sentences he had made the whole matter appallingly clear. The message that morning which had lured her into his hands; the false demand for the emerald, made in Mullett's name; even Philip would not question that, and the rescue she had so confidently expected would not come.

She gripped the back of the chair tightly with both hands, striving with all her will not to let him see how desperately frightened she was. He had risen also, and now came round the table towards her, and though every instinct prompted her to evade him she forced herself to remain still, feigning an indifference to his nearness which she did not feel. He halted just behind her and laid his hands on her shoulders.

"No, they will not come," he said quietly, as though she had spoken her thoughts aloud. "I have you fast, my dear, and you had better resign yourself to that fact." His hands slid down to her wrists, holding her prisoner against him; the mocking voice spoke softly, just above her head. "I have been very patient, Joanna! A faithful suitor for more than a year."

She stood rigidly in his arms, unyielding as a statue.

"Let us at least deal in honesty, Mr. Trayle," she said scornfully. "We both know that if I were not an heiress, I should not be here now."

A low laugh shook him.

"You are mistaken, my love! You would be precisely where you are now even if your father were a pauper. The only difference is that I should not marry you."

He bent his head, and she felt his lips against her cheek and then her neck, and in a sudden rush of terror and revulsion struggled against his hold. The violence of the movement took him unawares, so that she was able to free herself and put the width of the room between them. Just for an instant anger darkened his face, and then he recovered his composure and laughed.

"What a picture of outraged modesty!" he sneered. "It was a very different tale last night at the orchard gate."

Joanna did not deign to reply. She was breathing quickly and her face was very pale, but anger had revived now to dispel some of the fear which had numbed her brain since the realization of her plight. If Philip and her father had been tricked into following a false scent, then she must contrive to make her escape unaided.

The question which must be answered was where such an attempt would have the greatest chance of success. She stole a glance at the window, across which the curtains had not been drawn, and saw that it was dark now, and the edge of the moon just lifting above the trees at the end of

the garden. Perhaps it would be best to wait until they
were on their way to the coast. This house was isolated,
and occupied only by Gregory's servants, but during the
journey they would be obliged to pass through towns and
villages; if she could lull his watchfulness by pretended
acquiescence, she might succeed in attracting attention
and winning help from passers-by.

Trayle started to come across the room towards her,
and prudence was overwhelmed by the fear that he would
force further caresses upon her. She had paused by the
sideboard upon which the remains of supper still reposed,
and among the dishes lay a sharp, long-bladed knife. She
snatched it up, clutching it dagger-fashion in one small,
determined fist, and faced him with the desperation of a
hunted creature brought to bay.

"Keep your distance, Mr. Trayle," she said breathlessly, and he halted, looking more amused than dismayed.

"My dear Joanna," he expostulated, "you surely do not
suppose that I will permit you to use that murderous-
looking weapon upon me?"

"I do not know," she retorted, "but if you dare to
touch me again I shall most certainly try."

His brows lifted.

"I believe you would," he said with a laugh, and turned
aside to the fireplace and leancd his shoulders against the
chimneypiece. "Oh, put the confounded thing down, my
dear! I have no intention of engaging in an undignified
struggle, and there is not the least need for you to defend
your virtue in so melodramatic a fashion."

On the far side of the room the door was thrust quietly
open, and a third voice added itself to the conversation, a
voice which brought them both swinging round, Gregory
in incredulous fury, Joanna in equally incredulous relief.

"I am happy to hear it, Trayle," it said with deadly
quiet, "but perhaps Miss Selbourne would more readily
believe you if you matched your actions to your words."

XXII

Journey's End

For a moment or two a silence almost palpable possessed the room. Philip stood in the doorway as though he had materialized there out of the empty air, his clothes powdered with dust and a levelled pistol in his hand. Behind him, the lighted hall was empty and there had been no sound to give warning of his coming, neither of pounding hoofbeats nor of knocking upon the door.

"Philip!" Joanna let fall the knife and sprang towards him, and he put out his free hand to her, keeping his eyes on Trayle. "Oh, Philip, I did not think you would come! He said he had made you believe that Ned Mullet had captured me."

He glanced fleetingly down at her as she reached his side, and put his arm about her shoulders.

"I might well have believed it, sweetheart, but for one thing. Ned Mullett was arrested two days ago, and now lies in Bristol gaol." He looked again at Gregory. "If you had known that, eh?"

Gregory shrugged.

"At the moment it would interest me more to know how you entered this house. It displeases me to be taken unawares."

"It was simple enough! I thought it best not to proclaim my coming, and as I approached the house on foot I saw this lighted window. It was really very careless of you not to draw the curtains."

Trayle took out his snuff-box and helped himself to a pinch with great deliberation.

"I was not expecting any intruders," he drawled. "And then?"

"I forced my way in through the window of the adjoining room. I had seen enough to tell me that my presence was somewhat urgently required."

"I see!" Gregory flicked a speck of snuff from his coat. "You are very ingenious, cousin!"

Joanna's eyes widened.

"Cousin?" she repeated blankly, and Gregory laughed.

"I warned you, my dear, that Brinkbury has seen the last of Philip Digby. The gentleman you are so fondly embracing is the Earl of Varne."

"Philip!" She drew back a little, regarding him with astonishment and some disbelief. "It is not true?"

He smiled ruefully.

"I fear it is, my love! Can you forgive me?"

"Of course, but I do not understand. Why——" She broke off, for the sound of rapidly approaching horses was shattering the silence, their hoofbeats echoing in the overgrown drive and then on the open space before the house. Voices were heard, and then a thunderous knocking fell upon the front door. Gregory looked at Philip with raised brows.

"Reinforcements, cousin?" he inquired smoothly.

"You may call them that," Philip agreed. "I trust your servants will not hesitate to admit them."

He stepped aside from the door, drawing Joanna with him, and set his back to the wall as hasty footsteps approached from the rear of the house. Lister appeared in the doorway, an anxious query on his lips which perished there at sight of the intruder and his levelled pistol. His jaw dropped, and he looked from Philip to Gregory with bulging eyes.

"Sir Andrew Selbourne desires admittance, my friend," Philip said briskly. "Be good enough to open to him."

Lister cast a wildly inquiring glance at his master, who was once more leaning against the chimneypiece with an expression of detached, sardonic amusement in his dark face. Gregory made an airy gesture.

"Do as his lordship bids you, Lister," he said calmly. "As you can see, his orders are backed by unusual authority."

For a moment longer the man hesitated, and then he turned and went reluctantly to unfasten the door. No sooner was it open than Sir Andrew thrust past him into the hall, Simon and Oliver at his heels.

"Where is my daughter, you scoundrel?" he demanded

furiously. "By heaven, if she has come to any harm——!"

"Father!" Joanna had come into the hall and now ran to cast herself into Sir Andrew's arms. "Oh, Father, everything is all right! Philip was here before you."

"I told you, sir, that you had no cause for alarm," Simon remarked to Selbourne, and strolled past them to the doorway from which Joanna had emerged. "Plague on it, Philip, that damned brute you ride must be made of lightning! You had no difficulty here, I take it?"

"None whatsoever!" Philip put up his pistol and spoke briskly. "And now that you and Stonehurst are here we may settle this infernal business once and for all." He glanced at Gregory. "You agree to that?"

"With the greatest pleasure on earth," Trayle assured him. "As I told you when we parted, I have looked forward to this meeting with uncommon eagerness, although it is a privilege which I did not expect to enjoy quite so soon." Selbourne appeared in the doorway, an arm still about Joanna's shoulders, and Gregory bowed to him with mocking courtesy. "Ah, Sir Andrew! Allow me to bid you welcome to my house."

The older man's face darkened, but before he could reply Philip had intervened. Turning to Selbourne, he said quietly:

"Will you be good enough, sir, to take Joanna into another room? There is that to do here which is not fitting she should see."

Sir Andrew looked sharply from him to Gregory, and nodded his understanding. It was, he knew, quite useless to intervene, and although the thought of Trayle's reputation caused him the deepest foreboding, there was nothing for him to do but agree.

"As you wish, my lord," he said. "Come, Joanna!"

Gregory glanced at Lister, who was still hovering uneasily just outside the door.

"Conduct Sir Andrew and Miss Selbourne to the drawing-room," he said coolly. "I will, I trust, join them there in a little while."

Sir Andrew sought to lead his daughter away, but she

broke free of his hold and looked beseechingly at the Earl.

"Philip!" she said in a low, frightened voice, and he went quickly across to her and took her by the hand.

"Go with your father, dear heart," he said softly. "There is nothing more to fear."

She shook her head, and whispered his name again between white lips. He glanced at Sir Andrew, and then led her across the hall to the door which Lister was holding open for them. Within the room, while the servant kindled lights, they faced each other again, while Selbourne looked on with troubled eyes.

"Philip!" Joanna caught the front of his coat with both hands; there was a sob in her voice. "If you are going to fight him because of me, please, please do not! It is not worth it!"

He shook his head, covering her hands with his own.

"It is not only because of you, Joanna, though God knows, that would be cause enough! There is much besides which stands between us—your father will explain it to you. Be brave a little longer, my love! It will soon be over."

She gave a great sob and hid her face against his chest. For a moment or two he stood looking down at her, and then he dropped a kiss upon her hair and put her into her father's arms. Above the bowed fair head their eyes met, and Sir Andrew laid his hand awkwardly on Philip's shoulder.

"Have a care what you are about, my boy," he said gruffly. "They say he is a damnably fine swordsman."

A quick smile answered him, and then Philip turned and went out of the drawing-room and briskly crossed the hall. In the other room the furniture had been pushed to one side, and Simon, helped rather diffidently by Oliver, was measuring paces and rearranging lights, while Gregory, already stripped to shirt and breeches, looked on sardonically. He glanced round as Philip entered.

"You think of everything, cousin," he remarked caustically. "I am only astonished that you did not bring a surgeon with you also."

Philip smiled grimly and unfastened his coat.

"I doubt whether his services will be required," he retorted, "but whichever one of us survives the encounter will be glad that it took place before witnesses. The law takes a grave view of any duel which does not."

The preparations were soon completed, and they faced each other in the middle of the room. As they waited for Simon to give the word, they looked into each other's eyes and knew that this moment had been inevitable since the first instant of their meeting; that each fresh encounter, each move to thwart the other's schemes, had carried them surely and relentlessly one step closer to the time which now had come, when they must face each other with swords in their hands and the determination to kill in their hearts.

They began cautiously, and then Gregory opened the attack, only to be met by a guard he could not pierce, and driven back as Philip took the initiative in his turn. It was dangerous fighting, hard and swift, between two men who were both masters of swordplay. The two seconds stood motionless, their eyes following each movement of those flashing blades. Oliver was wide-eyed and a trifle pale, for he had never before seen such fighting and the grim purposefulness of the duellists filled him with awe; Simon watched with deep appreciation, nodding now and then in admiration of some particularly cunning thrust.

The clash and scrape of steel against steel, the pad of stockinged feet on polished boards, were the only sounds to break the silence. Gregory, his eyes narrowed, his lips set in a hard line, fought grimly, coldly determined to kill his opponent if it lay in his power, but slowly it was borne in upon him that in this slim young kinsman from across the sea he had at last met his master. He was beginning to tire, and his sword-arm ached intolerably from shoulder to wrist, but Philip seemed as fresh now as when they began to fight. He might have been made of steel for all the signs of fatigue he showed, and his point seemed to menace Trayle from half a dozen directions at once. Gregory set his teeth and fought grimly on, completely on the defensive now but still hopeful of finding an opening for a decisive thrust.

Suddenly such an opening seemed to offer itself, and with a flash of triumph he extended himself in a lunge which should have found his opponent's vitals, only to see, a fraction of a second too late, the trap into which he had been lured. Philip parried the thrust with incomparable skill, and before Trayle could recover, drove his own blade unerringly into the other man's heart.

Gregory's sword clattered to the floor, and then he seemed to crumple where he stood, and fell heavily as Philip sprang back. Halliard went quickly forward and dropped to one knee beside him, but Oliver stood paralysed, dazed by the suddenness of it all and feeling slightly sick. It was the first time he had seen a man die by violence.

Philip was breathing heavily and the sweat glistened on his brow. He wiped it away with his handkerchief and stood looking down at his cousin's body, a very grim expression in his face. Simon glanced up, and their eyes met.

"Dead?" Philip asked curtly, and Simon nodded.

"Yes, though it was a close fight," he replied, getting to his feet again. "He was a scoundrel, but a damned fine swordsman."

"Yes, he fought well!" Philip wiped his sword with the handkerchief and tossed the bloodstained stuff into the fire. "I do not think I have ever known a harder fight."

He sheathed the sword again and began to resume the garments he had laid aside, while Simon picked up Trayle's coat and spread it over the body. Then he glanced at Philip.

"What should be done now?"

"Best ask Sir Andrew," Philip replied curtly. He pulled on his second boot, rose to his feet, and thrust his arms into the coat which Oliver silently held up for him. "I will go to him now."

He crossed the hall, ignoring the servants who were clustered, white-faced and curious, at its farther end, and went into the drawing-room. Joanna had been sitting beside Sir Andrew on a couch, but when Philip entered she sprang up with a cry of relief and, heedless of her father's presence, flung herself into his arms. He held her close, but looked above her head at Selbourne.

"It is over, sir," he said quietly, "and I will be grateful if you will advise me how best to proceed now. The less noise the affair makes, the better for all of us."

"I will see to it," Sir Andrew replied gravely. "Some talk there must be, but we will endeavour to silence it as much as possible." He came forward and held out his hand. "My lord, I owe you an apology! Now that I know the reason for your secrecy, I could wish the events of last night undone, and the abuse I uttered then, unsaid."

Philip shook his head, gripping the proffered hand.

"The fault was mine, Sir Andrew," he replied. "I would have done better to take you into my confidence at the outset. It would have spared us all a deal of pain and anxicty."

"Well, well, that is over now, and youth is ever heedless!" Sir Andrew regarded them both benevolently, and patted his daughter's cheek. "You may dry your eyes now, my dear. He has come safely out of danger, and I will put no further obstacles in your way. You know the whole story now, but I don't doubt there is still a deal you have to say to each other. I will leave you to say it, and go deal with this other unhappy business."

He went out, and Joanna looked searchingly and with some anxiety at Philip, for though he still stood with one arm around her, he was not looking at her, nor had he made any response to her father's words. His face was grimly set, the lips compressed, the straight brows drawn together with a deep vertical furrow between, and the brilliant eyes were strangely sombre. She clasped his hand in both her own, and drew him to the couch and made him sit down there beside her.

"What is it, my dear?" she asked softly. "What is troubling you?"

The brooding gaze came to rest on her face.

"Did your father tell you that Bertram Colyton is dead?" She nodded, and he went on wearily: "For that I am responsible, though it was not my intention, God knows! And now Trayle, too, lies dead by my hand. He deserved death, and I should not regret it, and yet——" He broke off, making a helpless gesture with his free hand.

"They would have killed you, Philip," she reminded him quietly.

"Yes, I know! It was their lives, or mine, but—they were men of my own family, Joanna! The same blood ran in their veins as in mine." He bowed his head suddenly, laying his forehead against her shoulder. "That is what sickens me, I think! A man should not need to make war on his own kin."

With a compassionate and almost maternal gesture she put her arms around him, holding him close. One hand moved tenderly on the fiery hair.

"You are forgetting Francis, my dearest," she said gently after a moment. "He was determined to save your life, no matter at what cost to himself."

For a little while he did not reply, but then he lifted his head and she saw with relief that some of the trouble had faded from his face.

"Yes," he said in a low voice, "I had forgotten Francis! And I had forgotten you, my poor darling, and all that you have been through today. I should be offering comfort, not seeking it. Why do you not berate me for the selfish brute I am?"

A weary little smile quivered about her lips.

"I am too tired to be cross," she replied, "and I wish you would smile at me as you usually do, instead of looking so stern. It makes you seem like a stranger, and then I remember that you are the Earl of Varne, and not Philip Digby at all." She looked at him reproachfully. "Oh, why did you not tell me?"

"Sweetheart, it makes no difference, surely?" Philip was half anxious, half amused. "I am the same man, no matter by what name or title I am known. Your father has told you why it was necessary for me to come to Brinkbury under an assumed name."

"Yes, but I do not see why you had to go on pretending to me, and making believe you were poor, and all the rest of it. You did not think I would betray you?"

"No," he admitted slowly, "I did not think that." He was sitting now with one arm along the back of the couch, and the other hand imprisoning one of hers. He looked down consideringly at the slender, ringless fingers. "Joanna, do you remember the day we first met, when you questioned me about Richard Colyton, and speculated upon the possibility that he might come seeking a bride?"

"Yes, I remember," she replied in a puzzled voice. "You said that every marriageable girl would allow herself to be flung at his head." She broke off, her eyes kindling; when she spoke again her voice was indignant. "Philip, was that your reason? Did you really think that of me?"

"You denied it so very vigorously that I realized Richard Colyton would have no chance with you at all," he explained, and now she could see a familiar glint of laughter in his eyes, "and I confess that the temptation to deceive you was irresistible. Moreover, even before I left the Indies, I had been given such clear indications of the peculiar fascination a title holds for most women that, even before I discovered the real need for it, I had toyed with the idea of coming to Brinkbury in disguise."

"Well, of all the conceit!" Joanna tried to speak indignantly, but there was a tremor of laughter in her voice. "Philip, how could you?"

"It was no more than a jest at first," he said more seriously, "but after I met you, it became suddenly important to me to know beyond all doubt that the title and all the rest were of no account. Afterwards, when I could have told you, there were so many other things to be considered. I had to step warily, my love, and the fewer people to know my secret the better. Will you forgive me?"

"You know I will," she replied, her fingers tightening upon his, "and it is probably just as well you did not tell me, for I might have betrayed it accidentally, as I did about the emerald." She looked at him inquiringly. "What did become of the emerald, Philip? Is it still safe?"

"Yes, I have it here, and something else besides." He put his hand into his pocket and took out the ring of sapphires and pearls. "Your father brought them both to me at the inn last night." He lifted her hand to place the ring on her finger, but then paused, regarding her quizzically. "Will you wear it again, Joanna? You told me once that Varne could beg you on his knees to marry him, and you would refuse."

For answer she took the ring from him and slipped it on, and then lifted her face for his kiss. She was still in his arms when the door opened and Simon came into the room.

"I cry pardon for this intrusion," he said airily, "but I bring a message from Sir Andrew. He considers that as matters stand it will be best if he remains here for the present, and suggests that you, Philip, escort Miss Selbourne home in the coach which is even now standing at the door. Stonehurst has already been sent ahead of you with news of her safety."

"And you?" Philip inquired; Simon grinned.

"I remain here to give Sir Andrew any assistance he may need, and will return with him to Brinkbury. You may recall that there is a trifle of business to be settled between you and me."

"It can be settled now!" Philip thrust his hand into his pocket, and pulled out the little leather bag, and tossed it across to Simon. "That is what you have travelled so far to seek."

Halliard caught it dexterously and unfastened it, tipping the emerald out into his palm. Then he took it between finger and thumb and held it up to the light, so that it winked like a mocking, malevolent eye.

"The star of death!" he said softly. "I have waited a long while for you, my beauty!" For a moment he was silent, feasting his eyes upon the jewel, but then a fresh thought seemed to strike him and he looked with a quick frown at Philip. "Stay a moment, though! If this stone were set, would it not make a fitting wedding-gift for the Countess of Varne?"

Joanna blushed and shook her head.

"I would not wish to wear it, Mr. Halliard," she said firmly. "To me it seems an evil thing, beautiful though it is, and if you are not afraid of the ill-luck which seems to follow it, I pray that you will keep it."

Simon grinned.

"I will risk the ill-luck, madam, for such a prize as this," he assured her gaily, but Philip shook his head.

"Take my advice, Simon, and sell the confounded thing," he told him. "I have no doubt that you will squander the money within a twelvemonth, but that is better than risking a knife in the back from any rogue who chances to get wind of the jewel. I dare say that Coleford will advise you how to set about it." He got up and held out his hand to Joanna. "Come, my love, I will take you home."

She got up, but paused to offer Simon her hand.

"Good night, Mr. Halliard," she said. "Even though your business with Philip is settled, I trust that we shall still see you in Brinkbury soon."

He took the hand and held it for a moment, looking down at her with his lazy smile.

"Will there be a welcome, Miss Selbourne, for so dishonest a rogue as myself?"

She coloured, but met his eyes steadily.

"There will always be a welcome, sir," she replied simply. "You are Philip's friend."

He had the grace to look a trifle uncomfortable, but kissed her hand with unimpaired assurance and then went to open the door for her to pass through. As they emerged into the hall, Sir Andrew came out of the room opposite with Joanna's cloak over his arm. He put it about her shoulders, kissed her fondly, and charged her with a message for her mother. Then she and Philip entered the coach, farewells were said, and the cumbersome vehicle lumbered away along the drive towards the road.

For a time, as the coach made its slow way along the road which wound among the moonlit hills, Philip and

Joanna discussed the events of the day. There was still much to be explained, a good many matters to be made clear, and plans to be laid for a future which there was now no doubt that they would share. At length, however, Joanna's weariness overcame her. She fell silent, and her head drooped against Philip's shoulder. He thought her asleep, but suddenly she spoke again.

"Must I learn to call you Richard now?"

He shook his head.

"No, I have always been called Philip. Richard was my father's name as well as my own."

"I am glad!" Joanna's voice was drowsy, drugged with sleep. "It would not seem the same. You will always be Philip to me."

His arms tightened around her, but he did not speak, and after a little while her soft, even breathing told him that she slept. He leaned back against the soft cushions and looked out at the vista of rolling hills, frosty-bright under the moon, and a great contentment filled his heart and mind. Here among these quiet hills and valleys his future destiny lay; the years of restless wandering were behind him, and the recent weeks of cautious scheming had not been in vain. The journey was safely over. The Earl of Varne was coming home.